"A CRACKERJACK TREAT. WONDERFULLY WICKED...A BREEZY READ."

—*New York Daily News*

"HAPPY DAY! BERNIE RHODENBARR IS BURGLARING AGAIN—LIKE HIS AUTHOR HE IMPROVES WITH AGE."

—Tony Hillerman

"LIKABLE, CLEVER, FAST-MOVING ENTERTAINMENT...QUIRKY CHARACTERS, INVENTIVE PLOTTING AND LIVELY DIALOGUE."

—*Cleveland Plain Dealer*

"It is infrequent that a book causes one to laugh out loud but this one does . . . Bernie Rhodenbarr's funniest. Lawrence Block is in a superior class of his own. Thanks for a great one, Mr. B." —*Mystery News*

"Bernie Rhodenbarr is in terrific form. Hilarious, wonderful . . . fall-down funny Bernie can pick our lock any time."
—*Publishers Weekly*

"EVERYTHING MYSTERY READERS LOVE BEST . . . one of the most enjoyable mystery series we've ever read."
—*Denver Post*

"I can't remember the last book of any kind that made me laugh out loud. Bernie's takeoffs on the titles of Sue Grafton's mysteries are worth the price of admission alone. And the plot . . . is loopy enough to keep you reading." —*Chicago Tribune*

"A grand-slam fun fest that will lock a smile on your face from beginning to end . . . confirms Block's place at the mystery writing pinnacle." —*Macon Telegraph*

"Welcome back, Bernie the Burglar . . . with a plot that takes in everything from the value of rare baseball cards to the care and feeding of cats." —*Kentucky Advocate*

"AN ABSOLUTELY ABSORBING, WONDERFULLY MIND-TEASING CAPER by America's absolute Number One writer of mystery fiction." —Philip Friedman

"Yes. Heeding the moans and cries of his loyal readers, Lawrence Block has given us another Bernie Rhodenbarr mystery. My, it's nice to see Bernie again."

—*Washington Times*

"Very funny man, Bernie, whose friends and foes, equally bent and equally outrageous, make for a lively night's reading."

—*Hartford Courant*

"Bernie Rhodenbarr has returned to astound and beguile us. . . . *The Burglar Who Traded Ted Williams* . . . is a sparkling treat with Block's wit and energy."

—*Pittsburgh Post-Gazette*

"Block hasn't lost his light touch. Deliciously laid-back fare from a master who makes it all look easy. Bernie, it's been too long."

—*Kirkus Reviews*

"Lawrence Block's *The Burglar Who Traded Ted Williams* is a lemon soufflé—a great lemon soufflé—made entirely of ground-up razor blades and broken lightbulbs. It's lighter than air, the damn thing nearly floats, and it tastes better than any lemon soufflé ever made, but only one chef in the world, a great, hugely resourceful chef, could have made it. Lawrence Block is at his giddiest, funniest, and wildest in this book."

—Peter Straub

"Lawrence Block is addictive. Make room on your bookshelf. His novels become your friends." —David Morrell

"The long-awaited return of beloved crook Bernie Rhodenbarr is sure to be greeted by old fans with whoops of joy. . . . This is very funny, with a wonderful, complicated, highly improbable plot, hilarious dialogue and characters you wish you could invite over for supper." —*USA Today*

"The best Burglar book yet. . . . The dialogue is crisper and funnier, the plotting is superb, and, most important, Bernie still knows how to show us a good time." —*Mostly Murder*

"Here's the literary equivalent of a Beatles reunion. . . . We couldn't be more pleased, nor could Bernie's return be more extravagantly entertaining."

—*The Purloined Letter*

"A lighthearted tale, laced with plays on words, that will leave the reader smiling. Bernie is quick enough and clever enough to outfox those trying to frame him for a burglary he didn't do."

—*San Antonio Express-News*

"Bernie is so endearing, the reader has no choice but to applaud." —*Kansas City Star*

"A real steal. . . . Not for nothing was Block recently elected a grandmaster by the Mystery Writers of America."

—*Washington Post Book World*

"Side-splitting antics send readers on a wild and bumpy ride. . . . His canny survival instincts, combined with his irrepressible sense of humor, make Bernie Rhodenbarr one of detective fiction's most engaging heroes." —*Minnesota Star Tribune*

"The gent himself is enough to give burglary a good name."
—*Los Angeles Times Book Review*

"An absolute treat—the funniest, cleverest, in-jokiest lark of a mystery since, well . . . the amiably larcenous Bernie." —*Booklist*

"Bernie Rhodenbarr is back . . . as nimble-witted and nimble-fingered a delight as ever. Come on in, Bernie . . . I will count the spoons after." —Donald Westlake

"His survival instincts and sense of humor make Bernie Rhodenbarr one of detective fiction's truly singular heroes."
—*Alfred Hitchcock Mystery Magazine*

The Bernie Rhodenbarr mysteries
by
LAWRENCE BLOCK

Burglars Can't be Choosers

The Burglar in the Closet*

The Burglar Who Liked to Quote Kipling*

The Burglar Who Studied Spinoza*

The Burglar Who Painted Like Mondrian*

The Burglar Who Traded Ted Williams

The Burglar Who Thought He Was Bogart

***coming soon**

THE BURGLAR WHO TRADED TED WILLIAMS

A BERNIE RHODENBARR MYSTERY

LAWRENCE BLOCK

AN ONYX BOOK

ONYX
Published by the Penguin Group
Penguin Books USA Inc., 375 Hudson Street,
New York, New York 10014, U.S.A.
Penguin Books Ltd, 27 Wrights Lane,
London, W8 5TZ, England
Penguin Books Australia Ltd, Ringwood,
Victoria, Australia
Penguin Books Canada Ltd, 10 Alcorn Avenue,
Toronto, Ontario, Canada M4V 3B2
Penguin Books (N.Z.) Ltd, 182–190 Wairau Road,
Auckland 10, New Zealand

Penguin Books Ltd, Registered Offices:
Harmondsworth, Middlesex, England

Published by Onyx, an imprint of Dutton Signet,
a division of Penguin Books USA Inc.
Previously published in a Dutton edition.

First Onyx Printing, June, 1995
10 9 8 7 6 5 4 3 2 1

Printed in the United States of America

This one's for all the people who've come up to me over the past ten years to ask me if I was ever going to write another book about Bernie. If half of you buy it, I'll be rich.

It's also for Sue Grafton, a very classy lady indeed. And for Steve King, who wanted a book about cats.

And it's for Lynne. You want to know a secret? They're all for Lynne. . . .

This book is for all the people who've come up to me over the past ten years to ask me if I was ever going to write another book about them. If half of you buy it, I'll be rich.

It's also for Sue Chaloff, a very classy lady indeed. And for everyone who [illegible] a lot of [illegible].

And for [illegible]. You want to know [illegible]—they're [illegible].

The author is pleased to acknowledge the contributions of The Writers Room, in Greenwich Village, where much of the preliminary work on this book was undertaken, and of the Hotel Gaylord, in San Francisco, where it was written.

1

"Not a bad-looking *Burglar,*" he said. "I don't suppose you'd happen to have a decent *Alibi?*"

I didn't hear the italics. They're present not to indicate vocal stress but to show that they were titles, or at least truncated titles. *"A" Is for Alibi* and *"B" Is for Burglar,* those were the books in question, and he had just laid a copy of the latter volume on the counter in front of me, which might have given me a clue. But it didn't, and I didn't hear the italics. What I heard was a stocky fellow with a gruff voice calling me a burglar, albeit a not-bad-looking one, and asking if I had an alibi, and I have to tell you it gave me a turn.

Because I *am* a burglar, although that's something I've tried to keep from getting around. I'm also a bookseller, in which capacity I was sitting on a stool behind the counter at Barnegat Books. In fact, I'd just about managed to forsake burglary entirely in favor of bookselling, having gone over a year without letting myself into a stranger's abode. Lately, though, I'd been feeling on the verge of what those earnest folk in twelve-step programs would very likely call a slip.

Less forgiving souls would call it a premeditated felony.

Whatever you called it, I was a little sensitive on the subject. I went all cold inside, and then my eyes dropped to the book, and light dawned. "Oh," I said. "Sue Grafton."

"Right. Have you got *'A' Is for Alibi*?"

"I don't believe so. I *had* a copy of the book-club edition, but—"

"I'm not interested in book-club editions."

"No. Well, even if you were, I couldn't sell it to you. I don't have it anymore. Someone bought it."

"Why would anyone buy the book-club edition?"

"Well, the print's a little larger than the paperback."

"So?"

"Makes it easier to read."

The expression on his face told me what he thought of people who bought books for no better reason than to read them. He was in his late thirties, clean-shaven, with a suit and a tie and a full head of glossy brown hair. His mouth was full-lipped and pouty, and he'd have to lose a few pounds if he wanted a jawline.

"How much?" he demanded.

I checked the penciled price on the flyleaf.

"Eighty dollars. With tax it comes to"—a glance at the tax table—"eighty-six sixty."

"I'll give you a check."

"All right."

"Or I could give you eighty dollars in cash," he said, "and we can just forget about the tax."

Sometimes this works. Truth to tell, there aren't many books on my shelves I can't be persuaded to discount by ten percent or so, even without the incentive of blindsiding the governor. But I told him a check would be fine, and to make it payable to Barnegat Books. When he was done scribbling I looked at the check and read the signature. *Borden Stoppelgard,* he had written, and that very name was imprinted at the top of his check, along with an address on East Thirty-seventh Street.

I looked at the signature and I looked at him. "I'll have to see some identification," I said.

Don't ask me why. I didn't really think there could be anything wrong with him or his check. The lads who write hot checks don't offer you cash in an attempt to avoid paying sales tax. I guess I just didn't like him, and I was trying to be a generic pain in the neck.

He gave me a look that suggested as much, then hauled out his wallet and came up with a credit card and driver's license. I verified his signature, jotted down his Amex number on the back of the check, then looked at the picture on the license. It was him, all right, if a touch less jowly. I read the name, *Stoppelgard, Borden,* and finally the penny dropped.

"Borden Stoppelgard," I said.

"That's right."

"Of Hearthstone Realty."

His expression turned guarded. It hadn't been all that open in the first place, but now it was a fortress, and he was busy digging a moat around it.

"You're my landlord," I said. "You just bought this building."

"I own a lot of buildings," he said. "I buy them, I sell them."

"You bought this one, and now you're looking to raise my rent."

"You can hardly deny that it's ridiculously low."

"It's eight seventy-five a month," I said. "The lease is up the first of the year, and you're offering me a new lease at ten thousand five hundred dollars a month."

"I imagine that strikes you as high."

"High?" I said. "What makes you say that?"

"Because I can assure you—"

"Try stratospheric," I suggested.

"—that it's very much in line with the market."

"All I know," I said, "is that it's completely out of the question. You want me to pay more each month than I've been paying for an entire year. That's an increase of what, twelve hundred percent? Ten-five a month is more than I gross, for God's sake."

He shrugged. "I guess you'll have to move."

"I don't want to move," I said. "I love this store. I bought it from Mr. Litzauer when he decided to retire to Florida, and I want to go on owning it until *I* retire, and—"

"Perhaps you should start thinking early retirement."

I looked at him.

"Face it," he said. "I'm not raising the rent because I'm out to get you. Believe me, it's nothing personal. Your rent's been a steal since before you even bought the store. Some idiot gave your buddy Litzauer a thirty-year lease, and the escalators in it didn't begin to keep pace with the realities of commercial real estate in an inflationary economy. Once I get you out of here I'll rip out all that shelving and rent the place to a Thai restaurant or a Korean greengrocer, and do you know what kind of rent I'll get for a nice big space like this? Forget ten-five. Try fifteen a month, fifteen thousand dollars, and the tenant'll be glad to pay it."

"But what am I supposed to do?"

"Not my problem. But I'm sure there are places in Brooklyn or Queens where you can get this kind of square footage at an affordable rent."

"Who goes there to buy books?"

"Who comes *here* to buy books? You're an anachronism, my friend. You're a throwback to the days when Fourth Avenue was known throughout the world as Booksellers' Row. Dozens of stores, and what happened to them? The business changed.

Paperback books undermined the secondhand market. The general used-book store became a thing of the past, with the owners retiring or dying off. The few who are left are on the tail end of long-term leases like yours, or they're run by canny old codgers who bought their buildings outright years ago. You're in a dying business, Mr. Rhodenbarr. Here we are on a beautiful September afternoon and I'm the only customer in your shop. What does that say about your business?"

"I guess I ought to be selling kiwi fruit," I said. "Or cold noodles with sesame sauce."

"You could probably make this enterprise profitable," he said. "Throw out ninety-five percent of this junk and specialize in high-ticket collector items. That way you could make do with a tenth the square footage. You could get off the street and run the whole operation out of an upstairs office, or even out of your home. But I don't want to tell you how to run your business."

"You're already telling me to get out of it."

"Am I supposed to support you in a doomed enterprise? I'm not in business for my health."

"But," I said.

"But what?"

"But you're a patron of the arts," I said. "I saw your name in the *Times* last week. You donated a painting to a fund-raising auction to benefit the New York Public Library."

"My accountant advised it," he said. "Explained

to me how I'll save more in taxes than I'd have made selling the painting."

"Still, you have literary interests. Bookstores like this one are a cultural asset, as important in their own way as the library. You can hardly fail to appreciate that. As a collector—"

"An investor."

I pointed at *"B" Is for Burglar.* "An investment?"

"Of course, and a hell of a good one. Women crime writers are a hot item right now. *Alibi* was less than fifteen dollars when it was published a dozen or so years ago. Do you know what a mint copy with dust jacket will bring now?"

"Not offhand."

"Somewhere around eight-fifty. So I'm buying Grafton, I'm buying Nancy Pickard, I'm buying Linda Barnes. I have a standing order at Murder Ink for every first novel by a female author, because how can you tell who's going to turn out to be important? Most of them won't ever amount to much, but this way I don't have to worry about missing the occasional book that jumps from twenty dollars to a thousand in a few years' time."

"So you're just interested in investment," I said.

"Absolutely. You don't think I read this crap, do you?"

I pushed his credit card across the counter, followed it with his driver's license. I picked up his check and tore it in half, then in half again.

"Get out of here," I said.

"What's the matter with you?"

"Nothing's the matter with me," I said. "I sell books to people who enjoy reading them. It's anachronistic, I know, but it's what I do. I also sell them to people who get satisfaction out of collecting rare copies of their favorite authors, and probably to a few visually oriented souls who just like the way good books look on the wall flanking the fireplace. I may even have a few customers who buy with an eye toward investment, although it strikes me as an uncertain way of providing for one's old age. But I haven't yet had a customer who was openly contemptuous of what he was buying, and I don't think I want that kind of customer. I may not be able to pay the rent, Mr. Stoppelgard, but as long as it's my store I ought to be able to decide whose check I take."

"I'll give you cash."

"I don't want your cash either."

I reached for the book, but he snatched it away from me. "No!" he cried. "I found it and I want it. You have to sell it to me."

"The hell I do."

"You do! I'll file suit if I have to. But I won't have to, will I?" He got a hundred-dollar bill out of his wallet, slapped it on the counter. "You can keep the change," he said. "I'm taking the book. If you try to stop me you'll find yourself charged with assault."

"Oh, for God's sake," I said. "I'm not going to

fight you for it. Hold on a second and I'll get you your change."

"I told you to keep it. What do I care about the change? I just bought a five-hundred-dollar book for a hundred dollars. You damned fool, you don't even know how to price your own stock. No wonder you can't afford the rent."

2

"According to Oscar Wilde," I told Carolyn, "a cynic is a man who knows the price of everything and the value of nothing. I'd say that fits Borden Stoppelgard well enough. He doesn't even read the books but he knows what they're worth. I called a couple of the mystery bookstores, and the son of a bitch is right about the prices. *'A' Is for Alibi* has been bringing close to a thousand in decent shape. And my copy of *Burglar* was a five-hundred-dollar book."

"I have both of them."

"Really?"

"In paperback."

"In paperback they're worth something like a buck apiece."

"That's okay, Bern. I wasn't planning on selling them anyway. I have all the early books in paperback. I didn't start buying Sue Grafton in hardcover until the book about the photographer who took blackmail shots of the school principal and the nun. I forget the title."

" 'F' Is for Stop."

"Yeah, that's the one. I think it's the first book of hers I ever picked up in hardcover. Or was it the one about the exploitative sex therapist?"

" 'G' Is for Spot?"

"Great book. I know I've got that one in hardcover, and I think I've got the F one, too, but I didn't buy them for investment. I just didn't want to wait a year for them to come out in paperback. Bern? Do you suppose she's gay?"

"Sue Grafton? Gee, I don't think so. Isn't she married?"

She shook her head, impatient. "Not Sue Grafton," she said. "I'm positive *she's* straight. Didn't I tell you I met her at a signing last spring at Foul Play? Her husband was there, too. Real muscular guy, he looked like he could bench-press a Pontiac. No, I would say she's definitely straight."

"That's what I thought."

"No lesbian vibes at all. Hundred percent heterosexual, that's my take on the woman." She sighed. "What a waste."

"Well, if she's straight—"

"Definitely, Bern. No question."

"Then who were you wondering about?"

"Kinsey."

"Kinsey?"

"Kinsey Millhone."

"Kinsey Millhone?"

"What are you, an echo? Yeah, Kinsey Millhone. What's the matter with you, Bernie? Kinsey Millhone, leading private detective of Santa Teresa, California. Jesus, Bern, don't you read the books?"

"Of course I read the books. You think Kinsey's gay?"

"I think there's a good possibility."

"She's divorced," I said, "and she's involved with men from time to time, and—"

"Camouflage, Bern. I mean, look at the evidence, okay? She doesn't care about makeup, she's got this one all-purpose dress that she's still wearing ten books into the series, she's tough-minded, she's hard-boiled, she's sensible, she's logical—"

"Must be a lesbian."

"My point exactly. God, look at the men she gets involved with, like that shmendrick of a cop. Pure camouflage." She shrugged. "Now, I can certainly understand why she'd be in the closet. She'd lose a lot of readers otherwise. But who knows what she gets mixed up in between books?"

"Did you ask Sue Grafton?"

"Are you kidding? I could barely bring myself to speak. The last thing I was gonna do was ask her what Kinsey liked to do in bed. She signed her book for me, Bern. In fact, she inscribed it to me personally."

"That's great."

"Isn't it? I said, 'Miss Grafton, my name's Carolyn, I'm a real Kinsey Millhone fan.' And she inscribed it, 'To Carolyn, a real Kinsey Millhone fan.' "

"That's pretty imaginative."

"I'll say. Well, the woman's a writer, Bern. Anyway, I've got a signed copy of one of her books, but I don't suppose it'll ever be worth a thousand dollars, because there must be a ton of them. The line that day reached all the way to the corner. It's the book about the doctor. Have you read it yet?"

"Not yet."

"Well, you can't borrow my copy, because it's autographed. You'll have to wait for the paperback. Since you haven't read it I won't say anything about the murder method, but I have to tell you it's a shocker. The guy's a proctologist, if that gives you a hint. Why can't I ever remember the titles?"

" *'H' Is for Preparation.*"

"That's it. Wonderful book. I think she's gay, though, Bern. I really do."

"Carolyn."

"What?"

"Carolyn, she's a *character.* In a *book.*"

"I know that. Bern, just because somebody happens to be a character in a book, do you think she can't have a sexual preference?"

"But—"

"And don't you think she might decide to keep it to herself? Do you figure there aren't any closets in books?"

"But—"

"Never mind," she said. "I understand. You're upset about the rent, about maybe losing the store. That's why you're not thinking clearly."

It was around six in the evening, some three hours after Borden Stoppelgard had paid me a fifth of fair market value for my copy of the second novel about that notorious dyke Kinsey Millhone, and I was with Carolyn Kaiser in the Bum Rap, a shabby little ginmill at Eleventh and Broadway. While it may hearken back to the days when Fourth Avenue was given over largely to dealers in secondhand books, Barnegat Books itself is situated on Eleventh Street about halfway between Broadway and University Place. (You could say it's a stone's throw from Fourth Avenue, but it's a block and a half, and if you can throw a stone that far you don't belong on Fourth Avenue *or* East Eleventh Street. You ought to be up in the Bronx, playing right field for the Yankees.)

Also on Eleventh Street, but two doors closer to Broadway, is the Poodle Factory, where Carolyn earns a precarious living washing dogs, many of them larger than herself. We met shortly after I bought the store, hit it off from the start, and have been best friends ever since. We usually have lunch together, and we almost always stop at the Bum Rap after work for a drink.

Typically I'll nurse a bottle of beer while Carolyn

puts away a couple of scotches. Tonight, though, when the waitress came over to ask if we wanted the usual, I started to say, "Yeah, sure," but stopped myself. "Wait a second, Maxine," I said.

"Oh-oh," Carolyn said.

"Eighty-six the beer," I said. "Make it scotch for both of us." To Carolyn I said, "What do you mean, 'oh-oh'?"

"False alarm," she said. "Eighty-six the oh-oh. You had me worried for a second, that's all."

"Oh?"

"I was afraid you were going to order Perrier."

"And you know that stuff makes me crazy."

"Bern—"

"It's the little bubbles. They're small enough to pierce the blood-brain barrier, and the next thing you know—"

"Bern, cut it out."

"Most people," I said, "would be apprehensive if they thought a friend was about to order scotch, and relieved if he wound up ordering soda water. With you it's the other way around."

"Bern," she said, "we both know what it means when a certain person orders Perrier."

"It means he wants a clear head."

"And nimble fingers, and quick reflexes, and all the other things you need if you're about to go break into somebody's house."

"Wait a minute," I said. "Plenty of times I'll have

a Coke or a Perrier instead of a beer. It doesn't always mean I'm getting ready to commit a felony."

"I know that. I don't pretend to understand it, but I know it's true."

"So?"

"I also know you make it a rule not to drink any alcohol whatsoever before you go out burgling, and—"

"Burgling," I said.

"It's a word, isn't it?"

"And a colorful one at that. Here are our drinks."

"And not a moment too soon. Well, here's to crime. Scratch that, I didn't mean it."

"Sure you did," I said, and we drank.

We talked about my landlord, the book lover, and then we talked about Sue Grafton and her closeted heroine, and somewhere along the way we ordered a second round of drinks. "Two scotches," Carolyn said. "I guess I don't have to worry about you tonight."

"You can sleep easy," I said, "knowing that I'm half in the bag." I looked down at the tabletop, where I'd been busy making interlocking rings with the bottom of my glass, trying to duplicate the Olympics logo. "As a matter of fact," I said, "I had a reason to order scotch tonight."

"I always order scotch," she said, "and believe me, I always have a reason. But I've got to admit you had a particularly good reason after that scene with your friend Stoppelgard."

"That's not the reason."

"It's not?"

I shook my head. "I'm drinking," I said, "to make sure I don't commit a burglary tonight. For ten days now I've been fighting the urge."

"Because of—"

"The rent increase. You know, I never got into the book business to make money. I just figured I could come close to breaking even. I made my real money stealing, and the store gave me a respectable front and provided me with all the reading material I could possibly want. And I thought it would be a good place to meet girls."

"Well, you met me."

"I've met a lot of people, and most of the meetings have been pleasant ones. A nice thing about the book business is your clientele tends to be literate and your relationships with them are rarely adversarial, today's episode notwithstanding. And, amazingly, the store has actually become profitable as I've learned more about the business. Oh, it'll never be a gold mine. Nobody gets rich doing this. But for the past year I've been able to live on what I take home from the shop."

"That's great, Bern."

"I guess so. I never actually decided to give it up. I just kept putting it off, and then one day I realized it had been over six months since my last burglary, and then the next thing I knew it was a year. And I thought, well, maybe I've reformed, maybe the good moral upbringing I had as a child has finally taken hold, or maybe it's just adulthood creeping up on me, but whatever it was I seemed ready to be a decent law-abiding citizen. Then I found out what my new landlord wanted in the way of rent and I suddenly couldn't see the point of it all."

"I can imagine."

"The rent increase was on my mind all the time, and I couldn't figure out what to do about it. Believe me, there's no way to pick up an extra ten grand a month selling more books. What am I going to do, hike the price of the books on my three-for-a-buck table? So I found myself thinking, well, maybe I could cover the increase by stealing a hundred and twenty thousand dollars a year."

"To plow back into the business."

"I know it doesn't make any sense, but I just hate the thought of giving up the store. Still, I was all right until ten days ago."

"What happened ten days ago?"

"Maybe it was nine days."

"So what happened nine days ago?"

"No, I was right the first time. Ten days."

"Jesus, Bernie."

"I'm sorry. What happened was I was standing in line to get tickets for *If Wishes Were Horses*. I picked up a pair for the following night's performance, but the woman in front of me was getting tickets ten days in advance. She was wearing fur and a lot of jewelry, and she was having a very la-di-da conversation with another similarly pelted and bejeweled woman, and it struck me that I knew her name and address and that she and her husband would be away from the apartment on a particular September evening."

"Tonight's the night?"

"It is," I agreed, and held up a hand to get Maxine's attention, and made that circular motion you make to order another round. "Tonight's the night. When the curtain goes up at eight this evening at the Cort Theatre, the audience will include Martin and Edna Gilmartin, currently residing in Apartment 6-L at 1416 York Avenue."

"They make you give your apartment number when you buy theater tickets?"

"Not as of ten days ago. But I picked up some information from her conversation with her friend, and then I did a little research later on my own."

"You were planning to burgle the place."

"Not exactly."

"Not exactly?"

"I was thinking about it," I said. "That's all. I was keeping my options open. That's why Stoppelgard gave me such a turn at the beginning, mentioning burglars and alibis before I even realized he was talking about books." I stopped talking while Maxine brought our drinks, then took a sip of mine and said, "It would be stupid to go back to burglary, and it wouldn't work anyway. I can't steal myself solvent."

"Can you relocate?"

"Not unless I want to leave the neighborhood altogether. I checked on some vacancies around here, and the best I could do was a place way east on Ninth Street with half my present square footage and a base rental three times what I'm paying now, with escalators that will double that figure by the end of five years."

"That's no good."

"No kidding. I looked at lofts, too, but I need ground-floor space for the kind of store I have. I need the passerby trade, the people who start out browsing the bargain table and wind up coming inside. To duplicate what I've got I'd have to move clear out of Manhattan, and what's the point? No one would ever walk into the store. Including me, because I wouldn't want to go there either. I want to stay right where I am, Carolyn. I want to be two doors away from the Poodle Factory so we can always have lunch together, and I want to be a block from the Bum Rap so we can come here after work and get snockered."

"Are you getting snockered?"

"Maybe a little."

"Well, you're entitled," she said. "And it's good insurance against visiting the Gilhooleys tonight."

"The Gilmartins."

"That's what I meant."

"The Martin Gilmartins. If your name was Gilmartin, would you name your son Marty?"

"Probably not."

"I should hope not. What a thing to do to a kid."

"Well, at least you won't be picking their locks."

"Are you kidding? I never have so much as a beer before I go out. And I've had what, three drinks?"

"Three and a half, actually. You've been drinking mine."

"Sorry."

"No, that's okay."

"Three and a half scotches," I said. "And you think I could pick locks in this condition?"

"Bern—"

"I couldn't pick bagels," I said.

"Bern, not so loud."

"That was a joke, Carolyn. 'I couldn't pick locks, I couldn't even pick bagels.' Get it?"

"I got it."

"You didn't laugh."

"I figured I'd laugh later," she said, "when I have more time. Bern, the thing is you're talking kind of loud to be talking about picking locks."

"Or bagels."

"Or bagels," she agreed. "Either way, the volume control needs adjusting."

"Oh. I didn't realize I was shouting."

"Well, not shouting exactly, but—"

"But loud."

"Kind of."

"I didn't realize it," I said. "Am I talking loud now?"

"No, this is fine."

"You're sure?"

"Positive."

"It's funny how you can talk loud without even knowing it. It never happens on Perrier, I can tell you that."

"I know."

"Do you have any quarters?"

"Quarters?"

"Round things," I said. "George Washington on one side, a bird on the other. They still call them quarters, don't they?"

"I think so," she said. "Here's one, here's another. Is that enough, Bern? What do you want them for?"

"I'm going to play the jukebox," I said. "You wait right here. I'll be right back."

The jukebox at the Bum Rap is eclectic, which is to say that there's something on it to offend every taste. It leans more toward country and western than anything else, but there's some jazz and some rock and a single Bing Crosby record, with "Mother Machree" on the flip side of "Galway Bay." In the midst of all this are the two best records ever made—"I Can't Get Started With You" with a vocal and trumpet solo by Bunny Berrigan, and "Faded Love," sung by The Late Great Patsy Cline. They are wonderful recordings, and you do not by any means have to be drunk to enjoy them, but I'll tell you something. It doesn't hurt.

I finished Carolyn's drink while the records played, and I was chewing ice cubes by the time the second one was done. "How lucky we are," I told Carolyn. "How incredibly lucky we are."

"How so, Bern?"

"It could as easily have gone the other way around," I said. "We could have had Bunny Berrigan singing 'Faded Love' and The Late Great Patsy Cline singing 'I Can't Get Started.' Then where would we be?"

"You're right."

"No, *you're* right," I said. "You're right when you say that I'm right. You know what that means, don't you?"

"We're both right."

"We're both right," I said. "God, what a world. What an absolutely incredible world."

She laid a hand on top of mine. "Bern," she said gently, "I think we should think about getting something to eat."

"Here? At the Bum Rap?"

"No, of course not. I thought—"

"Good, because we tried that once, remember? Maxine popped a couple of burritos in the microwave for us. It took forever before they were cool enough to eat, and by then they were stale."

"I remember."

"For days," I said, "all I did was fart." I frowned. "I'm sorry."

"Don't apologize now, Bern. That was a year and a half ago."

"I'm not sorry I farted. I'm sorry I mentioned it. It's not terribly elegant, is it? Talking about farting. Damn, I just did it again."

"Bern."

"I don't mean I farted again. I mentioned it again, that's all. Isn't it amazing that I'll ordinarily go weeks on end without using the word 'fart,' and all of a sudden I can't seem to get through a sentence without it?"

"Bern, what I was thinking—"

"So I'd better not have any burritos tonight. I mean, if I can't even handle the whole concept verbally—"

"I thought Indian food."

"Hmmm."

"Or maybe Italian."

"Maybe."

"Or Thai."

"Always a possibility," I said. A thought started to slip past me on the right, and I extended a mental foot and sent it sprawling. "But I'm afraid tonight's out of the question," I said. "I must plead a previous engagement."

"You were going to cancel the Gilmartins," she said. "Remember?"

"Not the Gilmartins. My date's with Patience. Isn't that a great name?"

"It is, Bern."

"Deliciously old-fashioned, you might say."

"You might," she agreed. "She's the poet, right?"

"She's a poetry therapist," I said. "She has an MSW from NYU. Or is it an MSU from NYW?"

"I think you were right the first time."

"Maybe it's a BMW," I said, "from PDQ. Anyway, what she does is work with emotionally disturbed people, teaching them to express their innermost feelings through poetry. That way nobody will realize they're crazy. They'll just think they're poets."

"Does it work?"

"I guess so. Of course Patience is a poet, too, besides being a poetry therapist."

"Do people realize she's crazy?"

"Crazy? Who said she was crazy?"

"Never mind," she said. "Look, Bern, I think I'd better call her."

"What for?"

"To break the date."

"To break the date?" I stared at her. "Wait a goddam minute here," I said. "You mean to say you've got a date with her? I thought *I* was the one who had a date with her."

"You do."

"This isn't gonna be another Denise Raphaelson affair, is it?"

"No, of course not."

"Remember Denise Raphaelson?"

"Of course I remember her."

"She was my girlfriend," I said, "and then one day she was your girlfriend."

"Bern—"

"Just like that," I said. "Poof. Just like that."

"Bern, focus for a minute, okay? Pull yourself together."

"Okay."

"I want to call Patience to break your date because you're drunk and it wouldn't be a great idea for you to see her tonight. Do you understand?"

"Yes."

"You've just started seeing her, it's still early in the relationship, and you'd be making the wrong impression."

"I might fart," I said.

"Well—"

"Or mention farting, or something. So I'd better not see her." I took a deep breath. "You're absolutely right, Carolyn. I'll call her right now."

"No, I'll call."

"Would you do that? Would you really do that for me?"

"Sure."

"You're a wonderful person, Carolyn. You're the best friend any man ever had. Or any woman. You're an equal-opportunity friend, Carolyn."

"Just let me have her number, Bern."

"Oh," I said. "Right."

She went away, and a few minutes later she was back again. "All taken care of," she said. "I told her you had a nasty case of stomach flu and the doctor thought it was probably food poisoning. I said it looked as though you got a bad burrito at lunch."

"And we know what that'll do, don't we?"

"She was very sympathetic, Bern. She seems like a nice person."

"They all seem nice," I said darkly. "And then you get to know them."

"I guess that's one way to look at it. Bernie, where did these drinks come from? We never ordered them."

"It must be a miracle."

"You ordered them," she said. "You ordered them while I was on the phone."

"It's still a miracle."

"Bern—"

"Don't worry about a thing," I said. "If you can't handle yours, I'll drink 'em both."

"Oh, God," she said. "I don't think . . . Bern, what's that music?"

I cocked an ear. "Galway Bay," I said. "That's The Late Great Bing Crosby singing. I played it."

"No kidding."

"It turns out Maxine had quarters," I said, "with Washington on one side and a bird on the other. She let me have four of them for a dollar."

"Sounds about right."

"Well, I don't know. How's she gonna make a living that way? Be like selling *'B' Is for Burglar* for eighty-six sixty. How's she gonna pay the rent? God, don't you just love 'Galway Bay'?"

"No."

"Well, you'll like the next one. 'Mother Machree.' "

"Oh, God," she said.

3

"The rent's only part of it," I said. "There's more to it than that. I *miss* breaking and entering. Sometimes I forget how much I miss it, but the minute something comes along to raise the old anxiety level, well, this old burglar remembers in a hurry."

"What is it you miss, Bern?"

"The excitement. There's a thrill I get when I let myself into somebody else's home that's unlike anything else I've ever experienced. You tickle a lock and tease it into opening, you turn a knob and slip through a half-open door, and then at last you're inside and it's as if you're trying another person's life on for size. You're Goldilocks, sitting in all the chairs, sleeping in all the beds. You know, I never understood the end of that story. Why did the bears get so angry? Here's this sweet little blond girl sleeping like a lamb. You'd think they'd want to adopt her, and instead they're royally pissed. I don't get it."

"Well, she wasn't a very good houseguest, Bern. She ate their food, remember? And she broke the baby bear's chair."

"One lousy bowl of porridge," I said. "And when she ate it it was Just Right, remember? So by the time the bears got home it would have been Too Cold, just like the mama bear's. And I've always wondered about that chair, now that you mention it. What kind of chair supports a husky young bear but buckles under the weight of a little slip of a girl?"

"How do you know she was such a little slip of a girl, Bern? Maybe she was a real porker. Look how she tucked into that porridge."

"She was never chubby in any of the illustrations I ever saw. If you ask me, there was something wrong with the chair. It was ready to collapse the minute *anybody* sat on it."

"So that's your take on 'Goldilocks and the Three Bears,' Bern? The chair was defective?"

"Must have been."

"I like that," she said. "It adds a whole new dimension to the story. Sounds to me as though she'd have a damn good negligence case."

"I suppose she could have filed suit, come to think of it."

"Maybe that's why she ran all the way home. She wanted to call her lawyer before he left the office. I'll tell you one thing, Bernie. You proved your point."

"What point was that?"

"That you've still got burglary in your soul. Who else but a born burglar would see the story that way?"

"The negligence case was your idea," I said, "and only a born *lawyer*—"

"Watch it, Bern."

"The thing is," I said, "I'm pretty honest in ordinary circumstances. I call people back when they walk off without their change. When a waiter forgets to charge me for dessert I generally call it to his attention."

"I've seen you do that," she said, "and I've never understood it. What do you do when a pay phone gives you an extra quarter back? Send it to them in stamps?"

"No, I keep it. But I never shoplift, and I pay my taxes. I'm really only a crook when I'm out burgling. So I'm not a born thief, but I guess you're right, I guess I'm a born burglar. 'Born to Burgle.' That would be the perfect tattoo for me."

"Don't get a tattoo, Bern."

"Hey, not to worry," I said. "I'm not that drunk."

"Yes you are," she said. "But don't do it."

Truth to tell, I was barely drunk at all. We were in a no-nonsense Italian restaurant in a basement of Thompson Street two blocks south of Washington Square. We had ruled out Indian and Thai food because I didn't think my stomach could handle it, not after the attack of stomach flu Carolyn had invented for me. (Mexican, of course, was out of the question.) The fresh air on the way over from the Bum Rap had cleared my head considerably, and now, after a big plate of spaghetti marinara and two cups of espresso, I was pretty close to sober.

It was 9:17 when Carolyn waved at the waiter and made a scribbling motion in the middle of the air. I know this because I immediately glanced at my watch. "It's still early," I told her. "You want to have another espresso?"

"I didn't want the last one," she said. "No, I want to get home and check the cats and feed the mail. What's the matter?"

"Check the cats and feed the mail?"

"Is that what I said? Well, you know what I meant. Whatever it is, I want to go do it. It's been a long day."

"I know what you mean," I said. "Just let me make a phone call."

"Don't, Bern."

"Huh?"

"If you were going to call Patience, don't. I called her and broke the date for you, remember?"

"As if it were yesterday. I wasn't going to call her, but I suppose I could, couldn't I?"

"Don't."

"Miracle recovery, hit me like a ton of bricks and then it was over in nothing flat, blah blah blah. You think it's a bad idea, huh?"

"Trust me."

"I guess you're right. She'd just think I wasn't sick in the first place, and she'd probably figure I went out with some other woman. And, come to think of it, she'd be right, wouldn't she?"

I got up and walked past the waiter, who was struggling with a column of figures, and used the phone. When I got back to the table, Carolyn was frowning at the check. "I guess this is right," she said. "With handwriting like this the guy should have been a doctor." We split the check and she asked me if I'd made my call. "Because you weren't on the phone long," she said.

"Nobody home."

"Oh."

"I got my quarter back. But I didn't get an extra quarter, so I didn't have to wrestle with a moral dilemma."

"That's just as well," she said. "It's been a long day for both of us."

We headed west, crossed Sixth Avenue. As we were passing a quiet bar on one of the side streets, I suggested stopping for a drink.

"In that place? I never go there."

"Well, neither do I. Maybe it's nice."

She shook her head. "I looked in the door once, Bern. Old guys in thrift-shop overcoats, all of them carefully spaced a few stools apart. You'd think they were watching a porn movie."

"Oh."

"I don't think they'd let us in, Bern. Neither of us has been through detox even once. I think that's an entrance requirement."

"Oh. How about the place on the next corner? The Battered Child."

"All college kids. Loud, rowdy, spilling beer on everybody."

"You're hard to please," I said. "One joint's too quiet and the other's too noisy."

"I know, I'm worse than Goldilocks."

"There's a phone," I said. "Let me try that number again." I did, and nobody answered, and this time I didn't get my quarter back, either. I hit the side of the phone a couple of times with the heel of my hand, the way you do, and it held onto my quarter, the way it does.

"Dammit," I said. "I hate when that happens."

"Who'd you call?"

"The Gilmartins."

"They're at the theater, Bern."

"I know. The final curtain's not until ten thirty-eight."

"You really did research this, didn't you?"

"Well, it wasn't all that tricky. I went to the play myself, remember? So all I had to do was look at my watch when it was over."

"So why are you trying to reach them? Am I missing something here, Bern? You decided not to break into their apartment, remember?"

I nodded and lowered my eyes to gaze at the pavement, as if I expected to find my quarter there. "That's why I've been calling," I said.

"I don't get it."

"As soon as they're home," I said, "I'll be able to relax, because I won't be in any danger of acting on impulse. And as long as I'm with somebody, having a meal or a drink or a cup of coffee, I'm out of harm's way. That's why I made the date with Patience in the first place. I figured I'd be with her until they were home from the theater, and then I could go home myself."

"Unless you got lucky."

"If I just get through the night without committing a felony, that's as lucky as I want to get. I thought I'd make sure by having a drink after work, but I made a little too sure and got drunk, and you had to break the date for me. Which I appreciate, don't get me wrong, because I was in no condition to see her, but now it's"—I checked my watch—"not quite ten and the play doesn't end for another forty minutes and God knows what they'll do afterward. Suppose they go out for a late supper? They might not get home for hours."

"You poor guy." She put a hand on my arm. "You're really scared, aren't you?"

"I'm making a big deal out of nothing," I said, "but I guess you could say I'm experiencing a little anxiety."

"So walk me home," she said. "You can have a

drink or a cup of coffee and watch a little TV. You can try the Gilmartins every five minutes if you want, and you won't need a quarter. If they make a late night of it you can spend the night on the sofa. How does that sound?"

"It sounds wonderful," I said. "Thank God you're a lesbian."

"Huh?"

"Because you're the best friend anybody ever had, and if you were straight we'd get married, and that would ruin everything."

"It generally does," she said. "C'mon, Bern. Let's go home."

At a quarter to twelve I picked up Carolyn's phone for the umpteenth time—or was it the zillionth? I poked the redial button and listened to half a dozen rings before hanging up.

"I can't believe they don't have an answering machine," I said.

"Maybe they had one," she suggested, "until a burglar broke in and stole it. Are you about ready to bed down for the night, Bern? Because I'm starting to fade myself."

"I'm afraid the coffee worked too well."

"You're wired, huh?"

"Sort of. But you go ahead. I'll just sit here in the dark."

She gave me a look, then turned her attention back to the television set, where Charlie Rose was asking thoughtful, probing questions of an earnest chap who looked terribly knowledgeable and seriously constipated. I paid what attention I could, tearing myself away every five minutes to hit the redial button, and the fourth or fifth time I did this someone finally answered the phone. It was a man, and he said, "Hello?"

"Mr. Gilmartin?"

"Yes?"

"Well, thank God," I said. "I was starting to worry about you."

"Who is this?"

"Just someone with your best interests at heart. Look, you're home now, and that's what counts. How was the play?"

There was a sharp intake of breath. Then, "Do you have any idea what time it is?"

"I've got twelve-oh-nine, but I've been running a minute or so fast lately. Hey, lighten up, Marty. I just wanted to wish you and Edna the best. You get some sleep now, okay?"

I hung up and turned to see Carolyn shaking her head at me. "So I got carried away," I said. "So I had a little harmless fun at Marty G's expense. Well, I figured he owed me one. Look what I went through just to keep him from getting burgled tonight."

"I see what you mean. Are you going, Bern? You don't have to, you can still stay over."

I thought about it. It was late, and if I stayed the

night at Carolyn's West Village apartment I could walk to work in the morning. But I decided I wanted a change of clothes in the morning and my own bed that night.

Fateful decision, that.

I made a second fateful decision when a couple of drunken tourists beat me to a cab on Hudson Street. The hell with it, I decided, and I walked over to Sheridan Square and caught the subway. I rode uptown to Seventy-second Street, bought a copy of tomorrow's *Times,* and waited for the light to change so I could go home and read it.

"Excuse me . . ."

I turned toward the voice and was looking at a slender, dark-haired woman with a heart-shaped face. She had small regular features and a complexion out of a soap ad, and she was wearing a dark business suit and a red beret. She looked terrific, and my first thought was that I was going to be profoundly disappointed when she turned out to be selling flowers for the Reverend Moon.

"I hate to bother you," she said, "but you live here in the neighborhood, don't you?"

"Yes."

"I thought so. You looked familiar to me, and I'm pretty sure I've seen you around. I feel ridiculous saying this, but I just got off a bus and I was on my way to my apartment, and I had the feeling someone was stalking me. That sounds melodramatic now that I hear myself saying it, but that's what it felt like. And I live so close it seems silly to take a cab, and . . ."

"Would you like me to walk you home?"

"Would you? Unless it's completely out of your way. I'm at Seventy-fourth and West End."

"I'm on West End, too."

"Oh, that's great!"

"At Seventy-first Street."

"Oh," she said. "That means you'd be walking two blocks completely out of your way, and then two blocks back. That's an extra four blocks. No, I can't ask you to do that."

"Of course you can. People have asked far more of me than that."

"Are you sure? There's a cab now. Why don't I just take a cab?"

"To go two blocks? Come on."

"Well, if you were to walk me to West End," she said, "and then, when we did go our separate ways, I'd just have those two short blocks on my own, and—"

"Stop it," I said. "I'll walk you all the way home. I really don't mind."

Fateful, fateful.

She didn't usually get home this late, I learned. She'd had a class, and it ran a little later than usual, and then she'd gone out for coffee with a couple of her classmates, and the discussion got so spirited it had been easy to lose track of the time.

I asked what the discussion was about.

"Everything," she said. "We started out talking about one of the scenes we'd done earlier, and then we got onto the ethical implications of the Method, and then, oh, one thing led to another."

It usually does. "You're an actress."

"Well, it's an acting class," she said. "And maybe I'm an actress, but we don't know that yet. Which is one of the reasons I'm taking the class. To find out."

"And in the meantime—"

"I'm a lawyer. Except that's not quite true, either. What I really am is a paralegal, but I'm studying to become a lawyer. I'm taking classes on Mondays, Wednesdays, and Fridays at Manhattan Law School."

"And acting classes on Thursdays?"

"Tuesdays and Thursdays."

"And you work days as a paralegal?"

"Five days a week from nine to five at Haber, Haber & Crowell. And they just about always want me to come in Saturdays, and I almost always do. You're probably thinking I've got a very heavy schedule, and I do, but I prefer it that way, at least for now. I think I'm happier if I don't have a great deal of unscheduled time these days. I know that's cryptic and that one typically tells one's life story to a total stranger, but I'm a little shy about that, maybe diffident's a better word, a little diffident, and anyway you're not a *total* stranger because you live right here in the neighborhood. And this is West End Avenue, where we would go our separate ways if you weren't such a gentleman. You never told me your name. But then how could you? I've done all the talking. My name's Gwendolyn Cooper, and yours is . . ."

"Bernie Rhodenbarr."

"Short for Bernard. But people call you Bernie?"

"Usually."

"With Gwendolyn you get a choice. I can be Gwen or Wendy or even Lyn."

"Or Doll," I suggested.

"Doll? Oh, the second syllable. Doll Cooper. Or Dolly, but no, that doesn't really work. Doll Cooper. Can you see that on a playbill?"

"Easier than I can see it on a law school diploma."

"Oh, I'm afraid that's going to read 'Gwendolyn Beatrice Cooper.' Assuming I hang around long enough to get it. Doll Cooper. You want to know something? I like it."

"It's yours."

"Better than that, it's me. What do you do, Bernie? If that's not too invasive a question."

"I'm a bookseller."

"Like at Dalton or Waldenbooks?"

"No, I have my own store." I told her what it was called and where it was located and it turned out that was her favorite fantasy, to own and operate a used-book store.

"And in the Village," she said. "It sounds totally perfect. I bet you love it."

"I do, as a matter of fact."

"You must go to work every morning with a song on your lips."

"Well—"

"I know I would. Ah, here's where I live, the one with the canopy. Are you actually going to walk me to my front door? I wondered where the true gentlemen were these days. It turns out they're down in the Village selling books."

Her doorman was perched on a folding chair, his attention largely given over to a supermarket tabloid. The headline of the article he was reading hinted at a connection between extraterrestrials and the California lottery. "Hi, Eddie," she said.

"Hey, how ya doin'," he said, without raising his eyes from the page.

She turned to me, rolled her eyes, then turned to him again. "Eddie, do you know when the Nugents are coming back?" This time he actually glanced up at her, his own face unsullied by a look of comprehension. "Mr. and Mrs. Nugent," she said. "Apartment 9-G." As in spot, I thought. "As in gerbil," she said. "They went to Europe. Do you know when they're due back?"

"Hey, ya got me," he said. "Have to ask one of the day guys."

"I keep forgetting," she said, probably to me, since the tabloid had reclaimed his attention. "I'm in such a fog when I walk out of here in the morning that it's all I can do to find the subway. Oh, God, look at the time! I'll be in a worse fog than usual. Bernie, you're an angel."

"And you're a doll."

"I am now, thanks to you." She smiled, showing a mouthful of perfect teeth. Then she stood up on her toes, kissed the corner of my mouth, and disappeared into the building.

Three blocks south of there, I gave my own night doorman a nod and got a nod in return. I've been a little less effusive with the building staff ever since I found out the guy I'd been gamely practicing my Spanish on was from Azerbaijan. Nowadays I just nod, and they nod back, and that's as much of a relationship as anybody really needs.

I went upstairs to my own apartment. For a long moment I just stood there in the darkness, feeling like a diver on a high platform.

Well, at least I could get a little closer to the edge. Even curl my toes around it.

I turned on the light and got busy. I stepped out of my Florsheim wingtips and into an old pair of running shoes. From a cubbyhole at the rear of the bedroom closet I equipped myself with a little ring of instruments which are not, strictly speaking, keys. In the right hands, however, they will do all that a key can do and more. I put them in my pocket, and I added a tiny flashlight that throws a very narrow beam, and does not throw it terribly far. In the kitchen, in the drawer with the Glad bags and the aluminum foil, I found a roll of those disposable gloves of plastic film, much favored these days by doctors and dentists, not to mention those gentle souls for whom the word "fist" is a verb.

I used to use rubber gloves, cutting the palms out for ventilation. But you have to change with the times. I tore off two of the plastic gloves and tucked them in a pocket.

I'd been wearing a baseball jacket over a blue button-down shirt open at the collar and a pair of khakis. I added a tie and swapped the baseball jacket for a navy blazer. For a final touch I got a stethoscope from a dresser drawer and stuck it in a blazer pocket, so that the earpieces were just barely visible to the discerning eye.

On my way out the door I took a minute to look up a listing in the White Pages. I didn't call it, though. Not from my own phone.

At 1:24, dressed for success, I left my building. I walked up to Seventy-second Street, and then I walked a block out of my way to the corner where I'd met Doll Cooper. I dropped a quarter in a phone slot and dialed the number I'd looked up.

Four rings. Then a computer-generated voice, inviting me to leave a message for Joan or Harlan Nugent. I hung up instead and headed up Broadway to the Korean deli at Seventy-fifth Street, where I picked out enough groceries to fill a couple of bags. I went for low weight and high volume, choosing three boxes of cereal, a loaf of bread, and a couple of rolls of paper towels. No point in weighing oneself down.

I got out of there and took a left, walked a block to West End Avenue, turned left again, and walked to her building at the corner of Seventy-fourth. The same old stalwart was still manning his post. "Hi, Eddie," I said.

This time he looked up. He saw a well-dressed chap, tired from a long day removing spleens, performing one final domestic chore before settling in for some brief but well-deserved rest. Did he happen to note the stethoscope peeping out of the side pocket? Would he have known what it was if he did? Your guess is as good as mine.

"Hey, how ya doin'," he said.

I breezed past him and went up to call on the Nugents.

4

The elevator huffed and puffed getting me to the ninth floor, as if the operation that had years ago converted it to self-service had somehow sapped its strength in the process. I emerged at last into a conveniently empty hallway, turned to the right, walked past doors marked 9-D and 9-C, and saw the error of my ways. I did an about-face, walked on past the elevator, and found 9-G (as in Goldilocks) all the way at the end. I walked there, set down my bags of groceries on either side of the jute doormat, and tried to divine the presence of anyone within.

Because you never know. Maybe the Nugents had come home early. Maybe Harlan had got word of an emergency at the widget factory, maybe Joan couldn't bear to spend one more hour away from her beloved split-leaf philodendron. Or maybe Doll Cooper had got the apartment number wrong, and they lived one floor below in 8-G, just downstairs from the kung fu master who only left his apartment to walk his rottweiler.

I took out my stethoscope, fitted the earpieces in my ears, pressed the business end against the very heart of the door, and listened hard.

You didn't think the stethoscope was just camouflage, did you? If all I'd intended was to look like a doctor, I'd have carried a beat-up old Gladstone bag and pretended I was making a house call. No, I was using the stethoscope for the same reason a doctor does: to get a clue what was going on inside.

If 9-G had been a human being, I'd have closed its eyelids and put a tag on its toe. I couldn't hear a thing.

But what did that mean? The Nugents could be sleeping. The kung fu master could be sleeping. Even the rottweiler could be sleeping.

Let them lie, I told myself. *You don't have to be here, risking life and liberty in the pursuit of happiness. You can pick up your groceries and go home. You'll eat the bread and the cereal sooner or later. Who knows, maybe you'll actually* like *Count Chocula. And paper towels last forever, they've got almost as long a shelf life as Twinkies. So—*

I rang the bell.

It was a buzzer, actually, and with the stethoscope's assistance I heard it clear as . . . well, clear as a buzzer. I let up on it, listened to the silence, then buzzed again, a little longer this time. And listened to more silence.

That little Jiminy Cricket voice was silent now, too. I was on automatic pilot, doing what I do best.

Putting the stethoscope back in my pocket, taking out the little ring of picks and probes, and getting down to business.

It's a gift. Some guys can hit a curveball. Others can crunch numbers.

I can open locks.

Anybody can learn. I taught Carolyn once, and in a pinch she can open her apartment door without her keys. But for most people, even those who work at it, even the sort who make a precarious living at it, picking a lock is a very laborious process. You pick and pick and pick, almost as if you were trying to nag the lock into submission, and your fingers get clumsy and you get cramps in your hands, and sometimes you say the hell with it and jimmy the thing, or rear back and kick the door in.

Unless you happen to have the touch.

There were two locks on the Nugents' door. One was a Poulard, and you may have seen their ads, guaranteeing their product as pick-proof. The other was a Rabson; no guarantee, but a solid reliable lock.

I had them both open in under two minutes.

What can I tell you? It's a gift.

Strictly speaking, I don't think they should call it breaking and entering. If you're really good at it, you never actually break anything.

Unless there's a burglar alarm. Then, the instant you open a door or window that's wired into the circuit, you break the electrical connection. When this happens there's generally a high-pitched sort of whine, and you have a certain amount of time—generally forty-five seconds or thereabouts—to find the keypad and punch in the code that tells the system you've got every right to be there. After that you get the full treatment with bells and whistles and, sooner or later, a couple of private cops making an armed response.

By then, of course, any burglar in his right mind has gone home.

I took a deep breath, turned the knob, and opened the door.

No alarm.

Well, I couldn't know that for sure. There's also such a thing as a silent alarm. Open the door and there's no warning whine, no sound at all beyond the music of the spheres. There's a keypad concealed somewhere, but you've got no reason to go looking for it, and after forty-five seconds it's too late, because by that time an alarm has registered in the office of the security firm, and they turn up with guns in their hands while you're filling a pillowcase with the good sterling.

The thing is, hardly anybody installs a silent alarm these days, except as a supplementary system. What you want a burglar alarm to do is keep burglars out, not give you a shot at catching them once they're already inside. Most burglars, it pains me to say, are just looking for the easy dollar.

They've got no calling for the profession. The great majority, once they breach the system and hear the telltale whine, are out of there like a shot. A certain number, including the junkies and crackheads who get in by breaking a window or kicking in a door, will take a few minutes to grab a radio or go through a top dresser drawer. Then they're gone.

If the only alarm's a silent one, the burglar doesn't know it's there—which, after all, is the point of the thing. So the burglar goes about his business, and if he's a junkie or even if he's not, he'll very likely finish up and go home before the armed-response guys turn up. Even when traffic's light, it takes a while to answer a call. In rush hour, forget it.

Besides, a silent alarm is a pain in the neck for the householder. Because it's silent, there's nothing to remind you that you're supposed to key in your code. A certain amount of the time you forget, and the rent-a-cops turn up while you're sitting there switching back and forth between Leno and Letterman. After that happens a few times you stop setting the alarm in the first place.

Groceries in hand, I crossed the threshold and moved into the entering phase of breaking and entering. I nudged the door closed with my hip, cutting off the light from the hallway. It was pitch dark where I was standing, and silent as a tomb.

Lord, what a feeling! A quickening of the pulse,

a tingling in the fingertips, a lightness in the chest—but that doesn't begin to describe what I felt, and always feel in such circumstances. I'd told Carolyn about the excitement, the thrill of it all, but there was more. I felt an abiding sense of satisfaction, as if I was doing what I'd been placed on earth to do. I was a born burglar, and I was a-burgling, and whatever had led me to think I could possibly give it all up?

I set down my grocery bags and put on my disposable gloves. I got hold of my tiny flashlight, dropped it, and fumbled around on the floor for it, cursing the darkness. I found it, finally, and switched it on, then got to my feet and followed the straight and narrow beam all around the apartment. Once I'd established that every window was heavily curtained, I turned on a few lights and took another deliberate tour of the premises.

Walking from room to room, I felt like a gentleman farmer riding his fences, master of all he surveyed. But there was method in it. Long ago, in a nice apartment on East Sixty-seventh Street, I had amused myself looting a living room while the apartment's bona fide occupant was lying dead on the other side of the bedroom door. He had died, it must be said, of natural causes; someone had murdered him. The police, who conveniently turned up while I was still busy with my looting, jumped to the completely unwarranted conclusion that I ought to be listed as the proximate cause of death, and I had a hell of a time getting it all straightened out.

It's not the sort of thing anybody would want to go through twice, believe me. So I've learned to spend my first moments in a burglary checking around for dead bodies, and of course I never find any. They're like cops and cabs, never there when you're looking for them.

What I found instead was what realtors call a Classic Six, by no means a scarce item in prewar apartment buildings on the Upper West Side. An entrance foyer, where I'd groped for my flashlight. A living room, a formal dining room, a windowed kitchen. Two good-sized bedrooms, one with twin beds, the other a guest room which evidently doubled as an artist's studio for Joan Nugent. There was an easel with a half-finished painting of a man in harlequin drag playing the pipes of Pan. Pablo Picasso, eat your heart out.

That's six rooms right there if you count the foyer, but I don't think you do, because there was another room off the kitchen. I don't know what it was supposed to be originally. A pantry, I suppose, or else a maid's room. Now it was Harlan Nugent's den. There was a desk with a computer and a fax modem on it, and a bookcase that ran heavily to technothrillers, along with nonfiction along the lines of *How You Can Profit from the Coming Ice Age.* Above the desk hung a rural landscape which I was able to recognize as the work of Mrs. Nugent.

There was a moment, I have to admit, when I was overtaken by a feeling of infinite sadness. This was an unutterably serene apartment, with its heavy draperies and its thick carpet topped here and there by oriental area rugs, its graceful French furniture and torchère lamps, its old-fashioned wall molding and ceiling medallions, and even the art on its walls, the hand-tinted steel engravings of faraway places that shared wall space with Mrs. Nugent's oddly comforting thrift-shop acrylics. Why couldn't I relish for an hour or so the joy of illegal entry; then, having done so to my heart's content, why couldn't I leave everything exactly as I found it?

I suppose because photographic safaris are great for you and me, but they feel kind of lame to a born hunter. I could try telling myself to treat the Nugent apartment like a National Park, taking only snapshots, leaving only footprints, but it wasn't going to work. I was a burglar, and no burglar worthy of the name counts the night a success when he comes home empty-handed.

So I went to work. I started in the kitchen, where I unpacked the groceries I'd bought, wiped them free of fingerprints, and stowed them in the cupboards. (Maybe the Nugents would like Count Chocula.) Then I checked the refrigerator. It was empty of perishables, which suggested Joan and Harlan had gone off for a week or more. It was, alas, also empty of cash, as was the freezer compartment. A lot of people stash money in the fridge, and I guess it's as good a place as any, or at least it was until everybody started doing it. No cold cash in the Nugent icebox, however, so I moved on.

Nothing worth taking in the kitchen. There was an eight-piece canister set on the cupboard, white china with blue trim in a Dutch motif—windmills, tulips, a boy on ice skates, a girl with fat cheeks and one of those soup-bowl haircuts. One container held around thirty dollars in change and small bills, handy for tipping delivery boys, I suppose. I left it as I found it.

There was a locked drawer in the desk in the den, so it was the one I opened first. Locks like that are never terribly serious, and this one was child's play. Inside there was a diary, which I supposed was locked away so that Mrs. Nugent wouldn't get her hands on it. I read a few pages, hoping for a little prurient interest, and it may have been there for the finding, but not on the pages I happened to hit. There all I ran into was Harlan Nugent's personal ruminations on life and death, and as soon as I realized that's what I was getting I put the little book down like a hot brick. Pillaging the man's apartment was enough of an invasion of privacy for me. I couldn't bring myself to ransack his soul.

Besides the diary, the once-locked drawer held three manila envelopes a little larger than letter-size. The first one contained an insurance policy, the second a will. I did no more than look at each before returning it to its envelope, and I almost didn't bother with the third envelope, which would have been a mistake. It was full of money.

Hundred-dollar bills, and a thick sheaf of them. I took off my gloves to give the money a fast count, figuring it didn't matter if I left fingerprints on the bills. They'd be coming home with me.

Eighty-three of them, plus a stray fifty in the middle of the stack. $8,350 in perfectly anonymous used bills. A little off-the-books income old Harlan didn't want to report? Or was there a perfectly legitimate explanation? It is, after all, still legal for Americans to possess actual money.

Well, if it *was* unreported income, Nugent would bear its burden no longer. I pocketed the bills and returned the empty envelope to the drawer.

Then, just to show off, I took out my picks and locked the drawer after myself.

I moved a lot of pictures without uncovering a wall safe. I didn't find any loose bricks in the fireplace, either. Actually I didn't really expect to encounter a safe or a hidey-hole; if the apartment had had one, that's where he'd have stashed the $8,350, not in a desk drawer you could have opened with eyebrow tweezers.

There was some nice silver on top of the sideboard in the dining room, English by the look of it, Georgian if I had to guess. There was more of the same in the drawers. Over the years I've known three good customers for fine silver. One's dead, one's in jail, and the third retired to Florida two years ago. (He may still buy the odd soup tureen now and again, but you wouldn't want to shlep a load of stolen silver onto a plane. How would you get it through the metal detector?)

I passed up the silver, and some nice lace and linen, and went into the master bedroom, where Mrs. Nugent kept her jewelry in a miniature brass-bound chest on top of her Queen Anne dresser. The chest had a lock, but she hadn't locked it, which showed good sense on her part. I'd have opened it in a wink, and a cruder sort of yegg would have simply tucked the whole thing under his arm and hauled it off to open at leisure.

Some people have the same gift with gemstones that I have with locks. They barely have to look at a stone to know whether it came from the De Beers consortium in South Africa or the Home Shopping Network's once-in-a-lifetime Cubic Zirconium Jamboree. They can tell lapis from sodalite and ruby from spinel more readily than I can distinguish amber from plastic or hematite beads from ball bearings. (It doesn't really matter, neither one's worth stealing, but a person ought to be able to tell the difference.)

I don't have that gift, but when you've been stealing the stuff long enough you develop a certain sense of what to take and what to leave. When in doubt, you take. I passed up the pieces that were obvious costume. There was one necklace, for example, with a stone so large it would have had to be the Kloppman Diamond if it was real. There were earrings made of African trading beads. I got some nice things, and I could describe them in detail and even provide a ballpark estimate of their value, but why?

As you'll see, it turned out to be academic.

After half an hour in the Nugent apartment, I was ready to go home. I hadn't slept in any of the beds or broken any chairs, and there was no porridge anywhere to be found. I'd used my two plastic bags for the jewelry, plus a watch and some cufflinks of Harlan's, and then I'd tucked each bag into a pocket. Jewelry in each front trouser pocket, cash in the blazer's inside breast pocket, the stethoscope in an outside blazer pocket, my picks and flashlight tucked here and there—I may have cut an ungainly silhouette, but I had my hands free.

I took a last turn around my apartment, not in the hope of more booty but to make sure I hadn't left any traces of my visit. As usual, I'd been compulsively neat. I was ready to call it a night, and a long one at that, when my eyes settled on a door I hadn't noticed before. Another closet? The place was crawling with closets, and not a thing worth stealing in any of them.

The door wouldn't budge. And there was no keyhole, and thus no lock to pick.

What had we here? Was this a permanently sealed door leading to another apartment, a vestigial aperture from a time when this and the adjoining apartment had been a single unit? It seemed unlikely. The door was on a side wall of the guest room, Mrs. Nugent's studio. There was another door on that same wall leading to a large walk-in closet, into and out of which I had ambled a while earlier. Did the closet extend the whole length of the room, and had one of its two doors been closed off for some obscure reason?

I checked. The closet was deep and wide, but it only ran half the length of the wall. Was the sealed door one that led into the rear of a closet in the next apartment? It seemed like a strange way to do things, but old buildings get partitioned in curious ways over the years, so maybe it was possible.

What difference did it make?

Well, it was curious, that was all. And *I* was curious, and never mind what it did to the cat.

I got out my ring of picks and selected a flat steel strip four and a half inches long. I went up to the mystery door and slid my strip of steel between it and the jamb. I raised my hand to the top of the door, then lowered it again. I didn't encounter any resistance until I'd brought it down a few inches below my waist, right about where you'd expect to find a lock. I eased the steel strip out, drawing it downward to trace the outline of what seemed to be a bolt. Below the bolt, the strip had smooth sailing again all the way to the floor.

Curiouser and curiouser. If you were dividing one apartment into two, you didn't just close a door and bolt it. That was okay with adjoining hotel rooms, when you wanted to preserve the option of access, but it wouldn't do in this case, where you wanted privacy and security. At the very least, you'd seal the door all around with some sort of plaster compound.

Besides, the lock wasn't one of those add-on bolts you pick up at the hardware store. It was set right in the middle of a door two inches thick, which meant it was for a room designed to be locked and unlocked only from the inside. Closets don't have locks like that.

Bathrooms do.

Well, sure. There was a bathroom off the master bedroom, and a half bath off the foyer. ("Half-bath, half-human. They call him . . . Tubman!") So it made sense that there'd be one in the second bedroom as well. So that's all it was, another bathroom, and if I'd wanted to steal towels I'd have gone to the Waldorf, so the hell with it. I could just—

Wait a minute.

A bathroom in an empty apartment that happened to be locked from the inside?

I went back to the door and ran my hands over it, as if to assess its psychic energy. On the wall alongside it there was a switch plate set at shoulder height if your shoulders were set a tad lower than mine. I worked the single switch. No lights went on or off in the bedroom, and I couldn't tell if anything happened in the bathroom. No light showed beneath the door.

I flicked the switch back again, to undo whatever I might have done. I found a chair and sat down. I looked at the poor old harlequin in Joan Nugent's work-in-progress. On earlier inspection he'd looked sad. Now he looked confused.

Was someone in there? Had I alerted him by buzzing the buzzer, and had he responded by . . . by locking himself in the bathroom?

Why would anybody do that?

Well, say I wasn't the first burglar to come a-calling. I'd once been tossing a place when someone else broke in, and I'd found the whole thing something of a sticky wicket. I hadn't locked myself in the bathroom, but I might have, if it had occurred to me.

But did the apartment I entered look like one into which another housebreaker had recently broken? No way.

Still . . .

Logic, I thought. When all else fails, try logic.

All right. There were two possibilities. There was someone in the bathroom or there wasn't. If so, who could it be? A Nugent?

If you were a Nugent, or anyone else legitimately

present in the Nugents' apartment, you might or might not choose to answer a doorbell at an ungodly hour. But if you didn't go open the door, or at least peep through the peephole, would you instead lock yourself in the bathroom?

You would not.

Therefore if someone was there it was someone who didn't belong and who would sit on the john in the dark for half an hour to avoid detection. All I had to do was slip out and go home now and let the mystery visitor remain anonymous. Anybody in there had to be aware of my presence, and eventually he (or she; maybe it was Doll Cooper, for God's sake, trying out a third career) could emerge in his (or her) own good time. There was still silver for the taking, and thirty-odd dollars in the windmill canister, and, for all I knew, the legendary Kloppman Diamond.

I went around the apartment turning off lights. In no time at all the whole place was dark except for the overhead light in the foyer. I turned that off, too, and opened the front door and stuck my head out into the hallway.

And drew it back inside, and pulled the door shut, and padded noiselessly through the dark apartment, not even using my pen light. Moving slowly and silently, I slipped back into the guest room, where I hovered, barely breathing, and waited for the bathroom door to open.

* * *

Ten minutes passed, arguably the longest ten minutes of my life. By the time they'd crept by, it was glaringly obvious that the bathroom was unoccupied.

So why was it locked?

And what was inside?

The usual things, I told myself. A sink, a tub, maybe a stall shower. A commode. A medicine chest. Go home, I urged myself, and whatever's in there can stay in there, and who cares?

I did, evidently.

Because what I did—after I had turned on the light again, so that I could at least see what I was doing even if I couldn't satisfactorily explain it—what I did was get down on my hands and knees and try to pick the goddam lock. It was a nothing lock, it was a simple bolt of the sort you turn when you're in the john and you don't want someone to walk in on you. There were no tumblers, no pins, nothing, really, but a bolt that went back and forth when you turned the little gizmo on the back of the door.

I couldn't pick the sonofabitch to save my soul.

I could have popped it with one good kick, but I didn't want to do that. I was a man who'd once been called "the Heifetz of the picklock," and I certainly ought to be able to open a locked bathroom door. It wasn't Fort Knox, for God's sake. It was a bathroom, a *guest* bathroom, on West End Avenue.

Couldn't do it.

I flicked the switch again, the one at the side of the bathroom door, the one that had previously caused nothing to happen. Predictably, nothing happened.

Suppose I got married, suppose we had kids. Suppose one of them locked himself in the bathroom, the way the little bastards do, and then couldn't unlock the door and panicked. Suppose Daddy rushed to the rescue, picks in hand, and then suppose Daddy had to tell Mommy to call a locksmith, because *he* couldn't open the bloody door?

Ridiculous.

If it was my door, and my kid inside, I'd have taken it off its hinges. But that's a lot of work, and a real messy job. You always get chips of paint off the hinge and onto the carpet, a mute testament to one's continuing inability to draw back the bolt.

See, there was no way to work my kind of magic on the thing. All I could do was try to get a purchase on it with my tools and snick it back into the door. The gap between door and jamb was pretty snug, so I didn't have much room to work with. I could make a little progress, but sooner or later I'd be unable to maintain constant tension on the bolt, and my pick would slip and I'd be right back where I started, and not at all happy about it.

One of the steel strips on my tool ring is a cut-down hacksaw blade, and it would have gone through the bolt like a knife through butter. Not a hot knife, and not warm butter either, but it would have done the job. I ruled it out, though, for the same reason I wouldn't take the door off its hinges or kick it into the next county. I felt challenged, dammit.

I took off my pliofilm gloves. I dragged over a gooseneck lamp and positioned it to best advantage. I gritted my teeth and went to work.

And, by God, I opened the fucker.

With the bolt drawn and one hand on the doorknob, I paused to note the time. Astonishingly, it was getting on for four in the morning. How long had I taken to open the bathroom door? I didn't even want to know.

What I did want to do—needed to do, in fact—was use the bathroom, and I figured I'd earned the right. Its utilitarian aspects aside, the john was the massive anticlimax I'd figured it to be. The usual porcelain fixtures, a medicine cabinet with nothing in it more exciting than aspirin, a tub with a drawn shower curtain—

After all this buildup, you can see it coming, can't you?

Well, why not? It's obvious, isn't it? If a bathroom's that hard to unlock from outside, how could anybody have locked it in the first place? Why, duhhhh, whoever it was must have locked it from inside. And, unless that person had subsequently jumped out the window, leaving a terrible mess on the pavement below, where could he be but in the bathroom? Where indeed but in the tub, say, behind the floral shower curtain?

That's where he was and that's where I found him. Naked as the truth and dead as a pet rock, with a little round hole right in the middle of his forehead.

5

You're not here, I told the dead guy. *You're a figment of an overactive imagination, stressed beyond endurance by a rough day and a snootful of scotch and a nothing little deadbolt that took forever to open. You don't exist, and I'm going to close my eyes, and when I open them you'll be gone.*

It didn't work.

All right, I decided. In that case, *I* wasn't there. More precisely, I would erase all traces of my visit, and once I'd vanished into the night—what there was left of it—it would be as if I had never been there in the first place.

First, fingerprints. I'd taken off my gloves to get serious with the lock, and I hadn't yet troubled to put them back on. I did so now, and snatched up a washcloth and wiped everything I might have touched during my interlude of glovelessness. The lamp, the door, the knob on either side. The toilet seat, which I'd raised (and hadn't lowered afterward, what can I tell you, guys are like that). The flusher, which I'd flushed. The shower curtain, which I'd made the mistake of drawing open, and which I now returned to its original position. The light switch over the sink, which worked, and the light switch on the wall outside, which I tried again, and which still didn't seem to do anything. And other things like the towel bar and the hamper, which I probably hadn't touched, but why take chances?

I backed out of the bathroom and closed the door. I put Joan Nugent's gooseneck lamp back where I'd found it, took another look around her studio, and left it for the master bedroom, where I put all her jewelry back in her jewelry box. There was no way to make sure everything wound up in its original compartment, but I did the best I could. I'd been wearing gloves when I lifted the stuff and I was wearing them as I put everything back, so I didn't have to worry about prints.

I put Mr. Nugent's watch where I'd found it on his night table, and replaced his diamond-and-onyx cufflinks in the little stud box in his sock drawer. That left me with two empty shopping bags from the deli. I carried them into the kitchen and filled them up with the cereal boxes and paper towels they'd held when I entered the apartment. I wasn't entirely sure of the wisdom of this. Wasn't it risky to carry *anything* out of the building? And did I really have to worry about the cops canvassing all the neighborhood delis and bodegas, trying to trace two rolls of Bounty and a box of Count Chocula? I decided to be guided by a modified version of the National Parks Service motto, updated for hapless burglars. *Don't even leave footprints,* I told myself. *Don't even take snapshots.*

With my bags packed, I stood once again in the darkened foyer, filled this time with a different sort of anticipation. In another few minutes I'd be out of here, and I'd be leaving everything exactly as I'd found it—

Oh yeah? a little voice demanded. *What about the bathroom door?*

I just stood there. I gave it some thought, and then I gave it some more thought.

Then I took out my picks and went back to the guest room.

It was past five by the time I got out of there. I said good morning to Eddie as I sailed past him, face averted. "Hey, how ya doin'," he said, for a change. I walked briskly southward for three blocks, nodded to my own doorman, got nodded at in return, and went upstairs. I stopped at the compactor chute and disposed of my disposable gloves. I almost added the two sacks of groceries, but what the hell, they were mine, bought and paid for. I let myself into my apartment and put my groceries away.

I put away my burglar's tools, too, and my stethoscope. I hung up my tie and jacket, kicked off my sneakers, and threw everything else into the hamper. I had a shower which nobody could have called premature, then jumped into bed and fell asleep.

* * *

The phone woke me. It was Patience, my poetry therapist, calling to see if I was feeling better.

Oh, right, the food poisoning. "I'm still a little rocky," I said.

"You were sleeping, weren't you? I'm sorry I woke you. I tried you at the store, and when there wasn't any answer I was concerned. Have you seen a doctor?"

Had I? I couldn't remember what Carolyn had told her.

"Actually," I said, "I'm feeling a lot better."

"But you said you were still a little rocky."

"I'd say the crisis has passed," I said. "And as far as waking me is concerned, I'm glad you did. I should have been up hours ago." That seemed safe to say, if it was late enough for her to have tried me at the store. What time was it, anyway? God, eleven-fifteen. I *should* have been up hours ago.

"As a matter of fact," I went on, "I really have to get moving. But it's good you called, because I wanted to apologize for last night. I hated to cancel at the last minute like that."

"I'm just relieved you're all right."

"Could we reschedule, Patience? Are you free for dinner this evening?"

"This evening? Are you sure you're well enough, Bernie?"

"Absolutely," I said. "It's one of those twenty-four-hour food-poisoning things. I still feel the slightest bit rocky because it's only been about twenty-three hours, but an hour from now I'll be ready to wrestle alligators."

"Is the timing really that precise?"

"You can generally set your watch by it," I said. "I had the same thing two or three years ago, I got it from a brown rice knish from the health food store. Thought I was going to die, and then twenty-four hours later I was whistling show tunes. How about dinner tonight?"

"I have a client coming at seven," she said, "so I should be through by eight, but the session might run over. He's in the middle of a very tricky sonnet sequence and I hate to rush him. It's not like Freudian analysis, where you hurry them out the door after fifty minutes. I'd hate to risk stifling somebody's creativity."

"I know what you mean."

"So do you want to come here? Come at eight, and if we're not through you can sit in the waiting room and read a magazine. I'll definitely be ready by eight-thirty, and that's not too late, is it?"

"No, it's fine."

"We'll eat someplace in the neighborhood," she said. "No burritos, though."

"Please," I said. "Don't even say the B word."

It wasn't going to be my day to find out how I liked Count Chocula. I was in too much of a hurry. I shaved, dressed, and got out of there, not even pausing to trade nods with my doorman. I legged it over to Broadway and caught the subway. I would have taken a cab but at that hour the subway figured to be quicker, even with a change of trains at Times Square and a three-block walk from Fourteenth Street.

Why the hurry?

I usually open at ten, but it's not as though I generally have a mob of impatient bibliophiles banging on the steel gates. I have a standing lunch date with Carolyn, but I could have called to tell her I'd be late, or to go ahead and eat without me. I'd been up all night, and a hell of a night it had been. Why didn't I just spend the rest of the day in bed?

Good question.

I unfastened the big padlock, opened the steel security gates. I unlocked the several locks on my door, went in, flicked on the lights. Before I'd managed to take two steps inside the shop, the ravenous little bastard was rubbing himself against my pants leg.

"All right," I said. "Cut the crap, will you? I'm here."

He said what he always says. "Miaow," he said.

6

Look, it wasn't my idea.

And it happened very quickly. One day back in early June, Carolyn brought pastrami sandwiches and celery tonic to the bookstore, and I showed her a couple of books, an Ellen Glasgow novel and the collected letters of Evelyn Waugh. She took a look at the spines and made a sound somewhere between a *tssst* and a cluck. "You know what did that," she said.

"I have a haunting suspicion."

"Mice, Bern."

"That's what I was afraid you were going to say."

"Rodents," she said. "Vermin. You can throw those books right in the garbage."

"Maybe I should keep them. Maybe they'll eat these and leave the others alone."

"Maybe you should leave a quarter under your pillow," she said, "and the Tooth Fairy'll come in the middle of the night and chew their heads off."

"That doesn't seem very realistic, Carolyn."

"No," she said. "It doesn't. Bern, you wait right here."

"Where are you going?"

"I won't be long," she said. "Don't eat my sandwich."

"I won't, but—"

"And don't leave it where the mice can get it, either."

"Mouse," I said. "There's no reason to assume there's more than one."

"Bern," she said, "take my word for it. There's no such thing as one mouse."

I might have figured out what she was up to, but I opened the Waugh volume while I knocked off the rest of my own sandwich, and one letter led to another. I was still at it when the door opened and there she was, back again. She was holding one of those little cardboard satchels with air holes, the kind shaped like a New England saltbox house.

The sort of thing you carry cats in.

"Oh, no," I said.

"Bern, give me a minute, huh?"

"No."

"Bern, you've got mice. Your shop is infested with rodents. Do you know what that means?"

"It doesn't mean I'm going to be infested with cats."

"Not cats," she said. "There's no such thing as one mouse. There is such a thing as one cat. That's all I've got in here, Bern. One cat."

"That's good," I said. "You came in here with one cat, and you can leave with one cat. It makes it easy to keep track that way."

"You can't just live with the mice. They'll do thousands of dollars' worth of damage. They won't sit back and settle down with one volume and read it from cover to cover, you know. No, it's a bite here and a bite there, and before you know it you're out of business."

"Don't you think you're overdoing it?"

"No way. Bern, remember the Great Library at Alexandria? One of the seven wonders of the ancient world, and then a single mouse got in there."

"I thought you said there was no such thing as a single mouse."

"Well, now there's no such thing as the Great Library at Alexandria, and all because the pharaoh's head librarian didn't have the good sense to keep a cat."

"There are other ways to get rid of mice," I said.

"Name one."

"Poison."

"Bad idea, Bern."

"What's so bad about it?"

"Forget the cruelty aspect of it."

"Okay," I said. "It's forgotten."

"Forget the horror of gobbling down something with Warfarin in it and having all your little blood vessels burst. Forget the hideous specter of one of God's own little warm-blooded creatures dying a slow agonizing death from internal bleeding. Forget all that, Bern. If you possibly can."

"All forgotten. The memory tape's a blank."

"Instead, focus on the idea of dozens of mice dying in the walls around you, where you can't see them or get at them."

"Ah, well. Out of sight, out of mind. Isn't that what they say?"

"Nobody ever said it about dead mice. You'll have a store with hundreds of them decomposing in the walls."

"Hundreds?"

"God knows the actual number. The poisoned bait's designed to draw them from all over the area. You could have mice scurrying here from miles around, mice from SoHo to Kips Bay, all of them coming here to die."

I rolled my eyes.

"Maybe I'm exaggerating a tiny bit," she allowed. "But all you need is one dead mouse in the wall and you're gonna smell a rat, Bern."

"A mouse, you mean."

"You know what I mean. And maybe your customers won't exactly cross the street to avoid walking past the store—"

"Some of them do that already."

"—but they won't be too happy spending time in a shop with a bad odor to it. They might drop in for a minute, but they won't browse. No book lover wants to stand around smelling rotting mice."

"Traps," I suggested.

"Traps? You want to set mousetraps?"

"The world will beat a path to my door."

"What kind will you get, Bern? The kind with a powerful spring, that sooner or later you screw up while you're setting it and it takes off the tip of your finger? The kind that breaks the mouse's neck, and you open up the store and there's this dead mouse with its neck broken, and you've got to deal with that first thing in the morning?"

"Maybe one of those new glue traps. Like a Roach Motel, but for mice."

"Mice check in, but they can't check out."

"That's the idea."

"Great idea. There's the poor little mousie with its feet caught, whining piteously for hours, maybe trying to gnaw off its own feet in a pathetic attempt to escape, like a fox in a leg-hold trap in one of those animal-rights commercials."

"Carolyn—"

"It could happen. Who are you to say it couldn't happen? Anyway, you come in and open the store and there's the mouse, still alive, and then what do you do? Stomp on it? Get a gun and shoot it? Fill the sink and drown it?"

"Suppose I just drop it in the garbage, trap and all."

"Now *that's* humane," she said. "Poor thing's half-suffocated in the dark for days, and then the garbage men toss the bag into the hopper and it gets ground up into mouseburger. That's terrific, Bern. While you're at it, why not drop the trap into the incinerator? Why not burn the poor creature alive?"

I remembered something. "You can release the mice from glue traps," I said. "You pour a little baby oil on their feet and it acts as a solvent for the glue. The mouse just runs off, none the worse for wear."

"None the worse for wear?"

"Well—"

"Bern," she said. "Don't you realize what you'd be doing? You'd be releasing a psychotic mouse. Either it would find its way back into the store or it would get into one of the neighboring buildings, and who's to say what it would do? Even if you let it go miles from here, even if you took it clear out to Flushing, you'd be unleashing a deranged rodent upon the unsuspecting public. Bern, forget traps. Forget poison. You don't need any of that." She tapped the side of the cat carrier. "You've got a friend," she said.

"You're not talking friends. You're talking cats."

"What have you got against cats?"

"I haven't got anything against cats. I haven't got anything against elk, either, but that doesn't mean I'm going to keep one in the store so I'll have a place to hang my hat."

"I thought you liked cats."

"They're okay."

"You're always sweet to Archie and Ubi. I figured you were fond of them."

"I *am* fond of them," I said. "I think they're fine in their place, and their place happens to be your apartment. Carolyn, believe me, I don't want a pet. I'm not the type. If I can't even keep a steady girlfriend, how can I keep a pet?"

"Pets are easier," she said with feeling. "Believe me. Anyway, this cat's not a pet."

"Then what is it?"

"An employee," she said. "A working cat. A companion animal by day, a solitary night watchman when you're gone. A loyal, faithful, hardworking servant."

"Miaow," the cat said.

We both glanced at the cat carrier, and Carolyn bent down to unfasten its clasps. "He's cooped up in there," she said.

"Don't let him out."

"Oh, come on," she said, doing just that. "We're not talking Pandora's Box here, Bern. I'm just letting him get some air."

"That's what the air holes are for."

"He needs to stretch his legs," she said, and the cat emerged and did just that, extending his front legs and stretching, then doing the same for his rear legs. You know how cats do, like they're warming up for a dance class.

"He," I said. "It's a male? Well, at least it won't be having kittens all the time."

"Absolutely not," she said. "He's guaranteed not to have kittens."

"But won't he run around peeing on things? Like books, for instance. Don't male cats make a habit of that sort of thing?"

"He's post-op, Bern."

"Poor guy."

"He doesn't know what he's missing. But he won't have kittens, and he won't father them, either, or go nuts yowling whenever there's a female cat in heat somewhere between Thirty-fourth Street and the Battery. No, he'll just do his job, guarding the store and keeping the mice down."

"And using the books for a scratching post. What's the point of getting rid of mice if the books all wind up with claw marks?"

"No claws, Bern."

"Oh."

"He doesn't really need them, since there aren't a lot of enemies to fend off in here. Or a whole lot of trees to climb."

"I guess." I looked at him. There was something strange about him, but it took me a second or two to figure it out. "Carolyn," I said, "what happened to his tail?"

"He's a Manx."

"So he was born tailless. But don't Manx cats have a sort of hopping gait, almost like a rabbit? This guy just walks around like your ordinary garden-variety cat. He doesn't look much like any Manx I ever saw."

"Well, maybe he's only part Manx."

"Which part? The tail?"

"Well—"

"What do you figure happened? Did he get it caught in a door, or did the vet get carried away? I'll tell you, Carolyn, he's been neutered and declawed and his tail's no more than a memory. When you come right down to it, there's not a whole lot of the original cat left, is there? What we've got here is the stripped-down economy model. Is there anything else missing that I don't know about?"

"No."

"Did they leave the part that knows how to use a litter box? That's going to be tons of fun, changing the litter every day. Does he at least know how to use a box?"

"Even better, Bern. He uses the toilet."

"Like Archie and Ubi?" Carolyn had trained her own cats, first by keeping their litter pan on top of the toilet seat, then by cutting a hole in it, gradually enlarging the hole and finally getting rid of the pan altogether. "Well, that's something," I said. "I don't suppose he's figured out how to flush it."

"No. And don't leave the seat up."

I sighed heavily. The animal was stalking around my store, poking his head into corners. Surgery or no surgery, I kept waiting for him to cock a leg at a shelf full of first editions. I admit it, I didn't trust the little bastard.

"I don't know about this," I said. "There must be

a way to mouseproof a store like this. Maybe I should talk it over with an exterminator."

"Are you kidding? You want some weirdo skulking around the aisles, spraying toxic chemicals all over the place? Bern, you don't have to call an exterminator. You've got a live-in exterminator, your own personal organic rodent control division. He's had all his shots, he's free of fleas and ticks, and if he ever needs grooming you've got a friend in the business. What more could you ask for?"

I felt myself weakening, and I hated that. "He seems to like it here," I admitted. "He acts as though he's right at home."

"And why not? What could be more natural than a cat in a bookstore?"

"He's not bad-looking," I said. "Once you get used to the absence of a tail. And that shouldn't be too hard, given that I was already perfectly accustomed to the absence of an entire cat. What color would you say he was?"

"Gray tabby."

"It's a nice functional look," I decided. "Nothing flashy about it, but it goes with everything, doesn't it? Has he got a name?"

"Bern, you can always change it."

"Oh, I bet it's a pip."

"Well, it's not horrendous, at least I don't think it is, but he's like most cats I've known. He doesn't respond to his name. You know how Archie and Ubi are. Calling them by name is a waste of time.

If I want them to come, I just run the electric can opener."

"What's his name, Carolyn."

"Raffles," she said. "But you can change it to anything you want. Feel free."

"Raffles," I said.

"If you hate it—"

"Hate it?" I stared at her. "Are you kidding? It's got to be the perfect name for him."

"How do you figure that, Bern?"

"Don't you know who Raffles was? In the books by E. W. Hornung back around the turn of the century, and in the stories Barry Perowne's been doing recently? Raffles the amateur cracksman? World-class cricket player and gentleman burglar? I can't believe you never heard of the celebrated A. J. Raffles."

Her mouth fell open. "I never made the connection," she said. "All I could think of was like raffling off a car to raise funds for a church. But now that you mention it—"

"Raffles," I said. "The quintessential burglar of fiction. And here he is, a cat in a bookstore, and the bookstore's owned by a former burglar. I'll tell you, if I were looking for a name for the cat I couldn't possibly do better than the one he came with."

Her eyes met mine. "Bernie," she said solemnly, "it was meant to be."

"Miaow," said Raffles.

* * *

At noon the following day it was my turn to pick up lunch. I stopped at the falafel stand on the way to the Poodle Factory. Carolyn asked how Raffles was doing.

"He's doing fine," I said. "He drinks from his water bowl and eats out of his new blue cat dish, and I'll be damned if he doesn't use the toilet just the way you said he did. Of course I have to remember to leave the door ajar, but when I forget he reminds me by standing in front of it and yowling."

"It sounds as though it's working out."

"Oh, it's working out marvelously," I said. "Tell me something. What was his name before it was Raffles?"

"I don't follow you, Bern."

" 'I don't follow you, Bern.' That was the crowning touch, wasn't it? You waited until you had me pretty well softened up, and then you tossed in the name as a sort of *coup de foie gras*. 'His name's Raffles, but you can always change it.' Where did the cat come from?"

"Didn't I tell you? A customer of mine, he's a fashion photographer, he has a really gorgeous Irish water spaniel, and he told me about a friend of his who developed asthma and was heartbroken because his allergist insisted he had to get rid of his cat."

"And then what happened?"

"Then you developed a mouse problem, so I went and picked up the cat, and—"

"No."

"No?"

I shook my head. "You're leaving something out. All I had to do was mention the word 'mouse' and you were out of here like a cat out of hell. You didn't even have to think about it. And it couldn't have taken you more than twenty minutes to go and get the cat and stick it in a carrying case and come back with it. How did you spend those twenty minutes? Let's see—first you went back to the Poodle Factory to look up the number of your customer the fashion photographer, and then you called him and asked for the name and number of his friend with the allergies. Then I guess you called the friend and introduced yourself and arranged to meet him at his apartment and take a look at the animal, and then—"

"Stop it."

"Well?"

"The cat was at my apartment."

"What was he doing there?"

"He was living there, Bern."

I frowned. "I've met your cats," I said. "I've known them for years. I'd recognize them, with or without tails. Archie's a sable Burmese and Ubi's a Russian blue. Neither one of them could pass for a gray tabby, except maybe in a dark alley."

"He was living *with* Archie and Ubi," she said.

"Since when?"

"Oh, just for a little while."

I thought for a moment. "Not for just a little while," I said, "because he was there long enough to learn the toilet trick. You don't learn something like that overnight. Look how long it takes with human beings. That's how he learned, right? He picked it up from your cats, didn't he?"

"I suppose so."

"And he didn't pick it up overnight, either. Did he?"

"I feel like a suspect," she said. "I feel as though I'm being grilled."

"Grilled? You ought to be charbroiled. You set me up and euchred me, for heaven's sake. How long has Raffles been living with you?"

"Two and a half months."

"Two and a half *months!*"

"Well, maybe it's more like three."

"Three months! That's unbelievable. How many times have I been over to your place in the past three months? It's got to be eight or ten at the very least. Are you telling me I looked at the cat and didn't even notice him?"

"When you came over," she said, "I used to put him in the other room."

"What other room? You live in one room."

"I put him in the closet."

"In the closet?"

"Uh-huh. So you wouldn't see him."

"But why?"

"The same reason I never mentioned him."

"Why's that? I don't get it. Were you ashamed of him? What's wrong with him, anyway?"

"There's nothing wrong with him."

"Because if there's something shameful about the animal, I don't know that I want him hanging around my store."

"There's nothing shameful about him," she said. "He's a perfectly fine cat. He's trustworthy, he's loyal, he's helpful and friendly—"

"Courteous, kind," I said. "Obedient, cheerful, thrifty. He's a regular Boy Scout, isn't he? So why the hell were you keeping him a secret from me?"

"It wasn't just you, Bern. Honest. I was keeping him a secret from everybody."

"But *why,* Carolyn?"

"I don't even want to say it."

"Come on, for God's sake."

She took a breath. "Because," she said darkly, "he was the Third Cat."

"You lost me."

"Oh, God. This is impossible to explain. Bernie, there's something you have to understand. Cats can be very dangerous for a woman."

"What are you talking about?"

"You start with one," she said, "and that's fine, no problem, nothing wrong with that. And then you get a second one and that's even better, as a matter of fact, because they keep each other company. It's a curious thing, but it's actually easier to have two cats than one."

"I'll take your word for it."

"Then you get a third, and that's all right, it's still manageable, but before you know it you take in a fourth, and then you've gone and done it."

"Done what?"

"You've crossed the line."

"What line, and how have you crossed it?"

"You've become a Woman With Cats." I nodded. Light was beginning to dawn. "You know the kind of woman I mean," she went on. "They're all over the place. They don't have any friends, and they hardly ever set foot outdoors, and when they die people discover thirty or forty cats in the house. Or they're cooped up in an apartment with thirty or forty cats and the neighbors take them to court to evict them because of the filth and the smell. Or they seem perfectly normal, and then there's a fire or a break-in or something, and the world finds them out for what they are. They're Women With Cats, Bernie, and that's not what I want to be."

"No," I said, "and I can see why. But—"

"It doesn't seem to be a problem for men," she said. "There are lots of men with two cats, and probably plenty with three or four, but when did you ever hear anything about a Man With Cats? When it comes to cats, men don't seem to have trouble knowing when to stop." She frowned. "Funny, isn't it? In every other area of their lives—"

"Let's stick to cats," I suggested. "How did you happen to wind up with Raffles hanging out in your closet? And what was his name before it was Raffles?"

She shook her head. "Forget it, Bern. It was a real pussy name, if you ask me. Not right for the cat at all. As far as how I got him, well, it happened pretty much the way I said, except there were a few things I left out. George Brill is a customer of mine. I groom his Irish water spaniel."

"And his friend is allergic to cats."

"No, George is the one who's allergic. And when Felipe moved in with George, the cat had to go. The dog and cat got along fine, but George was wheezing and red-eyed all the time, so Felipe had to give up either George or the cat."

"And that was it for Raffles."

"Well, Felipe wasn't all that attached to the cat. It wasn't his cat in the first place. It was Patrick's."

"Where did Patrick come from?"

"Ireland, and he couldn't get a green card and he didn't like it here that much anyway, so when he went back home he left the cat with Felipe, because he couldn't take him through Immigration. Felipe was willing to give the cat a home, but when he and George got together, well, the cat had to go."

"And how come you were elected to take him?"

"George tricked me into it."

"What did he do, tell you the Poodle Factory was infested with mice?"

"No, he used some pretty outrageous emotional blackmail on me. Anyway, it worked. The next thing I knew I had a Third Cat."

"How did Archie and Ubi feel about it?"

"They didn't actually say anything, but their body language translated into something along the lines of 'There goes the neighborhood.' I don't think it broke their hearts yesterday when I packed him up and took him out of there."

"But in the meantime he spent three months in your apartment and you never said a word."

"I was planning on telling you, Bern."

"When?"

"Sooner or later. But I was afraid."

"Of what I would think?"

"Not only that. Afraid of what the Third Cat signified." She heaved a sigh. "All those Women With Cats," she said. "They didn't plan on it, Bern. They got a first cat, they got a second cat, they got a third cat, and all of a sudden they were gone."

"You don't think they might have been the least bit odd to begin with?"

"No," she said. "No, I don't. Oh, once in a while, maybe, you get a slightly wacko lady, and next thing you know she's up to her armpits in cats. But most of the Cat Ladies start out normal. By the time you get to the end of the story they're nuts, all right, but having thirty or forty cats'll do that to you. It sneaks up on you, and before you know it you're over the edge."

"And the Third Cat's the charm, huh?"

"No question. Bern, there are primitive cultures that don't really have numbers, not in the sense that we do. They have a word that means 'one,' and other words for 'two' and 'three,' and after that there's a word that just means 'more than three.' And that's how it is in our culture with cats. You can have one cat, you can have two cats, you can even have three cats, but after that you've got 'more than three.' "

"And you're a Woman With Cats."

"You got it."

"I've got it, all right. I've got your Third Cat. Is that the real reason you never mentioned it? Because you were planning all along to palm the little bugger off on me?"

"No," she said quickly. "Swear to God, Bern. A couple of times over the years the subject of a dog or cat has come up, and you've always said you didn't want a pet. Did I ever once press you?"

"No."

"I took you at your word. It sometimes crossed my mind that you might have a better time in life if you had an animal to love, but I managed to keep it to myself. It never even occurred to me that you could use a working cat. And then when I found out about your rodent problem—"

"You knew just how to solve it."

"Well, sure. And it's a great solution, isn't it? Admit it, Bern. Didn't it do your heart good this morning to have Raffles there to greet you?"

"It was all right," I admitted. "At least he was still alive. I had visions of him lying there dead with his paws in the air, and the mice forming a great circle around his body."

"See? You're concerned about him, Bern. Before you know it you're going to fall in love with the little guy."

"Don't hold your breath. Carolyn? What was his name before it was Raffles?"

"Oh, forget it. It was a stupid name."

"Tell me."

"Do I have to?" She sighed. "Well, it was Andro."

"Andrew? What's so stupid about that? Andrew Jackson, Andrew Johnson, Andrew Carnegie—they all did okay with it."

"Not Andrew, Bern. An*dro*."

"Andrew Mellon, Andrew Gardner . . . *not* Andrew? Andro?"

"Right."

"What's that, Greek for Andrew?"

She shook her head. "It's short for Androgynous."

"Oh."

"The idea being that his surgery had left the cat somewhat uncertain from a sexual standpoint."

"Oh."

"Which I gather was also the case for Patrick, although I don't believe surgery had anything to do with it."

"Oh."

"I never called him Andro myself," she said. "Actually, I didn't call him anything. I didn't want to give him a new name because that would mean I was leaning toward keeping him, and—"

"I understand."

"And then on the way over to the bookstore it just came to me in a flash. Raffles."

"As in raffling off a car to raise money for a church, I think you said."

"Don't hate me, Bern."

"I'll try not to."

"It's been no picnic, living a lie for the past three months. Believe me."

"I guess it'll be easier for everybody now that Raffles is out of the closet."

"I know it will. Bern, I didn't want to trick you into taking the cat."

"Of course you did."

"No, I didn't. I just wanted to make it as easy as possible for you and the cat to start off on the right foot. I knew you'd be crazy about him once you got to know him, and I thought anything I could do to get you over the first hurdle, any minor deception I might have to practice—"

"Like lying your head off."

"It was in a good cause. I had only your best interests at heart, Bern. Yours and the cat's."

"And your own."

"Well, yeah," she said, and flashed a winning smile. "But it worked out, didn't it? Bern, you've got to admit it worked out."

"We'll see," I said.

7

Well, it seemed to be working out. I'd had plenty of misgivings early on. I was sure I'd be tripping over the animal all the time, but he was remarkably good at keeping out of the way. He did his ankle-rubbing routine every morning when I opened up, but that was just his way of making sure I fed him. The rest of the time I hardly knew he was there. He walked around on little cat feet, appropriately enough, and he didn't bump into things. Sometimes he would catch a few rays in the front window, and now and then he'd make a silent spring onto a high shelf and ease himself into the gap between James Carroll and Rachel Carson, but most of the time he kept a low profile.

Few customers ever saw him, and those who did seemed generally unsurprised at the presence of a cat in a bookstore. "What a pretty cat!" they might say, or "What happened to his tail?" He seemed most inclined to display himself when the customer was an attractive woman, which made him something of an asset, functioning as a sort of ice-breaker. I don't know that he earned his keep in that capacity, but I'd have to list it as a plus on his résumé.

What paid the Tender Vittles tab, as far as I was concerned, was what he'd been hired for in the first place. Since Carolyn brought him into the shop, I hadn't found a single book with a nibbled spine. The rodent damage had ceased so abruptly and permanently I had to wonder if it had ever happened in the first place. Maybe, I sometimes thought, I'd never had a mouse in the store. Maybe the Waugh and Glasgow volumes had been like that when I got them. Or maybe Carolyn had snuck in herself and gnawed at the books, just so she could find a permanent home for the Third Cat.

I wouldn't put it past her.

Once I'd filled his dinner bowl and his water dish, I locked up again and went over to Carolyn's place. "I already ate," she said. "I didn't think you were going to open up today."

"That's what I figured," I said, "but I wanted to check. Let me grab something around the corner and I'll be right back. We have to talk."

"Sure," she said.

I went to the nearest deli and came back with a ham sandwich and a large container of coffee. Carolyn had a small brown dog on the grooming table. It kept making a sort of whimpering noise.

"Make yourself comfortable," she told me. "And is it all right if I finish up Alison while we talk? I'd like to be done with her."

"Go right ahead," I said. "Why's she making that noise?"

"I don't know," she said, "but I wish she'd stop. If she does it while the judge is looking her over, I think her owner can forget about Best of Breed."

"And what breed would that be?"

"She's either a Norfolk terrier or a Norwich terrier, and I can never remember which is which."

"And her name's Alison? No clue there."

"That's her call name," she said. "The name on her papers is Alison Wanda Land."

"I think I know why she's whimpering."

"Maybe it's because she misses her littermate, who didn't come in today because she's not scheduled to be shown this weekend. *Her* call name just happens to be Trudy, so do you want to guess what it says on her AKC registration?"

"It can't be Trudy Logan Glass."

"Wanna bet?"

I shuddered, then straightened up in my seat. "Look," I said, "go on fluffing Alison, but while you do I want to tell you what happened last night."

"No need, Bern."

"Huh?"

"Really," she said, "what makes you think you have to do that? You were the one who was doing all the drinking at the Bum Rap. I know I'm apt to have a blackout once in a while, but last night I didn't have enough booze to feel a glow, much less wipe out a few thousand brain cells. I remember everything up until the time you left, and there's nothing to remember after that because all I did was go to sleep."

"I want to tell you what happened to me."

"You went straight home."

"Right. And then I went out again."

"Oh, no. Bern—"

"Look, just let me tell it all the way through," I said. "Then we'll talk."

"I just don't get it," she said. "You worked so hard, Bern. You did everything possible to keep from breaking into the Gilmartin apartment."

"I know."

"And then, purely on the spur of the moment—"

"I know."

"It's not as if you had any reason to think there'd be anything there worth stealing. For all you knew, the Nugents didn't have a pot or a window."

"I know."

"And you were already through for the night. You were home safe in your own apartment."

"I know."

" 'I know, I know, I know.' So why did you do it?"

"I don't know."

"Bern—"

"Call it a character defect," I said, "or a mental

lapse, or temporary insanity. Maybe I was still a little bit drunk and all that coffee kept me from feeling it. All I can say is it seemed like a gift from the gods. I'd been a good boy, I'd resisted irresistible temptation, and they'd repaid me by sending a beautiful woman to lead me to an apartment just there for the taking."

"Figure she set you up?"

"First thing I thought of. Matter of fact, the possibility occurred to me before I even put my picks in my pocket."

"But you went anyway."

"Well, how could it have been a setup? She'd have had to know I was a burglar, and she'd have had to know I was going to be on that particular subway."

"Maybe she was on it herself. Maybe she'd been following you."

"All day? It doesn't seem very likely. And I don't think she was on the train, because I would have noticed her. She's the kind of woman you notice."

"Beautiful, huh?"

"Close enough. An easy eight on a ten scale."

"And she just happened to ask you to walk her home, and then she just happened to mention that Joan and Harlan were in Europe."

"I don't think she followed me," I said, "but she could have gone out to buy a quart of milk, say, and spotted me coming out of the subway. She said she recognized me from having seen me around the neighborhood, but I don't remember seeing her, so maybe she made that up. Suppose she knew I was a burglar, and she spotted me, so she got me to walk her home."

"If that was her home," she said. "Stay," she told Alison Wanda, and looked in the White Pages. "Cardamom . . . Chesapeake . . . Collier. Here we are, Cooper. . . . I don't see a Gwendolyn Cooper. There's a lot of G Coopers, and there's one at 910 West End, but that would have to be way uptown. What's the address of the Nugents' building?"

"Three-oh-four."

"Nope. I don't see any Coopers at that address."

"Maybe she spells it with a K."

"Like Kountry Kupboard? Let's see. . . . Gee, people really do spell it with a K, don't they? But not our Doll. Still, what does it prove? She could have an unlisted number, or she could be subletting or sharing an apartment with somebody, and the phone could be in another name."

"She knew the doorman."

"It sounds to me as though he's easy to know. You knew him, too, remember?"

"Good point," I said. "He's not the Maginot Line. She could have gotten past him whether she belonged in the building or not. But then where would she go?"

"The Nugent apartment."

"A quick entrance and exit? Maybe. Or she could have killed time in a stairwell waiting for me to go home and then just walked out herself. 'Bye, Eddie.' 'Hey, how ya doin'.' Piece of cake." I frowned. "But what's the point?"

"To set you up."

"To set me up to do what? Carolyn, any other night of my life I would have gone home and stayed home. Never mind that I've given up burglary. Say I was still an active burglar, even a hyperactive one. It's the middle of the night, and a mysterious stranger has just managed to let me know that the occupants of a particular apartment are out of town. What am I going to do?"

"You tell me."

"At the very least," I said, "I'm going to sleep on it. In the cold light of dawn I might do a little research, and if it looks extremely promising I might knock it off a day or two down the line. Probably in the early afternoon, when visitors look a whole lot less suspicious. Most likely, though, I'd wake up and decide to forget the whole thing. But the one thing I would never do is go in that very night."

"But you did."

"But I did," I acknowledged, "but how could she know I would?"

"Maybe she reads minds, Bern."

"Maybe she does. Maybe she read mine and saw that I was out of it. So she set me up, and I went for it. What's in it for her?"

"I don't know, Bern."

"Was I supposed to get caught in the Nugent

apartment? God knows I was a sitting duck. Ordinarily I get in and out of a place as quickly as I can, but not this time. If I'd stayed there much longer I could have claimed squatter's rights. If she'd tipped the police, they'd have had me dead to rights. The state troopers could have come on foot from Albany and got there before I left."

"Maybe you were supposed to do something inside the apartment."

"What?"

"I don't know."

"Neither do I. Whatever it was, I didn't do it. All I did in Apartment 9-G was kill time. I brought some groceries in and I took some groceries out."

"And gave your groceries a shake-shake-shake and turned yourself about."

"Turned myself inside out is more like it. When I saw the corpse in the bathtub—"

"Who was he, Bern?"

"Not Harlan or Joan."

"Well, I didn't think he was Joan."

"In this day and age," I said, "you never know. But there was a picture of the Nugents in Harlan's study, and the dead guy wasn't either of them. There were other pictures around the house, Nugent children and grandchildren, and he didn't turn up in any of the pictures. Probably not a long-lost relative, either, because I couldn't detect any family resemblance." I frowned. "There was something vaguely familiar about him, but I couldn't tell you what it was."

"What did he look like?"

"Mostly he looked naked and dead."

"Well, that explains it. You must have recognized him from a Norman Mailer novel."

I gave her a look. "I'd guess he was in his thirties," I said. "Dark hair, cut short and combed forward like Julius Caesar."

"No stab wounds, though."

"No, just a bullet hole in the forehead." I closed my eyes, trying to picture him. "He was thin," I said, "but muscular. A lot of dark body hair. His eyes were wide open, but I can't remember what color they were. I didn't really spend a lot of time looking at him."

"What was he doing there, Bern?"

"By the time I saw him," I said, "he wasn't doing much of anything."

"Maybe he was just looking for a place to kill himself," she said, "and he didn't have the price of a hotel room. So he broke in—"

"Through a Poulard lock?"

"It didn't stop you. All right, say he had a key. He got in, he took off all his clothes . . . Where were his clothes, Bern?"

"I guess he must have given them to the Goodwill. I certainly didn't run across them."

"Well, forget the clothes. He took 'em off, we

know that much, and then he got in the tub. Why the tub?"

"Who knows?"

"He got in the tub and shot himself. No, first he locked the bathroom door, and then he got in the tub, and then he drew the shower curtain shut, and *then* he shot himself."

"High time, too."

"But why, Bern?"

"That's the least of it. My question is, how did he do it? I suppose you could shoot yourself in the middle of the forehead if you put your mind to it. You could always use your thumb on the trigger. But wouldn't it be more natural to put the gun to your temple or stick it in your mouth?"

"The natural thing," she said, "would be to go on living."

"The thing is," I said, "I didn't see a gun. Now, I didn't go looking for one, either, and if he was standing up when he shot himself it's entirely possible that he dropped the gun inside the tub and then fell so that his body was concealing it. But it's also possible that there was no gun in the tub, or anywhere in the room."

"If there was no gun—"

"Then somebody else shot him."

"Doll Cooper?"

"Maybe," I said, "but there are eight million other people in town who could just as easily have done it. Either of the Nugents, for example, which would have given them a good reason to get on a plane."

"You think they did it?"

"I don't have a clue who did it," I told her. "It could have been anybody."

"Not you or me, Bern. We can alibi each other. We were together all evening."

"Except I don't know when he was killed. I don't know any of that forensic stuff about rigor mortis and lividity, and I didn't want to touch him to find out how cold he felt. He didn't smell too great, but corpses don't, even if they're fairly fresh. Remember the time a guy died in my store?"

"How could I forget? That was in the john, too."

"So it was."

"And we moved the body in a wheelchair. Yeah, I remember. He hadn't been dead long at all, and he wasn't too fragrant, was he?"

"No."

"So we can't alibi each other," she said. "That's a hell of a thing. How do you know we didn't do it?"

"Well, I know *I* didn't. It's the sort of thing I would remember. And I know you didn't because you're not the type."

"That's a relief."

"And that's all I have to know," I said, "because it's not my problem. Because I was never there."

"Huh?"

"I took no snapshots and left no footprints," I said. "Or fingerprints. Or cereal boxes. Nobody saw me enter and nobody saw me leave, unless you count Steady Eddie, and I don't. I took away everything I brought with me and put back everything I took. I even locked up after myself."

"You always do."

"Well, how much trouble is it? If I can pick a lock open, I ought to be able to pick it shut. And it's good policy. The longer it takes people to realize they've been burgled, the harder it is to catch the guy who did it."

"So you left everything exactly as you found it."

I didn't say anything.

"Bern? You left everything exactly as you found it, right?"

"I wouldn't say 'everything,' " I said. "I wouldn't say 'exactly.' "

"What do you mean?"

I reached out a hand and ruffled Alison's coat. She made that whimpering sound again. "I kept the money," I said.

"Bern."

"Well, I was going to put it back," I said, "and then I remembered that I'd taken off my gloves to count it, because if I was taking the money it hardly mattered if I got my prints on it. So I would have had to wipe off every single bill, and I'd have had to be thorough about it, and then I'd have had to pick the lock on the desk drawer, once to open it and a second time to close it again."

"So you took it."

"Well, I'd already taken it. What I did was keep it."

"Eight thousand dollars?"

"Close enough. Eighty-three fifty."

"And how long were you in there? Four hours? Call it two thousand dollars an hour. That sure beats minimum wage."

"Believe me," I said, "it wasn't worth it. I only kept the money because it was less trouble than putting it back. And it was pretty close to untraceable. The watches and the jewelry might lead back to the Nugent apartment, but money's just money." I shrugged. "I suppose I should have put it back, even if it meant wiping off each and every bill. But it was late and all I wanted to do was get out of there."

"But you took time to pick the locks. The ones on the outer door I can understand, but why lock up the bathroom? It took you forever to open that lock, and it must have been just as much trouble to relock it."

"Not quite. Locking's easier than unlocking with that particular mechanism, and I'd already made some surface grooves in the bolt the first time around. But it still took some time, I'll say that much."

"Then why bother?"

"Think about it," I said. "Say the cops come and they have to break the door down. They find a corpse in the tub with a gun alongside him. One little window, and it's locked, and so was the door until they forced it. If you're one of the cops, what conclusion do you draw?"

"Suicide," she said. "It couldn't be anything else. Bern? Wait a minute."

"I'm waiting."

"Suppose there's no gun."

"So?"

"Then it's not suicide, is it?"

I shook my head. "It's not," I said, "and what you've got is a locked-room homicide straight out of John Dickson Carr, and I'll be damned if I can figure out how the killer could have worked it. Now, I don't honestly think that's what happened, because it would have been impossible. I think the gun must have been out of sight somewhere, behind the body or underneath it. If it was suicide, I'd just as soon leave it as open-and-shut as possible. And if it was murder, some physically impossible kind of locked-room murder, why should I be the one to screw it up? Because if the door's open when the cops get there, then it's just another naked corpse in the bathtub. There's nothing special about it at all."

"I see what you mean."

"So that's why I locked up," I said, "and there may well be a flaw in my logic, but I was too worn out to spot it. The bathroom lock was easier to manipulate the second time around, but it was still a real pain in the neck, and it took time. Do you want to know something? I felt justified keeping the eighty-three fifty. I worked hard for it. I figure I earned it."

I chased the last bite of my sandwich with the last swallow of coffee and put the wrappings and the empty cup in the trash. Then I returned to watch Carolyn put the finishing touches on Alison Wanda's coiffure. "You must be exhausted after a night like that," she said. "I'm surprised you bothered to open up today."

"Well, Patience called, and that woke me up. And I had to come down and feed Raffles."

"Don't bother," she said. "When I saw you hadn't opened, I used my set of keys and gave him food and fresh water."

"When was that?"

"I don't know, eleven o'clock, something like that. Why?"

"Because he gave a damn good imitation of a cat on the brink of starvation when I opened up a little after twelve."

"You fed him again?"

"Of course I fed him again. His dish was spotless and he was wearing a hole in my sock."

"You're not supposed to overfeed them, Bern."

"Thanks," I said. "I'll keep that in mind."

I went back to Barnegat Books and opened up again. Raffles was rubbing against my ankle the minute my foot cleared the threshold.

"Yeah, right," I told him. "In your dreams, pal."

I hauled my bargain table outside and propped up the cardboard three-books-for-a-buck sign. Sometimes passersby lifted the odd volume, but at that price how much harm were they doing me? I'd have been more dismayed if one of them walked off with the sign.

I perched on my stool behind the counter and picked up my current book, *Clan of the Cave Bear.* (I'd read it once years ago, but if you don't think books are worth reading more than once you've got no business running a used-book store.) I still hadn't read the paper I'd bought when I got off the subway the night before, but neither had I brought it along when I left the apartment. That was just as well, because I didn't much want to know what was happening in the world. I was a lot more comfortable reading about a Cro-Magnon child being brought up by a couple of Neanderthals, which wasn't all that different from the way I remembered my own childhood.

Around two o'clock I made my first sale. It was only a buck but it broke the ice, and by three I'd rung up something like fifty dollars on the cash register. You don't get rich that way, you don't even break even that way, but at least I was selling books. And I suppose the cat could take credit for those sales, because if I hadn't had to feed him I wouldn't have bothered opening up.

And, like it or not, I was $8,350 ahead for having

dropped in on the Nugents. And I could do what I wanted with the money and forget what I'd gone through to earn it, because that chapter was over forever and I was in the clear.

Yeah, right. In your dreams, Bernie.

8

Trade picked up as the afternoon wore on, with a steady stream of people finding their way in and out of the shop. A number of them were just browsing, but I'm used to that; it is, after all, part of what a secondhand bookstore is all about. So is chitchat, and I got involved in a little of that, including a spirited discussion of what modern New York might have been like if the Dutch had retained their footing in the New World. My partner in that particular conversation was an elderly gentleman with a neat white beard and piercing blue eyes who had been browsing in the Old New York section, and damned if he didn't wind up spending close to two hundred dollars before he left.

As soon as he was out the door, a big man in a dark gray sharkskin suit drifted over to the counter and rested a meaty forearm on it. "Well, now," he said. "I got to hand it to you, Bernie. This place is turnin' into a regular literary saloon."

"Hello, Ray," I said. "Always a pleasure."

"That was real interestin'," he said. "What you an' Santa Claus there were talkin' about."

"Don't you think he was a little thin for Santa?"

"He'll fill out, same as everybody else. An' there's plenty of time. How many shoppin' days until Christmas?"

"I can never keep track."

"How about burglin' days, Bernie? How many of those between now an' when Santa pops in through the skylight?"

"Don't you mean down the chimney?"

"Whatever, Bernie. You'd be the expert on that, wouldn't you?" He flashed a grin that made the sharkskin suit seem singularly appropriate. "But it makes you think, what you an' the old guy were talkin' about. We could be standin' here, the both of us, an' we could be talkin' back an' forth in Dutch."

"We could."

"All these books'd be in Dutch, huh? I couldn't read a one of 'em. Of course, if I was talkin' Dutch with you, I guess I'd be able to read it, too. I'd have to if I was studyin' for the Sergeant's Exam, say, because all the questions'd be in Dutch." He frowned. "An' instead of cabdrivers who can't understand English, you'd get cabdrivers who couldn't understand Dutch, an' either way nine out of ten of 'em wouldn't know how to get to Penn Station. Be a whole new ball game, wouldn't it?"

"It would."

"But it sure is interestin', Bern. I was this close to hornin' in on your conversation, but then I figured why louse up a sale for you? You're a bookseller, you're well on your way to becomin' a literary saloon keeper, what do you need with a cop buttin' in and crampin' your style?"

"What indeed?"

He propped an elbow on the counter, placed his chin in his cupped hand. "You know, Bernie," he said, "you were talkin' a blue streak with Santa, an' now it's all you can do to hold up your end of the conversation. I see you got yourself a cat, stretched out in the window there tryin' to get hisself a tan. He got your tongue or somethin'?"

"No."

"Then how come I can't get a thing out of you but yes, no, an' maybe?"

"I'm not sure," I said. "Maybe it's because I'm trying to figure out what you're doing here, Ray."

"Bern," he said, looking hurt. "I thought we were friends."

"I suppose we are, but your friendly visits tend to have an ulterior motive."

He nodded. " 'Ulterior.' I always liked that word. You never hear it without hearin' 'motive' right after it. What's it mean, anyway?"

"I don't know," I admitted, and reached for the dictionary. There's a three-foot shelf of them in the Reference section, but I keep one close at hand,

and I flipped through it now. " 'Ulterior,' " I read. " 'One: lying beyond or on the farther side.' "

"Like the cat," he suggested. "Lyin' on the farther side of that row of shelves."

" 'Two: later, subsequent, or future. Three: further; more remote; esp., beyond what is expressed, implied, or evident; undisclosed, as an ulterior motive.' "

"Yeah," he said, nodding. "That sounds about right. Anyway, that's what you think, huh? That I got one of those?"

"Don't you?"

"Maybe I do," he said, "an' then again maybe I don't. It all depends how you answer a question."

"What's the question?"

"What the hell's the matter with you, Bernie? Are you losin' it?"

"That's the question?"

"No," he said, "that ain't the question. It's just the kind of thoughts go through the mind of a guy that's known you a long time, an' never yet knew you to make a habit of steppin' on your own dick. So that ain't the question. Here's the question."

"I can't wait."

"Why'd you call the guy?"

"What guy, Ray?"

" 'What guy, Ray?' I don't even need to check my notebook, because it's the kind of name tends to stick in your mind. Martin Gilmartin, that's what guy. Why the hell did you call him on the phone last night?"

There was suddenly a sinking feeling in the pit of my stomach, as if I'd somehow got hold of a bad burrito. "I don't know what you're talking about," I said.

I couldn't have been very convincing, because Ray Kirschmann didn't even trouble to roll his eyes. "I won't ask you why you broke into his place," he said, "anymore'n I'd ask that cat over there why he catches mice. It's his nature. He's a cat, same as you're a burglar."

"I'm retired."

"Yeah, right, Bernie. You could no more retire from bein' a burglar than he could retire from bein' a cat. It's your nature, it's what you are. So you don't have to explain why you robbed the guy's apartment. But why did you call him up afterward and taunt him about it?"

"Who says I did?"

"*He* says you did. Are you saying you didn't?"

"What else does he say?"

"That at first he didn't know what to make of it. Then he took a good look around the apartment, and he found out he'd been robbed."

"That's the second time you've used that word," I said, "and you should know better. You know what robbery is. It's the taking of money or property through force or violence, or the threat of force or violence."

"Here I am," he said, "back at the Academy, listenin' to a lecture."

"Well, it's maddening," I said. " 'He found out he'd been robbed.' You can't find out you've been robbed because you're aware of it while it's going on. Somebody sticks a gun in your face and tells you to give him your money or he'll blow your head off, *that's* robbery. I never robbed anyone in my life."

"You done, Bern?"

"I'm sorry," I said, "but words mean a lot to me. How did Mr. Gilmartin discover he'd been burglarized?"

"His property was missing."

"What kind of property?"

"As if you didn't know."

"Humor me, Ray."

"His baseball cards."

"Oh, for God's sake," I said. "What do you bet his mother threw them out?"

"Bernie—"

"That's what happened to mine. I came home from college and they were gone, and when I blew up she stood there and quoted St. Paul at me. Something about putting away childish things."

"Mr. Gilmartin had quite the collection."

"So did I," I remembered. "I had a ton of comic books, too. I liked the ones that taught you something about history. *Crime Does Not Pay,* that was my favorite."

"A shame you never got the message."

"As far as I could make out," I said, "the message seemed to be that crime paid just fine until the last frame. She threw out my comic books, too. You know something? It still bothers me."

"Bernie—"

"So I can imagine how Mr. Gilmartin must feel, and I'm not saying it was his mother who did it, but I think he ought to rule out the possibility before he goes around accusing other people. I can tell you one thing for sure, Ray. I had nothing to do with it."

"You denyin' that you called him last night?"

How could he possibly have known about the phone call?

"Maybe it's not a good idea for me to confirm or deny anything," I said slowly. "Maybe I ought to talk to my lawyer first."

"You know," he said, "that's probably exactly what you ought to do. Tell you what, Bern. I'll read you your Miranda rights, an' then you an' me'll head over to Central Bookin', an' we'll see about gettin' you mugged an' printed. Then you can give Wally Hemphill a call. If he ain't doin' laps around Central Park, maybe he can help you decide what to remember about last night."

"Don't read me my rights."

"You remember 'em from last time, huh? It don't matter, Bern. I gotta go by the book."

With the marathon coming up, Wally might not

be that easy to get hold of. Who else could I call, Doll Cooper?

"I guess there's no reason not to talk," I said slowly. "Since I didn't do anything wrong, why not clear the air?"

He smiled, looking more like a shark than ever.

First I locked the door and hung the "Back in Ten Minutes" sign in the window. I didn't want customers to disturb us while I straightened things out with Ray, and I could use a minute or two to get my thoughts in order.

On the one hand, it was ridiculous to get mugged and printed and thrown in a holding cell for a couple of hours for a crime that I'd had nothing to do with. At the same time, I had to be careful what I said or I'd simply be swapping the Gilmartin skillet for the Nugent bonfire.

I bought myself a few extra seconds by freshening the water in Raffles' bowl. I was tempted to feed him again while I was at it, and I don't suppose he would have given me an argument, but he'd already had one extra meal that day. At this rate his mousing days would soon be over.

"All right," I told Ray. "I'm ready to talk now."

"You sure you don't want to take a little time to rearrange the stock on your shelves?"

I ignored that. "I called Gilmartin," I said. "I admit it."

"Well, hallelujah."

"But it had nothing to do with a burglary. I really have retired, Ray, whether you're prepared to believe it or not. Look, I'd better start at the beginning."

"Why not?"

"Carolyn and I went out after work yesterday," I said.

"You always do," he said. "The Bum Rap, right?"

I nodded. "I've been under a little pressure lately," I said, "and I guess I let it get to me. The long and short of it is I had more to drink than I usually do."

"Hey, it happens."

"It does," I agreed, "but not to me, not that often, and I wasn't used to it. I got silly."

"Silly?"

"You know. Playful, goofy."

"I bet it was somethin' to see."

"You should have been there. Anyway, Carolyn and I spent the whole evening together. From the Bum Rap we went to an Italian restaurant for dinner, and then we went back to her place on Arbor Court. That's where I was when I called Mr. Gilmartin."

He nodded, as if I'd just passed some sort of test.

"I don't know how it started," I went on. "I was still a little drunk, I guess, and I got into this routine where I was finding funny names in the telephone book. I was picking out names and reading them aloud to Carolyn and making jokes."

"The two of you were makin' fun of people's names, Bern?"

"It was mostly my doing," I said, "and I'm not proud of it, but what can I say? It happened. Somehow or other the name Geraldine Fitzgerald came up. Remember her? She was a singer years ago."

"Is that a fact."

"Anyway, I said her name sounded to me like a recipe for a perfect relationship. Get it? Geraldine fits Gerald."

"Geraldine Fitzgerald," he said. "So?"

"Geraldine. Fits. Gerald."

"That's what I just said. What the hell's supposed to be so funny about that?"

"I guess you had to be there. I couldn't find a Geraldine Fitzgerald in the phone book, but I found a Gerald Fitzgerald, and I thought that was pretty funny."

"Yeah, it's a riot. Wha'd you do, call the guy up?"

A little warning bell went off. "I did," I said, "but nobody was home. So I flipped through the phone book some more, looking for doubled names like that."

"William Williams," he suggested. "John Johnson."

"Well, sort of, but the ones you just mentioned aren't particularly funny."

"Not real thigh-slappers like Gerald Fitzgerald."

"I know it doesn't seem all that amusing," I said, "when you're sober, but I wasn't. Eventually I found

Martin Gilmartin, and for some reason I thought that one was a real screamer. I should have known better, it was too late to call anybody, let alone a total stranger, but I picked up the phone and called him. He answered the phone, and I made some sort of joke about his name, real high-school humor, I'm ashamed to say."

"Did he get a good chuckle out of it, Bern?"

"He seemed a little flustered, so I joked with him some more and then hung up."

"Just like that."

"Pretty much, yeah."

"How'd you know he and his wife went to a play?"

Jesus. "Is that where they were? I knew he was out somewhere because I tried him a few times before I finally got an answer."

"Oh, yeah? Why'd you keep callin'?"

"Well, they make it easy these days," I said. "Carolyn's phone has this button that automatically redials the last number."

"A real time-saver."

"So when I finally got through," I said, "I guess I said something about being glad he was home, and I hoped he'd had a good evening. You know, some kind of smartass remark. But I didn't say anything about a play."

He let that pass. "Gilmartin says it was after midnight when you called."

"I would have said a few minutes before midnight," I said, "but I'll take his word for it. So?"

"What did you do after that? Call some more people?"

"No," I said. "Actually completing a call made me realize what a childish thing I was doing. Besides, it was late and I was tired."

"You stay the night at Carolyn's?"

"No, I went home."

"And you never left your house until morning, right?"

Uh-oh. "That's right," I said.

"You got home around one, musta been, and then you didn't set foot outside your apartment until you came down here and opened up earlier today."

"Right," I said. And just as he was about to say something I added, "Except for going to the store."

"When would that have been, Bernie?"

"Oh, I don't know. I don't remember noticing the time. I put the TV on and watched CNN for a little while, then realized I was out of milk for the morning. I went out and got a few things from the deli. Why?"

"Just curious."

"Well, I'm curious, too," I said. "According to what you said, Gilmartin got off the phone with me and went looking for his comic books and his Captain Midnight decoder ring."

"Just his baseball cards, Bern."

"You mean he didn't keep all his boyhood treasures in the same place? Never mind. Wherever he kept them, he looked for them and they were gone. Correct?"

"So?"

"They were gone then, right? At midnight or twelve-thirty or whenever it was, right?"

"What's the point, Bern?"

"The point," I said, "is that his baseball cards were already gone when I talked to him, so what possible difference could it make if I went to the deli at one or one-thirty in the morning?"

"If it don't make no difference," he said, "why did you have to go and lie about it?"

"Lie about it?"

"Well, what else would you call it?" He took out a pocket notebook, consulted a page. "You left your house at one-thirty. You got back at twenty minutes of six. That's better'n four hours, Bern. Where was this deli, Riverdale?"

"I guess I must have made another stop," I said. "On my way home from the deli."

"And it slipped your mind until this minute."

"No, it's been on my mind since the questioning started, and I didn't want to have to talk about it. I've been seeing someone, Ray."

"Oh, yeah? Anybody I know?"

"No, and you're not going to meet her, either. Look, you're a man of the world, Ray."

"This is gonna be a good one, isn't it?"

"She's married," I said. "We've had to sneak

around and grab moments when we can. Last night was one of those moments."

"I'm ashamed of you, Bernie."

"Well, I'm not proud of it myself, Ray, but—"

"Ashamed of you, trottin' out an oldie like that. You wouldn't want to give me her name, would you?"

"Ray, you know I can't do that."

"Too much of a gentleman, huh?"

"Ray, common decency requires—"

He held up a hand. "Spare me," he said. "You didn't go visit no woman last night, married or single. What you did, leavin' your place on the sly in the middle of the night, is you took the baseball cards you already stole from Martin Gilmartin—"

"See?" I demanded. "It *is* a silly name, drunk or sober."

"—an' you took 'em to a fence, an' you sold 'em. As far as when you broke into the Gilmartin place to steal 'em, my guess is it was sometime last night, because it was yesterday you had the argument with your landlord." He made a face. "Don't sputter like that, Bernie. If you got somethin' to say, go ahead an' say it. You gonna tell me you didn't have no trouble with the landlord?"

"We had a heated discussion about books," I said. "But you expect that sort of thing in a literary saloon. Anyway, his name is Stoppelgard."

"Borden Stoppelgard."

"So what has he got to do with Marty Gilmartin and baseball cards?"

"Gilmartin's married."

"Well, I swear it wasn't his wife I was in bed with last night."

"His wife's name is Edna."

"That's an okay name," I said. "Edna Gilmartin. Nothing the least bit funny about that."

"How about Edna Stoppelgard? What's that do for your funny bone?"

When Cornwallis was about to surrender his troops to George Washington at Yorktown, he ordered the band to play a tune called "The World Turned Upside Down." If I'd had a tape of it lying around I would have played it.

"Wait a minute," I said. "Gilmartin's wife used to be married to Stoppelgard?"

"Couldn't happen," he said. "There's a law against it. Although I suppose there's ways of gettin' around it, don't you figure?"

"Ways of getting around what?"

"The law against marryin' your own sister, but why would you want to? The only plus I can see is you wouldn't be arguin' every year about do you spend Christmas with your parents or hers." He shook his head. "Borden Stoppelgard is Martin Gilmartin's brother-in-law."

"You're making this up."

"All news to you, huh, Bernie? Nice try. Here's more news. Last night the Stoppelgards an' the

Gilmartins all went to the theater together, to see something about wishin' for horses. Then they all went out for supper, an' your name came up. Seems Stoppelgard was crowin' about the good deal he got on a rare book you sold him, an' how the prices'd be even better when you had your Goin'-Outta-Business sale."

"He said that, did he?"

"Then Gilmartin an' his wife went home, an' he got the call from you, but at the time he didn't know who it was. Even without knowin' it was you, first thought he had was somebody broke in, and the first thing he went an' looked for was his baseball card collection, an' it was gone."

"So he called the police."

"That's just what he did, an' the desk sent a couple of blue uniforms over, an' they took a report. It landed on my desk this mornin', an' I mighta let it lay there except he called up, an' the call got routed to me, an' I smelled somethin' funny."

"Somebody got a bad burrito," I suggested.

"He told me about the phone call," he said, "an' I figured any burglar'd be smart enough to make a call like that from a phone where it couldn't be traced back to him. But you learn to check these things out, because a burglar who's dumb enough to make that kind of call in the first place might be just stupid enough to make it from a friend's apartment, especially if the friend in question's a sawed-off little dyke who spends her life givin' poodles a shave an' a haircut."

"It's funny," I said, "the way you and Carolyn never did get along. Ray, I already admitted I made the phone call, so what's the big deal?"

"The big deal is I tried out your name on Gilmartin, an' he recognized it right away from his talk with his brother-in-law. 'I know who that is,' he says. 'He's a bookseller, an' not a very good one, either.' I tell him I know you, too, an' that ain't all you are. 'He's also a burglar,' I say, 'and there I'd have to say he's one of the best in the business.' "

"Thanks for the endorsement, Ray."

"Well, credit where credit's due."

"But if I'm such a high-level burglar—"

"One of the best, Bern. You always were."

"—then why would I waste my talents on a cigar box full of baseball cards?"

"More like a shoe box, according to Gilmartin."

"I don't care if it was a packing crate. For God's sake, Ray, these are little pieces of cardboard smelling of bubble gum. We're not talking about the Elgin Marbles."

"Marbles," he said. "That's what my mom got rid of, God rest her soul. I had a huge sack of 'em, too. I don't know if I had any Elgins, but I had a real nice collection."

"Ray—"

"Baseball cards aren't kid stuff anymore, Bernie.

Grown-ups buy 'em an' sell 'em. They're hot with investors these days."

"Like Sue Grafton."

"Does she collect 'em? I just read one book of hers, an' it wasn't bad. It was set on an army base durin' war game maneuvers."

"*'K' Is for Rations.*"

"Somethin' like that, yeah."

"I know some of the scarce cards are worth money," I said. "There's one famous one. Honus Wagner, right? And the card's worth a thousand dollars, maybe more."

"A thousand dollars."

"In perfect shape," I said. "If it's all beat up from flipping it against the wall, well, it would be worth a lot less."

He looked at the notebook again. "Honus Wagner," he announced. "Hall of Fame shortstop for the Pittsburgh Pirates. Back in 1910 they went an' put his picture on a card, except back then they gave 'em out in cigarette packs instead of bubble gum."

"But he didn't smoke," I recalled. "And he didn't want to have a bad influence on kids."

"So he made 'em withdraw the card, an' that's why it's so scarce today. You're a little low, though, when you peg it at a thousand bucks."

"Well, I was low on *'B' Is for Burglar,* too. What's it worth?"

"They auctioned one a couple of years back," he said, "an' it went for $451,000. Accordin' to Gilmartin, it'd bring well over a million in today's market. You honestly didn't know that, Bernie?"

"I didn't," I said, "and I'm not sure I believe it. A million dollars? For a baseball card?"

"The T-206 card. There's other Honus Wagner cards, not advertisin' cigarettes, an' they're not worth anythin' like that kind of dough."

"And Gilmartin had a T-206?"

"No."

"He didn't? Then who cares? Ray—"

"But he had lots of other good cards," he said. "He had the Topps 1952 set, with Mickey Mantle's rookie card. An' he had a lot of Ted Williams an' Babe Ruth an' Joe DiMaggio cards. I wouldn't mind havin' a card with Joe D on it, I got to admit it."

"If I ever get one," I said, "I'll swap you straight up for the Elgin Marbles."

"You got a deal, Bern. But the point is, Gilmartin didn't have Honus Wagner, but what he had was probably worth a lot more than what your mother gave to the sisterhood rummage sale. He had the whole lot insured for half a million dollars."

"Half a million dollars."

"An' he says it's worth more than that. That's why I was hopin' you took his cards, Bernie. We could do a little business, do us both some good. An' you took 'em all right, you poor sap, but you didn't know what you had. You took 'em sometime between eight o'clock an' midnight, an' you went out in the middle of the night to visit one of those wide receivers you know an' sold 'em cheap. You an' me, Bernie, we coulda done a deal with the insurance company an' split a hundred grand between us. I'll bet you didn't bring home a tenth of that last night."

"I didn't take the cards, Ray."

"You took 'em," he said. "You were mad at Stoppelgard. You prolly followed him to the Gilmartin place, an' then when they all went to the theater you went right in. You got back at Stoppelgard by knockin' off Gilmartin, an' you got in quick an' grabbed the first thing you saw that looked like it might be worth somethin'. An' instead of takin' the time an' trouble to find out what you had, you dumped 'em fast an' screwed yourself good." He sighed. "You got one chance of gettin' outta this clean. Have you got the cards?"

"No."

"Can you get them?"

"No."

"That's what I was afraid of," he said heavily. "Well, in that case, I got a card for you. Where'd I put the damn thing? Here we go. 'You have the right to remain silent. You have the right to consult an attorney. If you do not have an attorney . . .' "

9

"Before I forget," Wally Hemphill said, "I called your therapist. So that's one thing you don't have to worry about."

"Thanks," I said. "What therapist?"

"Patience Tremaine."

"*You* called her? I asked Carolyn to call her."

"Well, Carolyn asked me to call her, so I did. I told her Mr. Rhodenbarr had to cancel his eight o'clock appointment, and he'd be calling to reschedule as soon as he was able."

"That's what you told her, huh?"

"Right, I kept it crisp and professional. I've got to say she seems to take more of a personal interest in her clients than most of the shrinks I've known."

"She's not exactly a shrink," I said. "She's a poetry therapist."

"Oh, yeah? You been having trouble with your poems, Bernie?" He looked puzzled, then shrugged it away. "She seemed more concerned about your digestion than anything else. Something about knishes and burritos."

"Oh."

"But I cleared everything up for her. I explained that the cops had you in a holding pen charged with burglary, but that I was on my way to get a writ and I expected to have you out on bail in a couple of hours. Did I say something wrong?"

"Oh, I don't know, Wally. Don't you think you may have been overly discreet?"

"Bernie, she's your therapist, right? Obviously she knows your history and what you do for a living. How else could you expect to get anywhere in therapy?"

"How indeed?"

"Though she did seem taken aback, come to think of it. Maybe she was upset that you were actually arrested and charged with a crime."

"That must be it."

"People outside of the criminal justice system, they don't realize that's all part of the deal. Anyway, she'll be waiting for you to call."

"With bated breath, I'll bet. Wally, she's not my therapist. She's a woman I had a couple of dates with."

"Oh."

"We were just starting to get to know each other," I said. "As far as she knew, I was just a bookseller with a slight case of Delhi Belly. She had no idea I was a burglar."

"Well, she's got a pretty good idea now," he said. "Bernie, I'm sorry as all hell. I guess I really stepped in it."

"Forget it."

"Were you, uh, sleeping with her?"

"No," I said, "but I had hopes."

"Rats. I'm sorry, I really am. But hey, you'll call her in a day or two and you'll think of something to say."

"And so will she. Hers'll probably be something along the lines of 'Lose my number, asshole.' "

"I don't know," he said. "Talking to her, she didn't seem like the kind of girl to use bad language. Outside of that, you're probably right."

" 'If you do not have an attorney,' " Ray had intoned, " 'one will be provided for you.' "

Fortunately, that hadn't been necessary. I had an attorney. You can hardly be in business without one these days, and this is doubly true if your business comes under the broad heading of felonies and misdemeanors. You really need a lawyer you can call your own, and he ought to be the kind you have to pay. I'm sure the fellows and gals at Legal Aid do a commendable job for their clients, but I'm happier personally with legal counsel that's just a little more upscale.

Besides, a successful professional criminal with a Legal Aid lawyer is like a billionaire collecting So-cial Security. Maybe he's entitled to it, but so what? It's still tacky.

For years my lawyer was a man named Klein with an office on Queens Boulevard, a wife and kids in Kew Gardens, and a girlfriend in Turtle Bay, just around the corner from the United Nations. Then one day a couple of years ago I got arrested, through no real fault of my own, and when I went to call Klein I found out he was dead.

Poof, just like that.

So I called Wally Hemphill. I knew him from the park, where we would encounter each other evenings, dressed in shorts and singlets and shod in state-of-the-art running shoes. We would jog along together for a mile or so, chatting companionably about this and that, until he sped up or I slowed down. When I met him he was training for the marathon. That was several marathons ago, and he's never slowed down.

I, on the other hand, was a lot less dedicated. It's hard to remember why I started running in the first place, although it may have been a natural outgrowth of the instinct for self-preservation. It's nice to be able to run away if something takes it into its head to start chasing you. Still, I had never felt the urge to run twenty-six miles and change, or to transmute myself into a human whippet, and eventually the day came when running ceased to be one of the things I did and became instead one of the things I used to do, like reading comic books and collecting baseball cards. I still wear running shoes—they work just as well at low speeds—and I still own a few sets of running shorts and singlets, although I no longer get any use out of them. (If my mother lived with me, she'd probably throw them out.)

"I'm sorry it took so long," Wally was saying. It was a quarter after ten Saturday morning, some eighteen hours after Ray Kirschmann had read me my rights, and we were in an Ethiopian coffee shop on Chambers Street. I think the restaurant's previous owners must have been Greek, because they've still got spinach pie and moussaka on the menu.

Wally, who'd had an early breakfast before he came downtown, was working on a chocolate doughnut and a cup of coffee. I had coffee, too, along with a big glass of orange juice and a plate of scrambled eggs and salami and two slices of rye toast. Nothing builds an appetite like getting out of jail, even if you don't pass Go and collect $200.

"They were being obstructive," he explained. "Shunting you around from precinct to precinct like that so that I couldn't get you out until morning. It's a nuisance, but it's actually a good sign."

"How do you figure that?"

"What it tells me is they know they've got no case. What have they got? As far as evidence is concerned, they can demonstrate two things. One, someone called the Gilmartins from Carolyn's apartment around midnight Thursday. They can't even prove it was you that called, and the NYNEX records only show the one call that went through, so there's no indication you'd been trying the number for hours. Two, they've got your doorman's testimony that you left the building a little after one and didn't get back until just before dawn. Well, so what? Leaving aside the fact that I could tie the guy in knots on cross, they can't say you spent that time stealing Gilmartin's baseball cards, because he had already reported them missing. You don't have a working time machine, do you, Bernie?"

"I had one," I said, "but I could never get batteries for it."

"Their contention is you had the cards when you left your place and sold them during the night to person or persons unknown. But they have to do more than contend. Can they prove it?"

"No."

"Suppose they find the buyer?"

"There was no buyer, Wally."

"You know," he said, "I think I'm gonna have another of these doughnuts. You can't beat Ethiopians when it comes to doughnuts. You want one?" I shook my head. "It's good I run seventy miles a week," he said, "or I'd weigh three hundred pounds. Bernie, it might be a good idea if you beat them to the punch. Give up the fence."

"Give up the fence?"

"Rat him out."

"There was no fence," I said.

"I know it may strike you as unethical," he went on, "but standards aren't what they used to be. Even Mafia guys drop dimes on each other nowadays. Next thing they do is call their agent, set up a book deal and a miniseries. Incidentally, Bernie, when the time comes—"

"You're the guy I'll call, Wally."

"Naturally."

"Wally," I said, "there was no fence, because I never took the cards."

"Whatever you say, Bernie. Listen, if you *didn't* fence them—"

"I just said so, didn't I?"

"That case, I hope you got them someplace safe. One reason they kept you overnight was so they'd have time to get a warrant and search your apartment. They must not have found anything, because we'd know about it if they did. Wherever you put the cards—"

"I never took them."

"Bernie, I'm your attorney."

"Really? I was beginning to think you were the DA. I never took the cards. I didn't even know he had baseball cards, and they wouldn't have tempted me if I did, because who knew they were worth that kind of money?"

"I thought everybody knew. I must have a dozen

acquaintances who collect them. Lawyers, mostly. It's a great investment."

"So I understand."

"They go to dealers, spend their weekends at card shows. One woman I know never leaves her office. She sits at her desk, plugged into one of those computer bulletin boards, buying and selling as if she had a seat on the stock exchange. She pays by credit card and they Fed Ex the cards to her at the office. She walks them across the street to the bank and pops them in her safe deposit box. Her biggest hassle is deciding which client to bill her hours to. Bernie, say you did take the cards—"

"I didn't."

"This is hypothetical, okay? If you took them, or if you just happened to get hold of them, I could probably do an end run with the insurer that would include getting the charges dropped." He took a sip of coffee. "You really didn't take 'em, huh?"

"Don't tell me it's beginning to sink in."

"So why call Gilmartin?"

"If I'd just finished knocking off his apartment," I said, "that's the last thing I would have done. The thing is, I cased his apartment, and—"

"I thought you didn't know about the card collection."

"All I knew was he and his wife weren't going to be home that night. They lived in a good building in a decent neighborhood. It stood to reason I'd find something to steal."

"Makes sense."

"But I didn't go, Wally. I resisted temptation, and got a little bit tanked in the process. The real reason I called wasn't to tweak his tail, it was to make sure he and Edna were home safe so I didn't have to keep fighting the urge to pop his locks and make myself at home. When I finally reached him I joshed him a little, that's all. It seemed safe enough."

"And then you went home."

"Right."

"And then you went out again."

"Uh."

"What did you do?"

"Nothing you want to hear about, Wally."

"Bernie," he said earnestly, "I'm your attorney. Anything you tell me is a privileged communication. Anything you *don't* tell me is a potential stumbling block down the line. For instance, if you had told me that Patience Tremaine was someone you were involved with socially—"

"How could I tell you that? I never even had the chance to speak to you."

"Well, maybe that's not a good example. What did you do when you left your apartment in the middle of the night?"

"I let myself into another apartment, stole some money, and then came home."

"I wish you hadn't told me that, Bernie."

"You just said—"

"I know what I just said. I still wish you hadn't told me. When I was five years old I begged my older brother to tell me the truth about Santa Claus, and he wouldn't, and I begged and begged and begged, and finally he did, mostly to shut me up, I suppose. And the minute he did, I wished he hadn't. Nothing I could do about it, though. I knew there was no Santa Claus, and the knowledge has been with me for the rest of my life."

"It must have been awful."

"It was."

"So I guess you don't want to hear about the dead body."

"Oh my God."

"So I won't say anything."

He shook his head. "Ignorance may be bliss," he said, "but knowledge is power, and a good lawyer takes power over bliss any day. So let's hear it."

"Here's what I think will happen," he said. "They'll spend a few days investigating, and when they don't turn up anything further they'll drop all charges."

"Great."

"Unless they find out where you really went after you got home from Carolyn's. If that happens, I'd hate to be in your shoes." He paused to glance at my feet. "Saucony," he said, recognizing the logo on the shoes in question. "I almost bought a pair of those. How are they holding up?"

"They're fine. Of course, the only exercise they get is when I take them out for a walk."

"You never got back to running, huh, Bern? I don't know how you managed to stop. It's addictive, you know. They've done studies."

"I know."

"How'd you break the addiction?"

"I didn't," I said. "I just substituted another addiction for it. I found something even more addictive than running."

"What?"

"Not running," I said. "It's got to be the most addictive thing ever. Believe me, a few days of not running and I was hooked."

"I don't think it would work for me," he said. "I hope I never find out."

"Like Santa Claus."

"Right. Where was I?"

"If they find out, you'd hate to be in my Sauconys."

He nodded. "Because you won't have an alibi, and they'll have a witness or two and possibly some physical evidence, and the guy in the tub raises the stakes. A former president would say you were in deep doo-doo. His successor would probably advise you not to inhale."

"What should I do?"

"Just sit tight," he said. "Don't break into any houses."

"I wasn't planning to."

"Well, don't pull any unplanned burglaries, either. The money's not worth it. Speaking of money, Carolyn gave me ten thousand dollars."

A while back I had built a secret compartment into Carolyn's closet. It's small—you couldn't conceal a Third Cat there—but it's a perfect hiding place for money and valuables. I've always believed in maintaining a cash emergency fund, and it made sense to keep it not only where I could get hold of it, but where she'd have easy access. So I'd stashed ten grand in Carolyn's apartment, and she'd passed it on to Wally, as per my instructions.

"They wanted to set bail at half a million dollars," he said, "because that's the insurance coverage on the cards. I got that knocked down to fifty thousand, or five thousand in cash, which I posted. We'll get that back when they drop the charges. My thought is I ought to hang on to the other five as a retainer."

"Whatever you say."

"I've got to run," he said. "I'm sorry I screwed things up for you with Patience, but you can probably straighten all of that out. Just send her flowers."

"You think so?"

"They love it when you send them flowers. Don't

ask me why. You want to take care of the check? Otherwise it'll just wind up on your bill."

"I'll get it."

"Great. Don't rush, Bernie. Finish your meal. I'll be in touch."

10

I could have gone straight to the store and opened up, but not after a night in a cell. I went home and showered and shaved and put on clean clothes. So it was past noon by the time I got downtown again, and despite the act he put on I figured Raffles had already been fed. A note on the counter removed all doubt.

I dragged the bargain table outside and called the Poodle Factory. "I just opened up," I told Carolyn. "Thanks for feeding Raffles. And while I'm at it, thanks for calling Wally, and for getting the bail money to him, and for being a generally good scout."

"It's nothing, Bern."

"And thanks for calling Patience."

"Matter of fact," she said, "I got Wally to call her."

"How come?"

"I figured it would look better. Remember, I already called her once to break a date for you. If she gets two calls in a row from some woman she never met, what's she gonna think?"

"I see what you mean," I said, and explained the particular fashion in which Wally had canceled my presumed shrink appointment. "I'm not blaming you," I assured her. "You had the right idea, and so did Wally. It's just that something got lost in translation."

"You'd think I'd have enough to do," she said, "keeping my own love life constantly screwed up. You wouldn't think I'd have the time or the energy to ruin somebody else's. What can I say? I blew it, Bern."

"You broke even," I said. "You fed one cat and let another one out of the bag."

"What are you gonna say to her?"

"I haven't figured that out yet. In the meantime I sent flowers."

"Why would you do something like that?"

"Wally suggested it."

"He did? Well, what's the point of having a lawyer if you're not gonna take his advice?"

"That's what I figured."

"What kind did you send? An assortment?"

"No," I said. "I couldn't decide between cut flowers and a living plant. You know, something that would last."

"Something she'll still have long after she's forgotten ever having known you."

"That's the idea. I wound up springing for a

dozen roses and a plant, an African violet in a nice little pot."

"Red roses, I hope."

"Yes, as a matter of fact, but why?"

"And blue violets, right? Did you enclose a poem?"

"Oh."

"Listen, I gotta go, a woman just came in with a puli. You'll be there all afternoon, won't you?"

"Sure," I said. "Unless I get arrested again."

An hour later it looked as though I'd spoken too soon. I was ringing up a sale for one of my regular customers, an emergency-room physician at St. Vincent's. She drops in every Saturday and buys a dozen books at a time, all mysteries, all by hardboiled male writers. "There's nothing so relaxing," she told me once, "as blood and gore that's someone else's responsibility."

We were chatting about some of her favorites when Ray Kirschmann came into the shop. Normally he knows how to behave, biding his time when I've got a customer, but today he had a little snot from the DA's office for company, and he bulled his way right into the middle of our transaction and slapped a piece of paper on the counter.

" 'Scuse me, ma'am," he said, "but this here's a warrant authorizin' an' empowerin' me to search the premises."

"If you let me know what you're looking for," I said evenly, "perhaps I can save you some time."

"Now that's real considerate of you," he said, "but I know what I want an' I know where to find it, on account of I saw it here yesterday." He led the assistant DA to the Sports section, where he pulled one book off the shelf right away, then took his time selecting two more volumes. He handed all three books to his young companion, who brought them to the counter and set them down while he wrote out a receipt in perfect parochial-school penmanship.

" 'Received of Bernard Grimes Rhodenbarr,' " Ray read aloud. " 'Three books as follows. *Mr. Mint's Insider's Guide to Investing in Baseball Cards and Collectibles. Encyclopedia of Sports Card Values,* third edition. *Getting Started with Baseball Cards.*' I only saw the one yesterday, the Mr. Mint. You had the others stuck on the shelf below."

"That was to confuse you, Ray. Look, if you wanted the books, wouldn't it have been simpler to buy them? It strikes me as less trouble than getting a warrant. Price guides like that I practically give away, because by the time they get to my store they're apt to be seriously out of date. Now if you want something a little more current, I'd recommend the Barnes & Noble at Fifth Avenue and Eighteenth Street. They even discount their stock, although I know it's not quite the same as getting it for free, but—"

"These are evidence," the young fellow said. His name, according to the receipt he handed me, was J. Philip Flynn.

"Evidence," I said.

"Of prior knowledge," J. Philip Flynn said. He hefted the books. "You got something to put these in?"

I suppressed an impulse and handed him a shopping bag. Ray said, "Pretendin' you didn't know baseball cards was worth stealin', Bern. An' here you got not one but three books on the subject." He shook his head, awed by the perfidy of human nature.

"I've got half a shelf full of books on unarmed combat," I said, "but I don't know the first thing about taking a cop and a lawyer and knocking their heads together. I know this'll come as a shock to you, Ray, but there are actually a couple of books in the store that I haven't had time to read."

"Well, you'll have time soon," he said. "Plenty of time, way it looks to me."

And out he went, with J. Philip Flynn following in his wake. I turned to my customer and apologized for the interruption.

"Cops," she said with feeling. "It's Saturday. Twelve hours from now we'll be up to our clavicles in stabbings and gunshot wounds, and those two heroes are confiscating books. I thought at first they must be looking for kiddie porn, but those were books about baseball cards, weren't they?"

"I'm afraid so."

"I didn't know they were illegal," she said. "What is it, some carcinogen in the gum?" She raised a hand and waved the thought aside. "It's all crazy," she said. "Oh, hi, Raffles. Were you hiding from the nasty old policemen? Oh, you are a sweetie pie. Yes, you are! Yes, you are!"

"Miaow," said Raffles.

When the store's empty, or when the browsers strike me as trustworthy types, I'm apt to pick up a book and read. There's a little bell that tinkles when someone opens the door, but if I'm really caught up in my reading I don't always hear it.

Which is what happened around four-thirty. I was back in prehistory, sharing the heroine's dismay that those Neanderthals just didn't understand her, when the deliberate clearing of a throat just across the counter from me yanked me back to present time. I looked up from the primitive brutes on the page and into the swinish little eyes of Borden Stoppelgard.

"I suppose you want your change," I said.

"What, from the day before yesterday? No, of course not. You offered it to me then and I didn't take it. You think I'd make a special trip here for it?"

"Probably not," I said. "Unless you had to be in the neighborhood anyway to evict some widows and orphans."

"You've got me wrong, Rhodenbarr."

"Oh?"

"All wrong. What kind of man evicts widows and orphans in September? Christmas Eve, that's the time for it."

" 'Hark, the City Marshals Sing.' "

"My favorite Christmas carol," he said, with a hearty chuckle. He stepped closer to the counter. "As a matter of fact, I did make a special trip here this afternoon, but not to buy books. What I really want to do is apologize. We got off on the wrong foot the other day and it was my fault. I had the wrong idea about you."

"You did?"

"It's a constant hazard in my business, Rhodenbarr. I have to make snap judgments, and as a rule I'm pretty good at it. But nobody's a hundred percent, and every once in a while I put my foot in it."

"These things happen."

"Here's what I did," he said. "I walked in here, I checked out the store, I checked you out, and I jumped to a conclusion. I said to myself, Here's this poor sap busting his hump trying to clear twenty grand a year in a dead business. Be a good thing for him and everybody, I said to myself, when his lease is up and the laws of the marketplace put him out of his misery."

"Economic euthanasia," I suggested.

"That's a good way of putting it. But here's where I went wrong. I went strictly by appearances. And then I find out you're not an earnest nebbish of a bookseller after all. What you really are is a burglar."

"Uh, Mr. Stoppelgard—"

"Please," he said. "Borden."

"Uh."

"And what shall I call you? Bernard?"

Call me a taxi, I thought. I said, "Well, uh, people generally call me Bernie."

"Bernie," he said. "Bernie. I like that."

"Then I'll keep it."

"A burglar," he said, pronouncing the phrase the way a grandmother in Miami Beach might say "a doctor" or "a lawyer" or "a specialist." "This," he said, with a dismissive wave around him, "this is not the run-down mess it appears to be. On the contrary, it's a brilliantly executed false front. My congratulations, Bernie."

"Well, thanks," I said, "but—"

"The way I hear it, you're not just a garden-variety burglar, either. It seems you're something of a genius at what you do. The lock that can stop you hasn't been invented yet, according to that policeman, and there was more than a little grudging admiration in his voice, I have to tell you."

I was being buttered up. But why?

"So naturally you were upset at the thought of a rent increase. The store works for you because it's a subsistence enterprise with a very low overhead. Once the rent jumps anywhere near market value, you can't operate anywhere near the break-even point, not without changing your operation dramatically. The alternative is to shove money into the business from an outside source, and if you do that somebody's going to want to know where the money came from. And that's no good, is it?"

"No."

"What you need," he said, "is a renewal of your lease at the present rent for a substantial period of time. You don't have any kids, do you?"

"Not that I know of."

" 'Not that I know of.' I'll have to remember that one. No kids, then there's nobody you're going to have to leave the business to. You figure thirty more years is enough time to spend in the book business?"

"I would think that would be enough for anybody."

"Okay," he said. "Here's the deal. I'll renew your lease for thirty years at $875 a month. How does that sound to you?"

"Too good to be true. What's the catch?"

"Baseball cards."

"Baseball cards?"

"Better than coins and stamps. Better than French Impressionists. Better than Manhattan real estate, and a whole lot better than the New York Stock Exchange."

"Even better than women mystery writers?"

"You know it. Oh, it's volatile. You have to know

what you're doing. Buy garbage, and ten years from now all you've got is old garbage. Buy speculative stuff and you can make a killing or get killed, depending which way the wind blows. Say you had a big position in Bo Jackson rookie cards. Then he sustains what looks to be a career-ending injury. Where are you?"

"Where?"

"Up the well-known creek, Bernie, without the proverbial paddle. Bo's got the charisma, but he needs five or ten years in the bigs to put up the kind of numbers that will make him a superstar in the card market. Or say you bought Nolan Ryan during what was supposed to be his last season. Instead he decides to hang around for one more year, and while he's at it he throws another no-hitter. That wouldn't hurt the value of your portfolio, would it?"

"I guess not."

"Then there are the blue chips," he said. "Safer than T-bonds and a whole lot more profitable. Babe Ruth. Mickey Mantle. Joe DiMaggio. Or my own personal favorite, Ted Williams."

"You couldn't have seen him play," I said. "Unless you're a lot older than you look."

"No, he was before my time. But I don't have to see him swing a bat. All I need to do is look at his numbers. He was the last man ever to hit over .400 in major league ball." He followed this factoid with a blur of statistics—career batting and slugging averages, home runs, runs batted in, all the way to intentional walks. If you need to know this, check a baseball encyclopedia. "Teddy Baseball," he said reverently. "The Splendid Splinter. We'll never see his like again."

I didn't know what to say to that.

"He spent four years in the service, you know. During the Second World War. Think what it cost him."

"Think what it cost England."

"Four of the prime years of his playing career. Imagine what his numbers would look like if he'd been swinging away in Fenway Park all that time instead of serving his country. But it shows you the kind of a guy he was."

"A patriot?"

"A sap. But that's all water over the bridge, or under the dam, or wherever it goes."

"Up the creek," I suggested.

"Whatever. If he'd had those years, well . . ."

"I guess his cards would be worth more."

"His cards are seriously underpriced," he said flatly. "They go for a fraction of Mantle's cards, and for my money Williams was twice the ballplayer. Mantle's rookie card from the 1952 Topps set will cost you thirty thousand dollars in near-mint condition. All right, let's look at the Splendid Splinter's rookie card from the 1939 Play Ball set. Thirteen years older, and an infinitely scarcer set, and you can pick that card up in top condition for under five grand. But don't get me started."

"I won't."

"I collected baseball cards as a kid."

"So did I, until my mother threw them out."

"Mine knew better than to touch any of my possessions. Well, I grew up, I went into business, I put the cards away and forgot about them. Eventually I got married and we had a kid. Meanwhile my sister Edna got married."

"To Martin Gilmartin."

"When my kid was old enough to be interested, I gave him my old baseball cards to play with. I mentioned this to Marty, and it turned out he was a big collector himself. And that's when I found out about the investment potential of these cards."

"So you took them away from your kid."

"I borrowed a book from Marty," he said, "and I checked the kid's cards, and not too surprisingly there was nothing rare or valuable in the lot. They were in terrible condition, Scotch tape on some of them, others all beat up and scuffed and folded. But there was one, if it hadn't been in such bad condition, it would have been worth fifty bucks."

"Wow."

"What could I have paid for it? It seems to me you used to get a whole pack for a quarter, and that included the gum. They don't bother giving you the gum anymore, you know. They found out the kids just threw it away. Anyway, say I paid a nickel for that card, and now it was worth fifty bucks. Or at least it would have been if I'd taken decent care of it."

"Next time you'll know."

"Exactly what I told myself. 'This time,' I said, 'you take good care of your cards.' And I started collecting. I let my kid keep my old junk and I started right in buying quality, and . . ."

And the phone rang.

"Barnegat Books," I said.

"Hello, Bernie."

A woman's voice, familiar but hard to place. Then I reached out and nailed it.

"Well, hello, Doll. I didn't expect to hear from you."

"What a greeting! But you're the doll, Bernie. They're absolutely gorgeous."

"They are?"

"The roses are spectacular."

Oh, I thought. Wrong woman. "Patience," I said.

"And the African violet is the sweetest thing, but I have to warn you, I have a brown thumb. I can never keep plants alive."

"It's supposed to help if you talk to them."

"I know, but I never know what to say. Do you suppose this one likes poetry? I could read to it." She sighed. "I don't know what to say to you, either. Two nights in a row, two broken dates in a row, two different friends breaking them for you—or do you do voices, too?"

"Just Jimmy Stewart."

"I can hardly wait. Two different excuses, first a burrito and then a burglary. Both words are on the same page of the dictionary, but of course you know that. That's the page you break all your dates from, isn't it?"

"Patience—"

"We could make another date," she said, "but I'd only get a phone call advising me that you wouldn't be able to make it because you'd been eaten by a bugbear. Or bummed out, or bumped off, or some bumptious buckaroo had burst your bubble. The roses are truly beautiful."

"I'm glad."

"I was feeling terribly depressed. I get that way a lot. Most poets do, it's sort of an occupational illness. But then the flowers came and cheered me right up. So it's hard for me to stay mad at you. Are you really a burglar?"

"I can explain," I said.

"Whenever people say that, they can't. But I'll give you a chance. Tomorrow night there's going to be a poetry reading at the Café Villanelle on Ludlow Street. Do you know where that is?"

"Sort of."

"Two of my clients will be reading, and I promised I'd go. I may read something myself, I'm not sure. The reading's scheduled to start at ten o'clock, but it's all right to come early. It's all right to come late, too. It's even okay not to come at all."

"Patience—"

"What's not okay," she said, "is to have any of your legion of friends call with an excuse, no matter what letter it starts with. So maybe I'll see you tomorrow night, Bernie, and maybe I won't."

"You will."

"But if you don't come," she said, "do me a favor. Don't send flowers."

"So I started off small," he said. "Same as when I first got into real estate. You make some mistakes, but how else are you going to get the feel for what you're doing? You have to be willing to go in there and get your feet wet. You take your medicine, you pull up your socks, and you get right back up on the horse." He frowned, and who could blame him? "Bernie," he said, "you don't need to listen to all this crap."

"It's interesting."

"It's nice of you to say that, but let's cut to the chase, huh? We can do each other some good here. Each of us has something the other wants. I've got a storefront I can let you have for thirty years at half the price of a rooftop pigeon coop in Bensonhurst. And we both know what you've got."

"What?"

He grinned. "Marty's baseball cards."

11

"In 1950," I told Carolyn, "the Chalmers Mustard Company got up a special promotion. Every time you bought a jar of their mustard, you got a free coupon. If you mailed it in, they sent you three baseball cards."

"I never heard of Chalmers Mustard."

"You didn't grow up in Boston. Chalmers was strictly local, and I gather a major corporation acquired the company a few years ago, but back then it must have been hot stuff. If you bought a frankfurter at Fenway Park, you got Chalmers Mustard on it."

"Unless you said, 'Hold the mustard.' "

"There were forty of these cards," I went on, "and they all showed the same player, Ted Williams, who was the one thing in Boston hotter than Chalmers Mustard. They showed him in different poses and doing different things. Mostly hitting, of course, because that was what he was so good at, but also catching fly balls and trotting around the bases, and holding his cap in his hands while they played the 'Star Spangled Banner,' and signing autographs for little kids."

"I think I get the idea."

"In order to get all forty cards, you'd have had to buy a ton of mustard."

"Fourteen jars," she said. "And then you'd have two extras to trade for Dwight Gooden."

"He wasn't even born then. The thing is, you wouldn't necessarily get different cards every time you sent in a coupon, any more than you do nowadays when you buy a pack of baseball cards at the candy store. I gather they made more of some cards than others, and the high-numbered cards weren't distributed until late in the promotion. The idea was to make you buy as much mustard as possible."

"Sneaky."

"And not terribly effective, as it turned out, because kids got pretty tired of getting the same pictures of Williams every time the mailman showed up. And I guess their parents got tired of buying endless jars of mustard. There were no investors around at the time, either. So the whole thing sort of died out, with relatively few of cards #31 through #40 ever reaching the hands of collectors. That makes complete sets pretty hard to come by."

"And very valuable, I suppose."

"Not really," I said, "because this was strictly a regional issue, all of it tied to a single player, so it's not something you absolutely have to have in order to consider your collection complete. Most of the card encyclopedias don't even list it. And the cards themselves are pretty ugly, according to Stoppelgard. The photos are all black-and-white and the printing job leaves a lot to be desired. And the series is just too long. A dozen cards devoted to one player might be interesting, but forty is too many. So the series was never popular."

"What's it worth?"

"Hard to say. If you want a complete set, you pretty much have to hunt around and pick it up a card or two at a time. And you have to be careful about condition, because a lot of cards were poorly printed. I pressed Stoppelgard for a number, and he said that card #40 is genuinely rare, and would probably bring a thousand dollars. The common cards in the series bring anywhere from ten to twenty dollars, and cards #31 through #39 might go for a hundred apiece."

"So the whole set would be worth—"

"Something in the neighborhood of three thousand dollars. Pocket change, from Borden Stoppelgard's point of view, but that's not the point. The point is that Marty Gilmartin had the set and Stoppelgard didn't."

"And Stoppelgard wanted it?"

"Desperately. And Gilmartin wouldn't sell it to him. Gilmartin didn't give a hoot about Ted Williams, but he still insisted on holding on to the set, which struck Stoppelgard as a real dog-in-the-manger attitude."

"So he wants you to give him the set."

"Along with the rest of Gilmartin's baseball cards, in return for which I get a sweetheart deal on the store lease. I wish I'd had the damn cards. I'd have done the deal in a hot second."

"Really, Bern? I thought Gilmartin's collection was worth a million dollars."

"That's according to Gilmartin. It's only insured for half that, which means the insurance company would probably pay twenty or twenty-five percent of half a million to avoid having to pay the claim. If I let Ray be the go-between, he'd wind up with half, so what would that leave me? Fifty, sixty thousand dollars?"

"If you say so."

"I might do better fencing the cards myself," I said. "That might boost the take up into the low six figures. Well, as Stoppelgard pointed out, the new lease would be worth almost that much to me in the first year. You bet I'd have taken the deal."

"I don't suppose he believed you when you told him you didn't have the cards."

"I'm not sure."

"Oh?"

"I don't even think he cared," I said. "If I want to extend my lease, all I have to do is bring him half a million dollars' worth of baseball cards. It doesn't matter to him if they're Marty's cards. It doesn't even matter if the Chalmers Mustard set is part of the package, although that would certainly be a sweetener. But he doesn't care where they come from, and I don't suppose he really cares if they're baseball cards. He'd settle for Sue Grafton first editions if they added up to half a mil. You know what Scott Fitzgerald said."

"Was he Geraldine's brother?"

" 'The very rich are different from you and me,' Well, so are the very greedy. When he thought I was a poor but honest bookseller, all Stoppelgard wanted to do was get me out of his building. As soon as he found out I was a convicted felon, he was in a rush to be friends. Because he figures he can use me."

"Can he?"

"I hope so," I said. "Because what I want is to save the store, and for the first time in weeks I have hope."

I also had Perrier. We were at the Bum Rap, and I didn't want to drink anything that might slow my reflexes or blur my already questionable judgment. "It's not that I have anything planned beyond a quiet evening at home," I explained, "but I want to keep my options open."

"I understand, Bern."

"There's something about spending a night in a cell," I said, "that throws off your timing. When Patience phoned me at the store, I called her Doll. I got away with it. She thought I was being breezily affectionate."

"It never would have worked if you'd called her Gwendolyn."

"No."

"Bern? How come you thought it was Doll?"

"I don't know."

"Were you thinking about her?"

"Not consciously. I was in the middle of a conversation with Borden Stoppelgard. If I was thinking of anybody, it was probably Ted Williams."

"You don't suppose—"

"No," I said. "I don't."

"You didn't let me finish the question."

" 'You don't suppose they're both the same person?' That was the question, wasn't it? And the answer is no, I don't."

"Think about it, Bern."

"I don't want to think about it," I said, "because it's out of the question. They're two different women."

"How can you be so sure?"

"I saw them, Carolyn."

"Yeah, but did you ever see them both at the same time?"

"No," I said, "and I probably never will, but if I ever do it won't be hard to tell them apart. For starters, Doll's a brunette and Patience is a dishwater blonde."

"Ever hear of wigs, Bern?"

"Patience is a good four inches taller than Doll."

"High heels, Bern."

"Cut it out, will you? Patience looks as though she could have stepped out of a painting by Grant Wood or Harvey Dunn. She's tall and slender and she has a long *O Pioneers!* face and angular features. Doll has a heart-shaped face and very regular features and—"

"Hey, it was just a thought, Bern."

"They're two different women."

"Whatever you say. Just don't jump down my throat, okay? I had a rough day."

"I'm sorry."

"I was up half the night worrying about you, and then I had to give a wash and set to a puli with dreadlocks. Do you know what a challenge that is? Pulis and komondors, the Rastafarians of the dog world." She picked up her glass, found it empty, and gave it a look. "It's either have another of these or go home. I think I'll go home."

I rode uptown on the subway. I didn't pick up the paper, and nobody picked me up, either. I looked around, sort of hoping I'd see Doll Cooper lurking in a doorway somewhere, but I didn't. I walked home and nodded to my doorman, who nodded right back at me. Was he the same nodding acquaintance who'd reported my movements to the cops? I decided he was, and I decided his Christmas envelope was going to be a little light this year.

My apartment was as I'd left it. I'd been hoping

that elves might have come in and cleaned during my absence, and they hadn't, but neither had Ray Kirschmann come to give the place another toss. I put the TV on, and during the second set of commercials I called the Hunan Miracle and ordered dinner. In no time at all the kid was at my door with a bag full of sesame noodles and moo shu pork. After I'd paid and tipped him he smiled hugely and rushed off to shove menus under all my neighbors' doors.

I settled in for a quiet evening at home.

It was almost eleven when the phone rang.

I answered it. A woman's voice said, "Mr. Rhodenbarr?"

"Yes?"

"I'm not even sure you'll remember me, but you did me a huge favor the night before last."

"It wasn't such a huge favor. All I did was walk you home."

"You remember."

"You'd be hard to forget, Doll."

"That's right, you created a new name for me. I'd forgotten, because nobody's called me that since. When you said it just now it came out sounding like a line from Mickey Spillane. 'You'd be hard to forget, Doll.' You should be smoking an unfiltered cigarette and wearing a slouch hat, and there should be something bluesy playing in the background."

"A girl singer," I said, "working her way through 'Stormy Weather.' "

"Or 'Easy to Love.' Just as you're saying, 'You'd be . . . hard to forget,' you hear her in the background, singing, 'You'd be . . . so easy to love.' Nice touch, don't you think?"

"Very nice."

"I'm sorry. You know what I'm doing? I'm stalling. I have to ask you for another favor and I'm afraid you'll say no. Could I talk with you?"

"Isn't that what we're doing?"

"I mean face to face. I'm at the coffee shop at West End and Seventy-second. If you come down I'll buy you a cup of coffee. Or I could come up to your place."

I glanced around. The elves hadn't come, nor had I done their work for them. "I'll be right down," I said. "How will I recognize you?"

"Well, I still look basically the same," she said. "I haven't aged that much in the past two days. My outfit's different. I'm wearing—"

"Red vinyl hot pants and a Grateful Dead T-shirt."

"I'll be in a booth in the back," she said. "Come see for yourself."

12

Faded jeans, a cocoa-brown turtleneck, and a black leather biker's jacket with zipper pockets. No polish on her nails, no rings on her fingers. I slid in opposite her and told the waiter I'd have a cup of coffee. He brought it, and refilled Doll's cup without being asked.

"I have a few questions," I said. "How did you know my number?"

"I looked in the book."

"How did you know my name?"

"You told me, Bernie. Remember?"

"Oh."

"You told me your name was Bernie Rhodenbarr and you owned a used-book store in the Village. I couldn't call you there because I didn't know the name or address of the store, but you're the only B Rhodenbarr in the Manhattan phone book, and anyway I knew you lived at Seventy-first and West End, because you told me."

"Oh."

"You did me a favor," she said, "and you were totally sweet about it, and I figured maybe I'd give you a call sometime if I didn't happen to run into you in the neighborhood. And then when Marty told me about you—"

"Marty."

"Marty Gilmartin," she said. "You must know who that is. You stole his baseball cards."

"Wait a minute," I said.

"All right."

"I know who Martin Gilmartin is. And I didn't steal his baseball cards. Wait a minute."

"I'm waiting, Bernie."

"Good," I said, and closed my eyes. When I opened them she was still there, patiently waiting. "This is very confusing," I said.

"It is?"

"How do you know him?"

"He's a friend."

"Well, that clears it up."

"Sort of a special friend."

"Oh," I said.

Archly, I guess, because she colored. "I don't know how much you know about Marty," she said.

"Not a whole lot. I know where he lives, and I know what his building looks like because I went over and had a look at it, although I swear I never set a foot inside it. I never met him. I saw his wife once, but I never met her, either. I met her brother because it turns out he's my landlord, which made it a small world. It got a lot smaller when you mentioned his name."

She took a sip of her coffee. "Marty's crazy about the theater," she said. "He sees everything, and not just on Broadway. He's a member of the Pretenders, the actors' club on Gramercy Park. The playbills for half the off-Broadway theaters in town have him listed as a patron or supporter. He's extremely generous."

"I see."

"Marty's fifty-eight years old. He's plenty old enough to have a daughter my age, but he doesn't. He married late, and he and his wife didn't have any kids."

"So he's like a father to you."

"No."

"I didn't think so."

"When I met him," she said, "I was working at a midtown law firm called Haber, Haber & Crowell."

"You mentioned them."

"I know. I said I still worked there, but that's not true."

"Marty took you away from all that."

She nodded. "He was a client. I was a theatrical wannabe, taking classes and running around to auditions. They're very good about that at HH&C. They represent a lot of people in the theater, and they hire a lot of young actors and actresses as clerical workers and receptionists."

"And paralegals."

"I was never a paralegal. I worked reception desk and switchboard. Until, as you said, Marty took me away from all that. He was very nice to me, he took an interest in my career, he took me to lunch at the Pretenders and introduced me to people. And he said it was hard enough for a young person to get a foot in the door of the New York theater without having to hold down a full-time job at the same time. Which is the absolute truth, believe me."

"I'm sure you're right."

"And he said he'd like to pay my rent and give me enough money every month so that I could get by. It wouldn't be the lap of luxury, but it would keep me going while I found out whether I had a chance to make it in the theater."

"And all you had to do in return was go to bed with him."

"I was already doing that."

"Oh."

"He's an attractive man, Bernie. Tall and slender, flowing gray hair, very distinguished. Wonderful manners. He kind of swept me off my feet. When he made a pass at me, I was too honored to think about refusing." She lowered her eyes, gnawed at a thumbnail. "Even if I was sort of involved at the time."

"With Borden Stoppelgard," I guessed.

"Ughhh," she said. "Are you out of my mind?"

"Evidently."

"Borden Stoppelgard is pond scum, Bernie. You get warts from touching people like Borden Stoppelgard."

"I'm sorry I mentioned him."

"So am I. Marty thinks Borden is a joke. He has to put up with him because he's married to Borden's big sister. I only met Borden once, and believe me, that was enough."

"When was that?"

"Sometime in June. I was in a showcase presentation of an early P. J. Barry play. You know how that works, don't you? Nobody gets paid, but you can try to get people to come and see your work. Agents and people like that. Of course, ninety percent of the audience consists of the friends and relatives of the different members of the cast. But it's good experience, especially if the play's any good, and this one was excellent."

"And Marty brought the whole family?"

"He brought his wife," she said, "and he brought Borden and *his* wife. He gets a block of four patron tickets to every production at this particular theater, because he's one of their angels." She started to look away, then met my eyes. "That may have had something to do with my getting the part," she said levelly.

"Oh."

"I had dinner with the four of them after the show, along with a couple of other members of the cast. So I had a chance to form an opinion of Borden, and I already told you what it was."

"Pond scum, I think you said."

"I was giving him the benefit of the doubt. It would be just my luck to sound off like this and then have him turn out to be your best friend, but of course he's not, is he? He's your landlord."

"Right, and pond scum's the nicest thing anybody ever said about him. You said you were involved with somebody besides Gilmartin."

"I was," she said. "But I broke it off."

"When you started sleeping with Marty."

"No."

"When he started paying your rent."

"A little later than that, actually."

"When?"

"This past Monday."

"Oh."

"Or was it Tuesday? No, it was Monday night. I threw his keys at him and I stormed out the door. It was a great exit, but I should have held on to the keys. Bernie, can I ask you something?"

"Sure."

"Did you take Marty's cards? Look, in case you're afraid I'm wearing a wire, don't answer out loud. Blink once for yes and twice for no."

"I don't care if you're wearing a wire," I said. "The answer's no. No one else has believed me, so I hardly expect you to, but that's the answer."

"I believe you."

"You do?"

"I never thought you took them in the first place. I had a pretty good idea who took them the minute Marty mentioned they were gone, and before your name even came up. I think Luke took them."

"Good old Luke."

"I can't believe this. You know Luke?"

"Nope. Never heard of him. But I can probably guess who he is. Your boyfriend, right?"

"Not since Monday."

"That's when you threw the keys in his face."

"Actually I threw them across the room."

"Tell me about Luke," I suggested.

"I don't know where to start. He's an actor. He came to New York fresh out of high school and he's spent the past fifteen years trying to get a break. He's had some commercials and bit parts in a couple of soaps, and he had two lines in Sidney Lumet's last film, and he toured for three months in the road company of *Sour Grapes.* He pays the rent by tending bar and working for a couple of unlicensed moving companies. Gypsy movers, they call them." She frowned. "And he likes to see himself as a romantically shady character. One time he jumped out of bed in the middle of the afternoon and put on a suit and tie. I asked him where he was going. The supermarket, he told me. I said, you're dressing like that for D'Agostino's? You get more respect, he said, and he grabbed his attaché case and went out the door.

"Twenty minutes later he came back with a bag of groceries. A head of lettuce, a couple of potatoes, I forget what else. A couple of dollars' worth of groceries. Then he goes, Duh-dah! and opens the attaché case, and inside he's got two gorgeous strip sirloins an inch thick. You just have to know how to shop, he said."

"Isn't that how Jesse James used to do it?"

"At the time," she said, "I have to admit I thought it was pretty cool. And then when I started seeing Marty, the contrast between the two of them was kind of interesting."

"I can imagine."

"He's sort of a crook. I tried not to know very much about the various hustles he was working, but I know he's been doing a little small-time drug dealing. He takes a lot of pills himself, uppers and downers, and he pays for them by selling some of them to people he knows."

"Safer than selling to people you don't know."

"At first he thought it was really neat that Marty was paying my rent. He figured I had a hustle of my own going and that made us birds of a feather. He would refer to Marty as 'the old guy' or 'your meal ticket.' It started to bother him when he began to realize that I really cared for Marty, that the relationship was important to me emotionally."

"So he was jealous."

"Kind of, yeah."

"And then you had a fight and broke up with him."

"On Monday, and when Marty looked for his baseball cards Thursday night they were gone. I'm sure Luke took them. And it's all my fault."

"How do you figure that?"

"I told him about Marty's apartment, and the things he had in it. Marty took me there one afternoon last month. He and his wife were spending the week with friends in East Hampton, and he had come in for the day, and we went out to lunch and then he said he'd like to show me where he lived. It's not what you're thinking."

"Huh?"

"We didn't . . . do anything," she said. "I couldn't, not in his wife's house. I felt funny enough just being there. But it's a beautiful apartment, with a spectacular river view and gorgeous furnishings. When I was with Luke that night I couldn't stop myself from going on and on about what I saw."

"Including the baseball cards."

"They were in his office," she said, "in a polished rosewood chest lined with cedar. Marty used to keep cigars in it back when he still smoked, and when you opened it there was still a faint trace of the aroma of a good Havana cigar. The box wasn't even locked, and he kept it right on top of his desk. It was still there Thursday, Bernie, but when he lifted the lid it was empty."

"Somebody took the cards and left the box."

"I'm sure it was Luke. He got a lot more excited hearing about the baseball cards than when I told him about the bridges you could see from the living room window. He started talking about how valuable baseball cards were, and how easy it was to sell them. It seems he used to collect them as a kid, and—"

"Everybody did."

"Well, I didn't. Anyway, Marty's collection stirred up feelings of greed and nostalgia both at once. And when he had a chance to lash out at me and Marty, and make himself a bundle in the process—"

"He jumped at it."

"Right."

I thought about it. "All right," I said. "That's how you fit in, and Marty, and Luke. At least I've got a scorecard now, and everybody knows you can't tell the players without a scorecard. The thing is, there's no mirror handy. If I can't look in the mirror, how can I tell what number I'm wearing?"

"You lost me, Bernie."

"I'm the one who's lost. Why am I here? Why did you call me? What am I supposed to do?"

"Oh, that's easy," she said. "You're going to help me get Marty's cards back."

"I know what they say about coincidence," I said. "It's just God's way of remaining anonymous. But I can only swallow so much of it. Let's go back to Thursday night, okay?"

"Okay."

"Marty Gilmartin and his wife and Borden Stoppelgard and *his* wife—what's she like, by the way?"

"Nothing special. I just met her that one time, and I barely noticed her. I don't think she opened her mouth all evening."

"Anyway, the four of them went off to see *If Wishes Were Horses.* Did they like the play, incidentally? I asked Marty, but I might as well have asked Mary Lincoln what she thought of *Our American Cousin.*" I shrugged. "Never mind. They went to the play, and they finally came home, and I made an ill-considered phone call to the Gilmartin residence. That was just after midnight."

"Where does the coincidence come in?"

"It comes in about the time I get off the IRT a block from here and stop to buy a paper. And an extremely attractive young woman in corporate drag and a red beret singles me out and asks me to walk her home."

"That sort of thing must happen to you all the time, Bernie."

"It never happens," I said. "I've been buying the *Times* on the way home for years, and it never once happened in the past."

"I guess you were overdue."

"This woman," I went on, "just happens to be Martin Gilmartin's girlfriend. And, in her free time, she's also the girlfriend of the fellow who seems to have stolen Marty's baseball cards."

"I see what you mean about coincidence."

"If God really wants to keep his name out of it," I said, "he ought to wear gloves, because this one's got fingerprints all over it. But here's what I can't understand. How did you find out about the cards in time to pick me up at the corner newsstand? And how did you even know it was me, considering that nobody knew that until the cops checked the NYNEX records and found out the call had come from my friend Carolyn's apartment? And how could you know I'd be coming home by subway? I'd have taken a cab if a couple of rubes hadn't beaten me to it. How would you even recognize me? I don't get it. I don't get any of it, and . . . wait a minute, Doll. Where are you going?"

She was halfway out of the booth. "To get the check," she said. "I told you I'd buy the coffee, remember?" She put her hand on mine. "You'll see," she said. "I can explain everything."

Outside, we walked a long crosstown block to Broadway and stood on the corner watching people buy newspapers. "I didn't know about the baseball cards when I saw you," she told me. "And I didn't know who you were, and I didn't particularly care. All I knew was that you didn't look like an ax murderer. And I gave you a character test. I waited to see what paper you bought."

"Suppose I'd taken the *Post* instead?"

"If you'd picked up the *Post*," she said, "I'd have picked up somebody else. But I was perfectly sure you'd turn out to be a *Times* kind of guy. What I told you that night was the truth. I'd been to an acting class, I'd just gotten off a bus, and I didn't like the way it felt on the street. I never feel comfortable on the West Side, anyway. I know it's as safe as anywhere else but it just doesn't feel safe to me."

"Then why do you live over here?"

"I don't. I live on Seventy-eighth Street between First and Second."

"Who lives at 304 West End?"

"Lucas Santangelo."

"Alias Luke the boyfriend."

"Ex-boyfriend."

"You wanted a *New York Times* kind of guy to walk you to Luke's place. Why? To make him jealous?"

"I told you. I was scared to walk by myself."

"And out of all the guys around—"

"Bernie," she said, "look around, will you? And bear in mind that it was an hour later and in the middle of the week. There were fewer people out and most of them looked like . . . well, like that panhandler over there, and those two creeps in army jackets, and—"

"I see what you mean."

"I left some clothes at Luke's," she said, "and I'd

been calling him for a couple of days, trying to make arrangements to get my stuff back. But all I ever got was his machine. That didn't necessarily mean he was out, because sometimes he'll let the machine pick up and wait until he knows who it is before answering. So I finally decided to go over there. If he was home, maybe he'd be enough of a gentleman to let me have my things."

"And if he wasn't home?"

"Maybe I could get in anyway. Most of the time he doesn't bother to double-lock his door. I thought I might be able to open it with a credit card."

"That's not always as easy as they make it look on television."

"Now he tells me," she said, clapping her hand theatrically to her forehead. "It turned out to be impossible. I tried all three of my credit cards, and then I tried my ATM card, and that was a mistake because I must have crimped it a little. When I tried to get cash yesterday morning, the machine ate my card."

"Bummer."

"They gave me a new card. It was an inconvenience, that's all. Believe me, it was more frustrating standing in front of Luke's door with no way to get in. Why did I have to throw the keys? Why couldn't I have thrown an ashtray instead?"

"Or a tantrum. After you gave up trying to open the door, then what did you do?"

"I went home."

"Straight home?"

"Absolutely. I said good night to Eddie and off I went."

"Who walked you to the bus stop?"

"Nobody. I took a cab."

"Why didn't you take one in the first place?"

"I did."

"I thought you said you took a bus."

"I telescoped things a little. I took a bus home from acting class, and I tried Luke's number and got his machine again, and then I changed clothes to look ultrarespectable and took a cab from my apartment right through the park. I got off right in front of Luke's building and had the doorman ring his apartment. There was no answer. 'Well, I'll just go on up,' I said, but he wouldn't let me."

"Eddie stopped you? I'm surprised he even noticed you were there."

"*He* wasn't there. I got there a few minutes after midnight because that's when his shift starts, but he was running late. The fellow on duty was a young Haitian who's a real stickler for the rules. And I don't think he was too happy about having to stay late. He wouldn't let me in the building, so I walked over to Broadway to get a cup of coffee—the other coffee shop closes at midnight—"

"I know."

"—and I got a real creepy feeling on the way over there, as if someone was stalking me. I guess I was nervous about breaking into Luke's apartment. Then you turned up and walked me to my door, or to Luke's door, actually, and then I went in and then I came back out again and then I went home. The next day I found out Marty's baseball cards were missing. 'They even know who took them,' he said. 'The insolent son of a bitch called to brag about it and they were able to trace the call.' I couldn't believe Luke had been so stupid. And then I found out it was you."

"Thanks."

"I don't mean you were stupid. You had your own reasons for making the call, and why not make a joke out of it? You had no way of knowing Marty's cards would turn out to be missing."

"You're right about that. I didn't even know he had them in the first place." We had been walking back toward West End as we talked, and when we reached the corner we turned uptown as if by prearrangement, heading toward 304. "The way you tell it," I said, "there's hardly any coincidence operating at all. Just that Eddie happened to be late for work, and Luke happened to be away from his apartment, and I happened to be the first guy to come along and pick up the *Times*."

"That's right."

"I wish I knew how much of your story to believe. Is your name really Doll Cooper?"

"It is now, but you and I are the only people who

know it. You gave me the name, remember? Before that I told you my name was Gwendolyn Cooper, and it is."

"Can you prove it?"

She fished in her bag and produced a couple of plastic cards. "Here," she said. "A brand-new ATM card from Chemical. It was Manufacturers Hanover before the merger, and I loved going to a bank that you could call Manny Hanny for short. And here, my Visa card. It got crimped, too. See that corner? I tried to straighten it out but I think I only made it worse. I guess it'll be all right as long as I don't put it in any machines."

I gave the cards back to her. "You gave me the right name," I said. "How come?"

"The same reason you told me your name. We were two ships passing in the night. What reason would I have to lie to you?" She grinned. "Besides, Bernie, I wanted you to be able to get in touch with me."

"How? You're not in the phone book."

"I certainly am. G Cooper on East Seventy-eighth Street."

"But I wouldn't know to look there, would I? Because I was somehow under the impression that you lived at 304 West End Avenue."

"You could have called me at work."

"Where, at Faber Faber?"

"Haber Haber," she said, "and Crowell."

"You don't work there anymore, remember?"

"I sometimes get calls still at the office. They take messages for me. I said I was a paralegal because that's a lot more impressive than being a receptionist, and since I'm not either one, well, why not pick the one that sounds good?"

"You could have said you were a lawyer."

"I almost did," she said, "but I was afraid that might put you off. Some people don't like lawyers."

"Really?"

"I know it's hard to believe. Bernie, I fibbed a little, okay? At the beginning I treated it all as an acting exercise. Improv, you know? We do scenes like that all the time in class. But I wasn't really lying, any more than you lied to me by not mentioning that you're a burglar."

We had stopped walking now, half a block from Number 304. She nodded meaningfully at the building. "Listen," she said, "I've got a great idea. We could go there right now. I'm sure we can bluff our way past the doorman."

"Unless it's your Haitian friend."

"I could have sailed right past him, too, but I wanted him to ring the apartment first. We wouldn't have to do that this time. We could just walk in as if we lived there."

"And then what?"

"Then you could open Luke's door for me."

"Luke might not like that."

"I'm positive he's not there," she said. "You know what I bet happened? He stole Marty's cards early in the week. Then he got offered a job out of town. He would have jumped at it, too. But we can always ring his bell first, if you're nervous about picking his lock with him inside."

"Sure, that's a good idea," I said. "We'll ring his bell."

"And if he's there I'll just say I came to pick up my clothes. That's easy enough."

"And then we can drop in on the Nugents."

She frowned. "The Nugents? Joan and Harlan Nugent?"

"Those very Nugents. In 9-G."

"How do you know them?"

"I don't."

"Then why did you mention them?"

"You're the one who mentioned them."

"You just did, just a minute ago. 'And then we can drop in on the Nugents,' those were your very words. Remember?"

"Vividly. But you mentioned them two nights ago when we were standing in front of their building."

"I did?" She scratched her head. "Why would I do that? I barely know them."

"Well, you're still way ahead of me," I said, "because I don't know them at all. You asked Eddie when they were coming back from Europe."

"My God," she said. "You're right, I did. But that

was after you left, wasn't it?" She considered this, answered her own question. "Obviously not, or we wouldn't be having this conversation. The Nugents are an older couple. They live two flights up from Luke."

"In 9-G, if I remember correctly."

"You mean I even mentioned the apartment number? You must have thought—"

"That I was being invited to knock off their apartment," I finished for her. "That's exactly what I thought. But if you really didn't know I was a burglar—"

"How could I have known? When a man tells me he's a bookseller I generally take his word for it."

"Why did you mention the Nugents?"

"Because I wondered if they were back yet, that's all. Joan Nugent is an artist, and a couple of times we met in the hall and she asked me about posing for her. The last time I ran into her in the elevator she said she and Harlan were going to Europe, but that she would get in touch when she got back." She shrugged. "I don't know if I want to do it, though, if it would mean coming to this building and possibly running into Luke."

"Especially if you suspect him of taking the cards."

"It's more than a suspicion," she said. "I'm sure of it, and that's all the more reason why I'd like to get my stuff out of there before he comes back. Suppose his place gets raided and my things wind up in an evidence locker?"

"It could happen."

"I'd hate that." She put her hand on my arm. "So what do you say, Bernie? Want to be a real sweetie and show me how good you are at opening locks?"

13

Ten minutes later we were sitting in a Blimpie Base on Broadway, planning the commission of a felony. That set us apart from the other customers, who looked to have gotten well past the planning stage.

I started out by telling Doll I didn't want to have anything to do with it. I'd stayed away from burglary for over a year. Then all I'd done was think about knocking off an apartment and the next thing I knew I was spending the night in a cell.

"I'd like to help," I said. "You left some clothes in Luke's apartment and naturally you wanted them back. But it seems to me there are a couple of alternatives to illegal entry. You could wait until he gets back and give him a call, or you could hit Marty up for a loan and go shopping."

"Forget the clothes," she said.

"Exactly. Forget them and buy new ones."

Forget she'd even mentioned the clothes, she said. The big reason to break into Luke's apartment was to recover Marty's baseball cards. If Luke had left town in response to a call with an offer of work, he had probably rushed off before he had an opportunity to convert the baseball card collection into cash. Maybe he was in no rush, maybe he'd just as soon let the heat die down while he figured out the best way to sell them.

If we could just get into Luke's apartment, she was pretty sure we could find the cards. And if we could return them to Marty, that meant I'd be off the hook for burglarizing his apartment. The charges would be dropped, and wouldn't that be great?

"Well, it would certainly be nice," I told her. "But according to my lawyer they're probably going to have to drop the charges anyway, because he says they haven't got enough evidence to get an indictment, let alone a conviction. On top of that, do you see what I'd be doing? I'd be actually committing a crime in order to exonerate myself from one I didn't do. Somehow it doesn't seem worth it."

As a matter of fact, she went on, there might be something extra in it for me. She was pretty sure there'd be a reward. Marty, after all, was a generous man. His baseball card collection was near and dear to him. Surely I could count on being reimbursed handsomely for the risk I'd be running.

How handsomely, I wondered. Whatever Marty paid me would be coming out of his own pocket, and he'd already paid for the cards once. He wouldn't want to shell out for them all over again, would he?

"You know," she said, "he's already reported the loss to the insurance company, so I suppose they're already processing the claim. If I sat down with him privately and told him how you'd managed to recover the cards, well, maybe he wouldn't bother saying anything to the insurance company."

"I think I see what you're getting at."

"It wouldn't exactly be stealing," she said. "It would be more a case of letting things run their course, wouldn't it? If the insurance company paid half a million dollars to settle the claim, which is only fair because the cards really were stolen, well, Marty would have all that money to spend replenishing his collection. If he could do that by buying an almost identical collection from you for a quarter of a million dollars, say, he'd be ahead of the game."

"And so would I."

"Absolutely. We both would."

"Both of us, eh?"

"Fifty-fifty," she said. "I need you to open Luke's door and you need me to handle the arrangements with Marty. Bernie, that's more than a hundred thousand dollars apiece."

"I don't know about the percentages," I said.

"What could be fairer than fifty-fifty?"

"But is it really fifty-fifty? That's one way to look

at it, that you and I split what Marty pays out. But the whole pie is half a million dollars—"

"And Marty gets half of that, and we get the other half."

"That's if you count you and me as a team, Doll."

"I think we make a great team, Bernie."

"I'm sure we do, but there's another way to look at it, and that's that you and Marty are already a team, and your team winds up with three-quarters of the half million dollars."

We sat there for twenty minutes, arguing over money an insurance company hadn't yet paid for a box of baseball cards we hadn't yet seen. She gave ground grudgingly, and we wound up agreeing to a three-way split. Marty would pay each of us a third of whatever he got from his insurance company.

"But don't even think about going in there tonight," I said. "The public has this romantic idea of burglary as night work, but that's the most dangerous time for it. The later it gets, the worse it is. Right now it's past midnight, and the average person looks suspicious at this hour without even doing anything."

"But—"

"Look around you," I said. "Here are a bunch of perfectly nice people having coffee and doughnuts, and just because it's the middle of the night they look like riffraff and lowlife trash."

"That's what they are, Bernie."

"See? Case closed."

"But—"

"Tomorrow afternoon," I said. "The jeans and the jacket are great on you, but leave them home tomorrow. Dress up nice and meet me at the bookstore at two. We'll go straight from there."

I got to the bookstore the next morning at ten minutes of ten. The first thing I did was call Carolyn. "I'm at the store," I told her. "You said you'd walk over and feed Raffles for me, but you didn't have a chance yet, did you?"

"I'm still on my first cup of coffee."

"He's acting like a famine victim," I said, "but I've learned not to trust him, so I thought I'd better check. I'll feed him, so you don't have to."

"I was gonna come over around eleven. How come you opened up? You're always closed on Sundays."

"Well, maybe I've been making a mistake all these years," I said. "Maybe I've cost myself a bundle by closing on Sundays."

"You really think so?"

"No, but I'm meeting somebody here at two o'clock."

"You're four hours early."

"So? Everybody's got to be someplace. Come by and keep me company if you feel like it."

"I don't know," she said. "You really did have a quiet evening at home, didn't you? That's why you're so bright-eyed and bushy-tailed. I don't know if I can take it."

"Take what?"

"Your good mood."

I considered this. "You didn't have a quiet evening at home," I said.

"I was going to," she said, "but I stopped in at DT's Fat Cat. I figured I'd sleep better if I had a drink."

"Did you?"

"I slept fine," she said, "once they closed the place so I could go home. I may not get there, Bern, but I'll see you tomorrow for sure. Go feed the cat, he must be starving."

I filled his food dish, freshened his water, flushed his toilet, and came back and watched him eat. That reminded me I hadn't had anything myself since last night's moo shu pork, so I went to the deli and picked up a couple of bagels and a container of coffee. After I had my bargain table set up outside I settled in behind the counter and ate my breakfast. The cat came over and sat on my lap for a while, watching me eat, but eating only held his interest when he was the one doing it. He leaped down onto the floor and sat there as if waiting for something to happen.

I finished one bagel and crumpled the paper it had come wrapped in. The noise caught Raffles' attention and he reacted, the way they do. I let him stare in my direction. The minute he looked away I crumpled the paper some more, then tossed it past him. Except it didn't get past him, because he sprang to his right and snagged the ball of paper on one hop. Then he batted it to and fro, chasing it up one aisle and down another and slapping it silly. Finally he decided it was dead and wasn't going to come back to life, so he turned and walked away from it.

"Bring it back," I said, "and I'll throw it again."

I swear he gave me a look, and I swear the unvoiced thought that accompanied it was something along the lines of *What the hell do you think I am, a fucking Labrador retriever?*

His game, his rules. I unwrapped the other bagel, crumpled the paper, and put the ball in play.

Carolyn never showed up, which gave her something in common with most of humanity. I spent a couple of hours crumpling up sheets of paper and trying to throw them past Raffles. Then at a quarter of two the door opened, and it was Doll.

She was all dolled up, too, in a navy-blue dress and high heels. The dress was a perfect choice; it made her look as respectable as a Junior League luncheon while leaving no doubt whatsoever that she was a female member of her species, and that it was a distinctly mammalian species at that.

"You look great," I told her. "That's the perfect outfit."

"Is it all right? I tried on the leather hot pants

and the Deadhead T-shirt, but wouldn't you know it got shrunk the last time I washed it? I was afraid it made me look too chesty."

"That would never do."

"No," she said. "You look great yourself, Bernie. You should put on a tie and jacket more often. Bernie, why are there balls of paper all over your floor?"

I looked around for Raffles, but he was hiding. I crumpled a sheet of paper and his head came into view. "Now watch," I said, and I threw the ball to his left, and the little rascal sprang up and batted it down.

"You have a cat," she said.

"I don't exactly have him," I said. "He just works here. He's not a pet or anything like that."

"What is he?"

"An employee, that's all."

"And what's this, a fringe benefit? On Sundays the help gets to play catch with the boss?"

"We're not playing," I said. "It's to sharpen his reflexes." I walked around picking up paper balls, not for the first time. "He won't fetch," I said.

"He's not a dog, Bernie."

"His words exactly. If he could talk, I mean." I threw a ball for him. "Look at that," I said. "I swear he could play shortstop. Ozzie Smith would have been proud of the move he made on that last one. Of course, Ozzie Smith would have whirled and pegged to first instead of trying to kill the ball.

That's why Ozzie's playing in the bigs and Raffles is snagging mice in a bookstore."

"What happened to his tail?"

"You know how they're always chasing their tails? Well, you see how fast his reflexes are. He was chasing his tail one day and he actually caught it."

"And he killed it?"

"No, he scooped it up on one hop and rifled it to first base. What's so funny?"

"You are."

"It's just nerves, Doll," I assured her. "I'll settle down once we get there."

The cab ride uptown didn't do much to settle either of us. We were blessed with a driver who clearly believed that his best hope lay in reincarnation, and the sooner the better. Neither of us said much, except perhaps in silent prayer, until we pulled up right in front of 304 West End Avenue. I can't imagine the doorman would have challenged a well-dressed couple who arrived by taxi, but the fellow on duty barely noticed us. His attention was taken up by a little old lady who wanted to know what all the fuss had been about that morning.

"Cops in the hallways," she said. "On a Sunday morning yet. This was always such a nice building."

They'd come and gone, he told her, before he went on duty. We were waiting for the elevator when the old woman said, "So what did she do, kill her husband? Stupid! Does she think they grow on trees?"

The door opened and we rode up to the seventh floor. Doll asked me what I thought the woman was talking about. Domestic violence, I said, was what it sounded like to me. On the other hand, I suggested, maybe the old lady was nuts. She'd been carrying on about cops in the hallways, and I certainly hadn't seen any. If the doorman didn't care, why should we?

I turned the wrong way when we got out on seven, but Doll caught my arm and steered me in the right direction. Luke Santangelo's lock yielded to me as to an old lover. In a matter of seconds we were inside.

"I guess you haven't lost your touch," she whispered.

I flexed my fingers. "Once you learn," I whispered back, "you never forget. It's like drowning."

"You mean swimming."

"Or falling off a bicycle," I said. "Same thing." I donned my plastic gloves, double-locked the door, fastened the chain lock, and put on the light. Doll pointed at my gloves and mimed putting on a pair of her own.

"Sorry," I said. "I wasn't thinking. I only brought the one pair. Anyway, you couldn't have worn gloves all the other times you were here, so the place must be full of your fingerprints. A few more won't matter."

"I guess you're right."

"Besides, you don't think Luke's going to dust the place for prints, do you?"

"No, but—"

"So let's just find what we're looking for and get out of here."

That was easier said than done. She went first to the closet, and she did a pretty commendable job of ransacking it, yanking garments off hangers and tumbling boxes down from the top shelf. I guess that's the way to search a place if you're in a hurry, but it's never been my style. I tend to walk lightly upon the earth, especially in other people's houses.

"These are mine," she said, holding a couple of sweaters and a pair of jeans. "But who cares?" She tossed them onto a wooden chair and spun around to glare at the open closet, her hands on her hips. "Come on, Bernie! I thought you were going to check the dresser."

"I did."

"How come you didn't just pull out all the drawers and empty them in the middle of the floor? Isn't that what burglars do?"

"Some do, I guess. This one doesn't."

"Well, you're the expert," she said, "but it seems to me—"

"Slow down," I said. "Take a breath."

"I know they're here," she said. "I guess I had this picture in my mind. You would open the door and we'd walk in and there they'd be, right out in plain sight. I expected to see Marty's rosewood humidor sitting on Luke's coffee table. But of course he left the humidor, didn't he?"

"How would he have taken the cards? He didn't just stuff them in his pockets."

"I don't know. Maybe he'd pack them in a shopping bag."

"And walk out of Marty's building that way?"

"Why not? He could just—Bernie, the attaché case! That's what he would have used."

"I hope the cards don't wind up smelling like meat."

"Meat? Oh, right, I told you how he used it for shoplifting. But I'll bet that's what he did. He put on his one decent suit, he shaved his larcenous little rat face, he packed up his attaché case, and—"

"What's the matter?"

She ran to the closet. "Where's his suit? Shit. Son of a bitch."

"What's the matter?"

"His suit's gone. You don't see a suit, do you? The son of a bitch took it with him."

"You said he probably got an acting job out of town. Maybe they told him to bring a suit because the part called for it."

She shook her head. "Bad casting. If the part called for a suit, you'd get a different actor. Did he take the attaché case? That's the real question, isn't it?"

"Where did he keep it, Doll?"

"In the closet," she said. "Isn't that where you'd keep it?"

"I might. What other luggage did he have?"

"I don't know. We never went anywhere together. All he really wanted to do was go to bed. The bed!"

"What about it?"

"Under it," she said, diving to the floor. I stood by as she fished things out—an olive-drab duffel bag, a maroon backpack, a carryall of light blue parachute nylon. There were other things, too—a couple of athletic shoes, a tennis racket, a sock. No attaché case.

"Shit," she said. "I give up. They're not here. If he had the cards in the first place."

"You think he didn't?"

"I don't know what to think. I was positive, but now I don't know. And if he did have them, they're not here now."

"We don't know that."

"We don't? This is a tiny little one-bedroom apartment, Bernie. And we searched it from top to bottom. Why are you looking at me like that?"

"Sit down," he said. "I'll show you how to search a place."

The thing is, you can't just dash around. You have to proceed methodically, taking it a room at a time, going through each room in a deliberate fashion. You don't necessarily spend more time that way but you spend it wisely, and when you quit a place you know you haven't missed anything.

Within reason, that is. If you put a little thought and effort into it, you can hide stuff so that it won't be found other than by a crew of professionals with time on their hands. Of course, the right dog will sniff out drugs or explosives in nothing flat, but otherwise you're safe.

I was willing to assume, though, that Luke had not enlisted a carpenter to build in some really good hiding places, in a baseboard, say, or as a false back to a cupboard or closet. The fact that he had three large bottles of pills in his freezer and a plastic bag full of some dried herb underneath the sugar in his sugar canister suggested to me that he probably stuck to the tried and true. Most people do.

I spent half an hour at it, and when I was done I'd have been prepared to swear that there was neither an attaché case nor a quantity of baseball cards in that apartment. I didn't say a word during the entire half hour, and, after a few conversational ventures that I ignored, neither did Doll. When I gave up at last and let my shoulders sag in defeat, I realized that she was staring at me with something akin to awe. I asked her what was the matter.

"You've done this before," she said.

"What do you mean?"

"I mean I'm impressed, you're obviously a pro at this. What did you think I meant?"

I shrugged. "I don't know what I thought," I said. "It's frustrating. The best sort of burglary is when you know exactly what you're looking for and just where it is, and you go in and it's there and you take it and you're gone."

"That's how I thought this was going to be."

"I know. So did I. The second-best burglary is when you go in without any expectations whatsoever, and there's the thrill of discovery whenever you find something. But this is the worst kind, because . . . well, no, that's not true, is it? The worst kind is when you get caught."

"Don't even say that, Bernie!"

"The next-to-worst kind," I said, "is when there's something you're looking for and it's not there, and even if you do find something else you don't really give a damn because it's not what you wanted. Here."

"What's this?"

"It's a hundred and twenty dollars," I said. "It's exactly half of what he had stashed in an empty jelly jar in the fridge. There was some change, too, but I left it. Go ahead, take it. We're partners, remember?"

"It seems strange to take it."

"It would seem stupid to leave it. I think we should get the hell out of here. You checked the duffel and the carryall, didn't you? And the little red backpack?"

"I reached inside them. Why?"

"Check 'em good," I said. "One reason I've been going through things so thoroughly is I don't know exactly what we're looking for." I picked up the duffel bag, opened the long zipper, ran my hands around the inside. "Maybe he stuffed the attaché case, cards and all, into a locker somewhere. Maybe he gave it to a checkroom attendant and walked away with a claim check."

"Wouldn't it be in his wallet?"

"Probably," I said. I tossed the duffel bag aside and grabbed the carryall. "Check the backpack," I told her. "It's got a whole batch of compartments, same as this stupid thing. We might as well be thorough."

And I set about being thorough, and so did she, and wouldn't you know it?

"Bernie," she said, dropping the backpack to the floor, turning to me with something in her hand. "Bernie, what's this?"

"Let's see," I said. "Well, it's a baseball card, isn't it? And an old one, too, from the looks of it. Black-and-white photo on the front. Lousy printing, too, but the card's in good shape, wouldn't you say?"

"Bernie—"

" 'A Stand-up Triple!' And there's our hero, standing up at third base. Recognize the guy?"

"Which one?"

"Well, not the third baseman or the umpire. The other guy, the one planted on third with his hands on his hips and a belligerent glare on his face. I never saw him play, but I can recognize him." I turned the card over. " 'Chalmers Mustard.' Can we smell the mustard? No, but I swear there's the faintest trace of Havana tobacco."

"From Marty's humidor."

"I don't think there's any question about it," I said. "The card's from a special Ted Williams series. It's a specialized item, so it's not worth a fortune, but it's rare. And Marty owns it, or at least he did until your friend Luke paid him a visit." I gazed ruefully at the hunk of cardboard, then tucked it away in my breast pocket. "Half of this is yours," I said, "but I'd just as soon keep it intact for the time being. The cards were here, Doll. This proves it. Luke took them and brought them here." I sighed. "And then the son of a bitch took them somewhere else."

14

"Here we are," I said. "The 1950 Chalmers Mustard Ted Williams series. 'A lengthy—some would say overlong—set of cards produced and distributed locally in Boston. Public interest flagged as the season wore on, and the later cards received a tepid reception, perhaps reflecting their subject's lukewarm performance on the playing field.' " I looked up. "I guess the Splendid Splinter had an off year. I didn't know that ever happened to him. I saw a baseball record book a minute ago. We could look it up."

"Do we have to?"

"I guess not," I said. "What difference could it make, anyway? I just thought it would be easy to do, since we're here."

We were at Shakespeare & Co., a bookstore six or seven blocks north of Luke Santangelo's ransacked apartment. We'd walked up Broadway, made our way through the mob of Sunday noshers waiting to get into Zabar's, and were now checking things out in a baseball card encyclopedia. It billed itself as complete, and I could believe it. The thing weighed as much as Hank Aaron's bat.

Every newsstand along our route had had a supply of sports card price guides in magazine form, but they were pretty much limited to the post-1948 sets issued by the more prominent national manufacturers. Our card fit the time frame, but it was much too local and esoteric for the magazines to give it space. The books Ray Kirschmann had found at my store would probably have had the Chalmers set listed, but Ray and that po-faced lout of an ADA had confiscated them.

Just as well. They were out of date, anyway. And I wouldn't have wanted to make another trip to the store. I'd have just wound up feeding the cat again.

"And here's our card," I said. " 'A Stand-up Triple!' Number thirty-four, and that makes it one of the good ones."

"What's it worth?"

"A hundred and twenty dollars. That's in NM condition. It's only thirty bucks in VG. NM is near mint, and VG is very good."

"What's ours?"

"I guess it's near mint. I don't know how they grade these things, but that's what I would call it."

"When you come right down to it," she said, "who cares? After all we went through today, we've got a piece of cardboard that's worth somewhere between thirty and a hundred twenty dollars. Suppose we wanted to sell it. What could we get for it?"

"Gee, I don't know, Doll."

"Twenty dollars?"

"I'm sure we could get twenty."

"Fifty?"

"Probably not. It's worth more than that, but the average dealer wouldn't break out into a cold sweat at the sight of it. It's just one card out of a set that most collectors aren't interested in. If we took it to Boston—"

"Oh, great," she said. "We'll grab the shuttle to Boston so we can get a hot fifty dollars for the fucking card."

"I wasn't suggesting we do that. I was speaking hypothetically."

"I know. I'm sorry I snapped. Let's get out of here, okay? And put the book back before they arrest you for shoplifting."

What a thought. "I think I'll buy it," I said.

"For God's sake, why?"

"I guess the money's burning a hole in my pocket. You know, my half of the two-forty from Luke's jelly jar. Anyway, I like books. And this one brings back memories. I collected baseball cards when I was a kid, did I happen to mention it?"

"Yes," she said. "You happened to mention it."

* * *

We wound up walking all the way to her place.

Did I mention that it was a beautiful day? It was a perfect September afternoon, and we took a rambling walk across Central Park. The minute we crossed Central Park West and entered the park, the landscape shifted from Norman Mailer (or maybe Norman Bates) to Norman Rockwell. Families spread checkered cloths on the lawn and opened picnic baskets. Lovers walked hand in hand, sat close on benches, or lay unashamed in one another's arms. Toddlers toddled, infants mewled and puked, and boys hurled sticks for dogs to fetch. (You'd be wasting your time trying that with a cat.)

Now, I know perfectly well it was an illusion. I even knew it at the time. Half the kids making wheelies on their bikes had very likely acquired those bikes at gunpoint from other kids. Half the folks gazing placidly into the middle distance were too stoned to blink. Some of the lovers would murder their partners by nightfall, while others were doing all they could to spread disease and increase the population. The families were dysfunctional, the toddlers were incest survivors in the making, and all the dogs had fleas.

But the illusion worked all the same. We bought into it, walking those tree-lined paths, leaving them to trip lightly over the greensward. We were no longer a pair of unrepentant felons griping about the minimal return yielded by our criminal enterprise. Instead we became a charming young couple, with a spring in our step, with a song on our lips, and with love and not larceny in our hearts.

Somewhere along the way we stopped and took seats on a slatted green bench. On another bench opposite us, an old woman with a shawl sat feeding Cracker Jack to a couple of gray squirrels. We watched for a while. Then I started talking (it doesn't matter what about) and Doll listened (it doesn't matter how closely). I finished whatever I was saying and put my arm around her, and she turned to look up at me.

And we kissed.

We clung together, breathless, until we had to pause for breath. I looked across the path and caught the old lady watching us. She beamed at me, threw the last of the caramel corn to the squirrels, clucked at them or at us, and waddled off.

"Oh, Bernie," Doll said.

I stood up. She started to rise, but I stopped her with a hand on her shoulder. "You wait here," I said.

"Where are you going?"

"I'll be right back. Wait for me."

"Oh, I will," she said.

As if divinely guided, I followed the path around its first bend. Before I'd gone fifty yards I came upon a young Asian couple with their two children. They had finished their picnic and repacked their straw hamper, all but the picnic blanket. The man and woman were giving it a shake and preparing to fold it. The kids were watching, fascinated.

"That's a wonderful blanket," I told the young father. "I'll give you fifty dollars for it."

As I walked off, the blanket over my shoulder, I could hear the little girl asking why the man had taken their blanket. "The man got lucky," her brother suggested. "Charles!" their mother cried. "Did you hear what he said? Where do they *learn* things like that?" "Where indeed?" Charles said, and I moved on out of hearing range.

Doll was where I'd left her. "A blanket," she said as I hove into view. "Bernie, you're a genius."

And she rose and took my arm, and we went off to spread our blanket beneath the trees.

We left the park at Ninetieth Street and Fifth Avenue, quitting Norman Rockwell's world for Norman Schwarzkopf's (or maybe it was Norman Lear's). I still had the baseball card encyclopedia in the Shakespeare & Co. shopping bag, and Doll had the articles of clothing she'd salvaged from Santangelo's apartment, but we'd left the picnic blanket for whoever needed it next. If we were back in urban reality now, we yet retained a glow imparted by our bucolic idyll. It had us holding hands when we crossed streets, which was something we hadn't done before our sojourn.

We stopped along the way at an Italian place on

Second Avenue. They had half a dozen tables set up on the sidewalk, and we sat at one of them and drank coffee and split a sandwich of cheese and Parma ham on focaccia. Doll recommended it, as she'd picked the place. We were on her turf now, just a few blocks from her apartment.

She grabbed the check when it came. "No arguments," she said. "You paid for the blanket."

"The best fifty dollars I ever spent."

"You're a sweet man, Bernie."

"You're not so bad yourself."

"I just wish . . ."

She let the thought trail off. "If wishes were horses," I said, "burglars would ride. But they're not and we don't. This afternoon was a gift, Doll."

"I know."

Her building on Seventy-eighth turned out to be an Italianate brownstone closer to First than Second. At the stoop she said, "This is where I get off. Do you want to come up for a few minutes? The place is a mess, but I can stand it if you can."

In the vestibule, I scanned the column of buzzers while she fumbled in her purse for her keys. The buzzer for 5-R said *G Cooper* on the little card. Doll started to fit her key in the lock, then asked me if I'd care to get out my tools and show off my skills.

"I don't even need tools," I said. "You could crack this thing with a popsicle stick." I got a plastic calendar from my wallet, my annual gift from a man named Michael Godshaw who lives in hope that someday I'll buy a life insurance policy from him. It's a more flexible plastic than most credit cards. And if I wrecked it, so what?

I didn't, though. I opened the door at least as quickly as Doll could have managed with the key. "No excuse for that," I said. "The lock's a decent one, but you really need a strip of steel attached here or a two-year-old could card his way in. Any locksmith can do it for you. Don't even bother asking the landlord. Just hire somebody to do it."

When you live in a fifth-floor walk-up you get used to the stairs. But I didn't and I hadn't, and it had been a long day. I didn't quite pause for breath at the landings, but I thought about it.

Her own door was secured by three locks, one of them a Fox police lock. It looked safe enough, and neither of us was in a mood to test it. She unlocked all three locks and led me inside. There were two rooms, one of them an eat-in kitchen with a tin-topped table and two caned chairs, the other what the English call a bed-sitter, meaning, I suppose, that you can sit in it or go to bed in it, whatever your pleasure. I suppose you could do anything else you wanted there, too, including swing a cat, but just barely.

"Sit down," she said. "I'll make some coffee. Or would you rather have a glass of wine?"

I told her that sounded good. I was done burgling for the day, so why not? She came back from the kitchen with two glasses of something red and gave one of them to me. "Cheers," I said. "I guess the elves dropped by earlier. I hope they got to my place."

"What are you talking about?"

"You said your place was a mess. It looks to me as though elves came in and cleaned it."

"Oh," she said. "Well, this is as messy as it gets, actually. I tend to be neat."

"I noticed that tendency earlier," I said. "On West End Avenue."

"I wanted to make a mess there," she said. "I was mad at him for taking Marty's cards."

"You were even angrier by the time we got out of there."

"I know. I still think we should have flushed the pills and the dope down the toilet."

"Why not paint satanic slogans on the walls while we were at it? Why not set the bed on fire?"

"Gee, I didn't even think of that," she said.

She put on the TV and we sat side by side on the narrow bed and watched it. (Maybe that's why they call it a bed-sitter. The bed's there, and you sit on it.) We watched the tail end of *60 Minutes* and switched to one of the PBS channels to watch a British miniseries based on a John Gardner espionage novel. The characters all wore moth-eaten cardigans and lived in bed-sitters, so you knew it was cultural.

It ended, finally, and she changed the channel. She went into the kitchen for more wine, even as a woman with one of those patented anchor-woman smiles was saying, "—identification of the nude corpse on the Upper West Side. Film at eleven."

Doll came back with the wine and said, "What was that? Something about a nude corpse?"

"Headless Corpse in Topless Bar," I said, quoting everybody's favorite *Post* headline. "Film at eleven. What time is it, nine?" I looked at my watch. "Ten? Is it really ten o'clock?"

"That's what I've got."

"That was a two-hour program? I thought it was just a very long hour. Oh, hell."

"What's the matter?"

"I'm late. Hell."

"Late for what?"

"I have to go to a poetry reading on the Lower East Side," I said. "It starts at ten."

"You're not making that up," she said. "No one would. Don't forget your book."

"Oh, right. Thanks."

"You're welcome. And Bernie? I had a nice time today."

"Me too, Doll."

She reached out a hand, gave mine a squeeze.

Either of us could have said something. Neither of us did.

I left, and as I reached the fourth-floor landing I heard her door swing shut.

15

Once, briefly, there was a Second Avenue subway. Back in the seventies they dug up the street for miles. Then they ran out of money, so they left everything just long enough for most of the retailers to go out of business. Then they filled in all the tunnels they'd dug, and then they went home. By taxi.

Which is how I went downtown. A subway would have been quicker and cheaper, but then I'd have missed my chance to tell Hashmat Tuktee how to find Ludlow Street when I wasn't all that certain myself. He was newly arrived from Tajikistan, was Hashmat Tuktee, and he grinned at everything as if he still couldn't believe his good fortune. "I am Tajik," he told me. "You probably think I am Uzbek."

"Not in a million years."

"You know my country?"

"I know it when I see it on a map. It's the one that's shaped like a rabbit."

This may not have been the right thing to say, although it's perfectly true. "We are a proud people," he said, grinning furiously. "Very proud." He stamped down on the accelerator and we flew for eight or ten blocks. Then we caught a light and he stamped down just as hard on the pedal. He swung around and grinned at me. "Tell me," he said. "What is rabbit?"

"An animal of great power and wisdom."

"Ah," he said.

I knew Ludlow Street crossed Delancey, so that meant it ran north and south. I figured it probably started or ended at Houston, having ended or started at Canal, but I wasn't exactly sure—

You don't have to know all this. We took Second Avenue to Houston and found Ludlow and crept along it until I spotted Café Villanelle, a dim little storefront tucked in between a burned-out building and an empty lot. Hashmat Tuktee beamed at the sight of it.

"Like my city," he said. "Like Dushanbe."

"Really?"

"Have fighting there now. Burn buildings, break windows. We are a proud people."

"I've heard that."

"Great fighters," he said, showing his teeth. "Fight like rabbits."

A villanelle, as you probably recall, is an old French verse form in which two lines take turns ending all of the stanzas, and then wind up as the last couplet of the final stanza. (There's got to be a better way to explain it, but I'm obviously incapable of it.) Dylan Thomas wrote a couple of villanelles, including "Do Not Go Gentle into That Good Night." More recently, Marilyn Hacker has made interesting use of the form.

I didn't hear any villanelles that night at the eponymous café, or anything with much in the way of traditional form. There were some arresting images ("I'll paint the roof of your mouth with menstrual blood!"), some noteworthy rhymes ("Mother, your ovaries / Are nothing next to Madame Bovary's"), and now and then something with a faintly familiar ring to it ("How do I hate you? Let me fucking count . . .").

The room itself was small and dark. The walls and ceilings were black, and the sole illumination was provided by black candles set in empty cat food cans. There wasn't much of a crowd, so I had no trouble finding Patience and getting a seat next to her.

I don't know how long we were there. I looked at my watch a couple of times. If the light had been better, I might have reached for my wallet and looked at my calendar. Some of the poets recited their work in a deliberately uninflected monotone. Others declaimed and emoted. One fellow with a high forehead and lank shoulder-length hair sang some poems, accompanying himself on the guitar.

He only knew a couple of chords, but then he was only using two melodies, "The Yellow Rose of Texas" and "Moonlight in Vermont."

Nothing lasts forever. Eventually the woman who seemed to be in charge of the proceedings announced that the evening's program was concluded, but that those who were up for it were welcome to hang around for an informal session. My heart sank at the prospect, but Patience was already getting to her feet, and I followed her out to the street.

An empty cab came along just as we cleared the Villanelle's doorway. God knows what he was doing there. My guess is he was lost. I stuck out a hand and found him, and we got in and Patience gave him her address.

She lived on Twenty-fifth Street between Park and Madison, two flights above a shop that trades in reconditioned sewing machines. We didn't say much on the way there. She seemed detached, shut down. In her apartment she made a pot of herbal tea and filled two cups. It tasted as though it could cure just about anything.

"I'm sorry, Bernie," she said, standing at her window and gazing out at a blank wall. "You were sweet to come, but I never should have dragged you all the way down there. It was awful, wasn't it?"

"It wasn't so bad. I thought you were going to read."

"I didn't feel up to it. That's not a great room to read in."

"Well, black candles."

"It's funny, but I always expect a black candle to have a black flame. But of course they never do."

"No."

"The poems were ghastly, weren't they?"

"Well—"

"They're good therapy," she said. "It's wonderful that they're able to bring all that emotion to the surface. And having them perform is a very valuable part of the process. They really put themselves out there that way. Some of those people won't be the same after a night like this."

"I can believe it."

"But the poems themselves," she said, "are enough to make you weep."

"They weren't all that bad. The guy with the guitar—"

"Not all of those poems were his. A lot of them were Emily Dickinson's. You can sing almost anything of hers to the tune of 'The Yellow Rose of Texas.' And you can sing any and all haiku to 'Moonlight in Vermont.' "

"Really?"

"Sure. 'Haiku's such a bore / Sheer pretentious balderdash / Stick it in your hat.' Try it yourself, Bernie."

" 'Wonder why the Japs / Think they're writing poetry / They're just marking time.' "

"That's the idea. Nothing to it, really. 'Pomp and circumstance / Prairie dogs and cauliflower / Moonlight in Vermont.' "

"I kind of like that one, Patience. 'Prairie dogs and cauliflower.' "

"I don't know," she said. "Maybe I should write it down."

I took a cab home from Patience's loft. When I got to my door I heard the phone ringing, but by the time I was inside it had stopped. I hung up my blazer. I'd taken off my tie earlier, at the Villanelle, where even without it I'd felt more than a little overdressed. I got it from my pocket and frowned at it, wondering if the wrinkles would hang out. I hung it up to give them a chance and the phone rang.

It was Doll. "Thank God," she said. "I've been calling and calling."

"What's the matter?"

" 'Film at eleven.' You must not have seen the news."

"No."

"Turn it on now. You have cable, don't you? Turn it on. Right now, I'll hold on."

"What am I supposed to turn on? CNN? Headline News?"

"Channel One. You know, the twenty-four-hour local news channel. Turn it *on*."

"Hold on," I said.

First I had to watch as a professionally sympathetic reporter interviewed survivors at a tenement fire off Boston Road in the Morrisania section of the Bronx. Then they cut to a light-skinned black woman doing a stand-up in front of a building that looked familiar. She reported that the nude corpse found as the result of an anonymous tip in a luxurious Upper West Side apartment had been identified as that of Lucas Santangelo, thirty-four, of 411 West Forty-sixth Street. The dead man, an unemployed actor, had no known connection to the owner-occupants of the apartment, a Mr. and Mrs. Harlan Nugent, who were in any case out of the country, according to neighbors in the building.

"Death appears to have been the result of a single gunshot wound," she said, "but whether it may have been self-inflicted seems to be an open question at this stage. My hunch is that there's more to come on this one, Chuck."

"Thanks, Norma, and now for a look at tomorrow's weather—"

I killed the set and went back to the phone. "Wow," I said.

"When we went there," she said, "they must have already hauled him out in a body bag."

"Are you sure?"

"Don't you remember what the old lady was saying about cops in the hallways? What do you think she was talking about?"

"I thought she said some woman killed her husband."

"So she got it wrong. They hadn't identified him yet."

"The address they gave—"

"Way west on Forty-sixth Street. It's a rooming house. He stayed there for a couple of weeks when he first moved to New York years ago. The thing is, the apartment on West End was never in his name. It was one of those things where he was subletting it from a rent-controlled tenant. That's how he could afford to live there. Bernie, what are we going to do?"

"I don't know about you," I said, "but I'm going to go to sleep. I was going to shower first, but I think I'll let that go until morning."

"But—"

"You're upset," I said, "because he was your boyfriend. But I never even met the guy."

"My fingerprints are all over his apartment."

"You just said the apartment's in somebody else's name. Maybe they'll never get there."

"They'll get there," she said. "They'll talk to the right person at the rooming house and find out he didn't live there anymore, and then they'll call the Actors Equity office and get the right address. Shit, all they really have to do is look in the phone book. Lucas Santangelo, 304 West End. Even the cops ought to be able to figure that out."

I wasn't so sure of that, but I let it pass. I told

her that she might get drawn into the case, if anybody happened to volunteer the information that she had been romantically involved with the dead man. If that happened, all she had to do was tell them an abbreviated version of the truth. "You didn't know him that well," I said. "He was one of several men that you were friendly with—"

"God, that makes me sound like a tramp."

"—and you broke up with him recently, and saw him for the last time a week ago. If you left fingerprints in his apartment, well, so what? I'd be surprised if they gave his apartment a second look. I gather they think he may have killed himself."

"Why would he do that?"

"I don't know why anybody would do it," I said, "but it's something people seem to do all the time. Maybe it just struck him that his life wasn't working out."

"Right, he had half a million dollars' worth of baseball cards in his attaché case and it depressed him so badly that he shot himself. Where would he get a gun?"

"Maybe he had one all along."

"You searched his apartment top to bottom this afternoon," she said. "Did you see a gun?"

"No, I didn't," I said. "On the other hand, you couldn't really expect him to put it back in his sock drawer after shooting himself upstairs in 9-G."

"I didn't think of that," she said softly.

"No, because you're too upset to think clearly.

I'm not upset, but I'm certainly exhausted. It's been a long day."

"It's been almost twelve hours since I met you at your bookstore."

"And I'd already put in half a day by then. I opened up around ten."

"So you've been up since what, eight o'clock?"

"Something like that."

"I should let you go to sleep," she said. "I guess I just want to be reassured that there's nothing I have to worry about."

"Is that all? That's easy. There's nothing you have to worry about, Doll. Get some sleep yourself. I'll talk to you tomorrow."

I got undressed and decided I wanted a shower after all, no matter how late it was or how long I'd been up. Afterward I put on a robe and checked the pocket of my blazer for "A Stand-up Triple!" The back of the card enumerated all the three-base hits Ted Williams had had in the years through 1949, and told which years he'd had them in, and whether he'd secured them in Fenway or on the road. There was no indication, though, as to how many had been stand-up triples of the sort illustrated on the card's face and how many times he'd had to slide.

Damn, I thought. Inquiring Minds Want to Know . . .

I sighed, and got out the step stool, and stood on

it while I removed the little screws that held the panel that makes the back wall of my closet appear to start a few inches sooner than it does. I could have put my picks and probes to bed in the compartment I thus opened, but I decided not to. I'd gotten used to having them on my person lately. I don't know that I'd have felt naked without them, but I decided to go on providing pocket space for them for the next little while.

I could have helped myself to all or part of Harlan Nugent's $8,350, too. It was still there, where I'd tucked it away Friday morning. Sooner or later I'd want to relocate it to Carolyn's hidey-hole, in case she had to bail me out again. But that could wait.

So what I did instead was take out a tan attaché case of Hartmann's best belting leather, its corners reinforced in brass. The case sported matching brass hardware, including a pair of clasps, each with its own three-number combination lock.

I carried it into the living room and sat down on the couch with it. Luggage locks in general are more for show than security. Anyone with enough brute strength to pull the ring top off a can of Dr Pepper can knock them loose with a hammer, or pry them off with a screwdriver. A gentler soul can simply run the numbers. There are, after all, only a thousand possibilities, and how long can it take? It's tedious, starting with 0–0–0 and 0–0–1 and 0–0–2, but once you get going there's not much to it. If you worked at a positive snail's pace of five seconds per combination, you'd run twelve in a minute, 120 in ten minutes, and you'd be all the way to 9–9–9 in what, an hour and a half?

Since the mechanisms are pretty simple, they're also easy to pick, which is what I'd done. Having done so, I'd reset both combinations to 4–2–2, which was the house number of my boyhood home. (That's where *my* baseball cards used to be, once upon a time.) I opened them now so that I could put "A Stand-up Triple!" with its companions.

I know, I know. You're wondering where the attaché case came from. Didn't Doll and I just spend part of the afternoon searching fruitlessly for it?

Well, much as it pains me to admit it, I haven't played entirely fair with you. My day actually got underway a little earlier than you (and Doll Cooper) may have been led to believe. See, I left out a few things in the telling. . . .

16

I was somewhere, God knows where, picking a lock. Had I been an Iraqi, I might have called in the mother of all locks, because every time I seemed to have opened it I found another more intricate mechanism within. At last the final set of tumblers tumbled, giving me access not to a house or apartment but to the inner recesses of the lock itself. I had done it, I had broken into the lock, and I could wander around in its labyrinthine chambers where no mere human had ever gone before, and—

The burglar alarm went off. Loud, piercing shrill. Where was the keypad? What was the combination? How could I get out of here?

I rolled over, sat up, blinked, and glared at the alarm clock. There was no keypad to cope with, no combination to be entered. There was a button to push, and I pushed it, and the awful ringing stopped.

But not without having done its job. I was awake, with no hope of finding my way back into the seductive machinery of the dream. You could wait all your life for a dream like that, and then it finally comes along, and there you are, abruptly delivered from it as if by an obstetrician with a golf date in an hour. Maybe if I settled my head on the pillow, maybe if I just thought about locks for a moment—

No.

It was six in the morning, and time for my Sunday to start. I put on a singlet and a pair of nylon running shorts. I pulled my socks on, reached for my Sauconys, then set them aside and got an old pair of New Balance 450s from the closet. I never wore them anymore because they were falling apart, but you couldn't touch them for comfort.

I put a few things in a fanny pack and hooked it around my waist. I found a terry-cloth sweatband and put it on, picked up a blue-and-white checkered hand towel and tucked that into the waistband of my fanny pack. I let myself out of my apartment, locked up after myself, and put my keys in the fanny pack and zipped it shut.

Outside, the sky was just lightening up, which was more than I could say for myself. I started off walking briskly, and that seemed to me as much as ought to be required of anyone. If a man needs to move any faster than that, let him take a cab.

At Seventy-second Street, I forced myself to turn left, toward Riverside Park and the Hudson River. I walked for another twenty or thirty yards, then made myself ease into a slow trot.

You're doing it, I told myself. *You're running. You fool, you're running!*

Not for very long, however. I trotted for half a block or so, then switched back to my brisk walking pace. By the time I got on the asphalt park path I was trotting again, and fifty yards down the line I was walking.

It's remarkable the extent to which a healthy and reasonably active young man can allow himself to get out of shape. It's even more remarkable the way he can hold two irreconcilable ideas in his mind at the same time. As I huffed and puffed my way around the park, I marveled at the fact that I'd once been masochistic enough to put myself through this pointless and hideous ritual every single day. And, even as I was thinking this, a part of my mind was toying with the prospect of getting back into the horrible swing of it. Just an easy two or three miles a day, I was actually telling myself. Three times a week, say. Just enough to work up a sweat, keep the blood moving, tone the old cardiovascular whatsit. What was so bad about that?

Sweat beaded on my brow, gathered under my arms, dampened the front of my singlet. Well, that was the object, wasn't it? I'd signed on for this farce with the sole intent of working up a visible lather of perspiration, not pushing myself to the brink of coronary catastrophe. I could take it down a notch now, gear down to my old brisk walk, and then in the final stretch—

"Hey, Bernie! What a surprise, huh?"

"Wally," I said.

"Today's my weekly long run," he said. "I figure from here to the Cloisters and back is pretty darn close to a half marathon. And coming back it's mostly downhill."

"Piece of cake."

"You said it. What I'd really like to do, I'd like to do it twice, go for a full twenty-six miles. But then I'd run the risk of peaking too soon."

"You don't want to do that."

"Not with the marathon coming up the first Sunday in November. You think you'll run it next year, Bernie? You could, you know. Just increase your distance a little bit every week and before you know it twenty-six miles is just a walk in the park. Bernie, you're walking. What's wrong?"

"Nothing."

"Why'd you suddenly stop running?"

"I'm practicing for the marathon," I said. "You said it'll be a walk in the park, and that's what I'm doing, walking in the park."

"Pick it up a little," he urged. "We'll take a nice easy run up to Eighty-first Street. Then you can walk back home. How does that sound?"

It sounded terrible. "It sounds wonderful," I assured him, "but I don't want to peak too soon."

I guess he saw the wisdom in that. He took off,

heading gamely uptown, and I found my way out of the park and retraced my steps to Seventy-second and West End. I was walking now, and not too briskly, either, but the part of the system that controls perspiration was a little late getting the message. The sweat was still pouring out of me, and my shorts and singlet were soaked.

Good.

Maybe, I thought, I could have avoided running altogether. Maybe I could have simply soaked my clothes in the sink before putting them on. Then all I'd have had to do was pour a cup of water over my head and I'd be a perfect study in verisimilitude.

Oh, well.

At West End I turned north, not south, and started jogging again. There's something about the sight of the finish line that gets the old adrenaline flowing, and I guess I put on a burst of speed at the end without having intended to. When I reached the entrance of 304, my heart was pounding and I was gasping for breath, even as I mopped my face with the blue towel.

I chugged right past the doorman and into the elevator.

Luke Santangelo's door didn't present much of a problem. There was just one lock, and I picked my way through it with ease. He'd double-locked it, though, so I wouldn't have been any more able than Doll to get past it with a credit card.

Inside, I gave the place a quick check to make sure I wasn't sharing the premises with any other persons, living or dead. This was a simpler process than it had been Thursday night in 9-G. Unlike the Nugents' Classic Six, 7-B was a less-than-classic one-bedroom apartment. There was only a single bathroom and no one had been so inconsiderate as to lock its door, let alone die in it. When I had established as much I returned to the living room and put on the pair of gloves I'd stowed in my fanny pack.

Then I got down to business.

When I left Luke's apartment I was wearing a suit. It was the only one in his closet, a three-button charcoal pinstripe with a label indicating it had been bought (or, considering what I knew about Luke, stolen) from Brooks Brothers. We were about the same size, Luke and I, but the pants were a little tight in the seat and waist and the jacket was a little large at the shoulders.

Maybe if I got back to running three times a week, I thought, and did an upper-body workout with free weights on the days I didn't run—

I found a shirt that fit me, freshly ironed. He'd forgotten to tell them "no starch." He had half a dozen ties hanging on a nail, and I don't know where he'd stolen those, or why he'd bothered. I picked the one with red and black stripes.

His shoes were small on my feet, but I hate the

way running shoes look with a suit, although it's a costume with which Wally Hemphill seems perfectly happy. I tried on all three pairs of leather shoes in his closet and settled on the black penny loafers as the most nearly comfortable of the lot, hoping I wouldn't have to wear them for very long.

His attaché case was under the bed, along with some other luggage. The attaché was the only one that was locked, and the only one that seemed to contain anything. I picked it open and found, to my gratification if not greatly to my surprise, that it was full of baseball cards. I'd thought I might add my sneakers and running gear, but there wasn't any room.

Before I closed the attaché case, I chose a single baseball card and found a temporary home for it in a pocket of the maroon backpack. I took a quick turn around the apartment, but I did not linger long. I had my picks in a pocket of the suit jacket, where I could get at them easily, and I took off the pliofilm gloves just before I quit the apartment and slipped them into another pocket. I had the attaché case in one hand, and I had a canvas tote bag over one arm. It contained my sneakers and running clothes and fanny pack, and it bore the logo of the Mercurial Wombat, a gift shop in Tucumcari, New Mexico.

There was a tenant in the hallway, a woman waiting for the elevator, but if she looked in my direction all she could have seen was a man locking his door. It wasn't my door, and I wasn't using a key, but there was no way for her to know that. Before I'd finished, the elevator came and whisked her away. Then I took a silk hanky from the breast pocket of my suit, wiped my prints from the doorknob, and walked to the end of the corridor, where a door led to a staircase.

I climbed the two flights to the ninth floor, made sure the hall was empty, and walked the length of it to the Nugents' door. I hadn't rung Luke's bell, but I leaned long and hard on their buzzer, giving anyone inside plenty of time to put on a robe and come to the door. When no one did, I let myself in. I didn't bother letting my eyes accustom themselves to the darkness this time around. I put my picks away, donned my gloves, and turned on a light.

The apartment hadn't changed much in the fifty hours or so since my last visit. I took a quick look around, then went straight to the guest room. The harlequin on the easel looked as depressed as ever, and who could blame him?

The bathroom door was still locked. I knocked on it, and on the adjoining wall. I tapped the switch plate and fiddled with the switch, the one that didn't seem to turn on a light in either the guest room or the bathroom.

I drew my tool ring from my pocket, selected the appropriate instrument, and unscrewed the two screws that held the switch plate in place. I lifted it off and set it aside. It was a dummy, with no switch box in the wall behind it. The switch itself was attached to the plate and came away with it, leaving a rectangular opening about four inches high and three inches wide. I put my hand in and tapped the rear of the little compartment, running my fingers over the surface. I had my gloves on, so it took me longer than it might have to identify what I was touching as the unglazed side of a square of ceramic tile.

What had we here? A hiding place? Not likely, because the interior of the opening wasn't framed. Anything you stashed here would drop down to the bottom of the wall and you wouldn't be able to get it out.

I put a little pressure on the tile. It was hinged on top and it swung back, and I caught the scent of the dead man in the bathtub. The bathroom door fit snugly enough to have held the smell within, but I'd broken the seal when I pushed the tile, and two days of aging had ripened him wonderfully. I steeled myself, reached all the way in, and unlocked the door.

I made myself go in there. I drew the shower curtain and took a look at the fellow, just to refresh my memory. He was quite as I remembered him, if a good deal more pungent. I still couldn't tell if there was a gun in the tub with him, and I still didn't care enough to move him to find out. I left the bathroom door open and went to the master bedroom, where I spent a moment or two. I went back to the bathroom and took hold of the door, swinging it to and fro, not so much to air the place out as to let the aroma fill the rest of the apartment. It wasn't the sort of task you want to devote a great deal of time to, and I didn't. Before long I left the bathroom, closed the door, and reached in through the secret passageway to turn the lock.

I withdrew my arm and the hinged tile swung right back into place. I replaced the dummy switch plate and screwed in the screws. I went into the master bedroom again and scooped up the watches and jewelry I'd been so careful to put back two nights ago. This time it all went straight into the attaché case. Then, in Harlan Nugent's closet, I picked out a well-polished pair of shoes, black cap toes by Allen-Edmonds. They were much easier on my feet than Luke's penny loafers, which I'd actually kicked off shortly after entering the Nugent apartment. (They went better with the suit, too.) I put the loafers in the closet, in the space on the shoe rack previously occupied by the cap toes.

I turned off all the lights, let myself out, locked up, and went home.

After I'd showered and shaved and rinsed out my running clothes, I got dressed again, this time in some clothes of my own. I put on my blue blazer and a pair of gray slacks, and I packed up all of Luke's clothes along with Harlan Nugent's shoes in a pair of plastic shopping bags. I could have hung everything in my closet, but why take chances? The shirt had a laundry mark, and there might well be something identifiable about the suit. They have this DNA testing nowadays, so God knows what they can or can't find out. Besides, it's not as if I would ever have worn any of the stuff again. The suit didn't fit right, the shirt had an unbecoming collar style, and the tie was a real loser. The shoes were a temptation, the first $300 shoes I'd ever had on my feet, and I sort of felt like keeping them around. But they were a half-size too large, and that made it a little easier to give them up.

I hid the attaché case behind the panel in my closet, along with the Tucumcari tote bag. I tucked my picks in one pocket, my gloves in another, and I put on a much nicer tie than I'd taken from Luke's place, and I locked up and left.

I walked east on Seventy-first, and at the corner of Broadway I found a pay phone and dialed 911. "Hi," I said. "Say, I just had a delivery at West End and Seventy-fourth and there was a real nasty smell coming from one of the apartments. I was in the military, and it's a smell you don't forget once you smelled it. Somebody's dead in there, I'd put money on it." The operator asked my name. "Naw, I don't want to get involved," I said. "You got to put something down on your form, put Joe Blow. The apartment's 9-G, that's G as in George, and the building's number 304 West End Avenue. I tried reporting it to the doorman but I don't think he got it.

Could be his English isn't too good. 9-G, 304 West End. Something dead in there, I'd be willing to bet on it. Bye."

The first uptown train to come along was an express, and I rode it one stop to Ninety-sixth Street. I went out through the turnstile and started walking down Broadway. The first panhandler I met was a woman, the second a large man. I gave each of them a dollar. The third was a man about my size, and I gave him my two shopping bags. "What's this?" he demanded. "Hey, what's this?"

"Wear it in good health," I told him, and turned around and went back to the subway.

By ten o'clock I was in the store, helping Raffles develop his mousing skills. A few hours later I was back in Luke's apartment, trying to look as though I was there for the first time. I'd been careful to leave his $240 in the jelly jar earlier. This time I took it, but you'll recall that I split it down the middle with Doll.

That's called ethics.

By the time I got home my half of the $240 was largely depleted. I'd spent twenty bucks for a baseball card encyclopedia and fifty for a blanket, and as the night wore on I kept shelling out for cabs and coffee. And now it was two in the morning, and I'd been awake for twenty hours, and was I bedded down with my head on my pillow? I was not. Instead, I was sitting on my couch examining baseball cards and looking them up in the encyclopedia.

Some kids never grow up.

17

"This is an interesting combination," Carolyn said, inspecting her sandwich. "Corned beef, pastrami, turkey and—"

"Smoked whitefish."

"And cole slaw and Russian dressing, all on a seeded roll. Nice. I don't think I ever had it before. Is it named for anybody?"

"They call it the Pyotr Kropotkin," I said. "Don't ask me why. Normally it comes on rye bread, but I thought—"

"Much better on a roll. Where's your sandwich, Bernie?"

"I'm just having coffee," I said. "I've got a lunch date in an hour."

"You didn't have to bring me a sandwich, Bern. You could have just called and I'd have gone somewhere on my own. But I'm glad you came by, because I never got out of the house yesterday. It's a funny thing, but every time I spend four or five hours at Pandora's or the Fat Cat, I'm a complete wreck the next day."

"I wonder why that is."

"Well, the rooms are very smoky," she said. "A lot of the regulars smoke, and the ventilation's not good at all."

"That must be it."

"And in the course of a long evening I'll almost always have a piece of pie or a candy bar, something sweet like that. And you know how I'm subject to sugar hangovers."

"I know."

"So I spent the day at home. I reread a Kinsey Millhone. The one about the high school kid who has an affair with his gym teacher's wife, and then she gets him to kill her husband. I just gave away the ending, so I hope it's one you already read."

" *'T' Is for Sympathy?* I read it when it first came out."

"You remember the scene where Kinsey's shooting baskets with the girls' gym teacher?" She rolled her eyes. "Case closed, Bern. So how'd it go yesterday? You sell any books?"

"Well, it's a long story," I said.

"Wow," she said. "It's real complicated, isn't it? Did you know the dead guy would turn out to be Luke?"

"I knew there had to be a connection," I said. "There were too many 'just-happeneds' from the beginning. When a corpse just happened to be in the apartment Doll Cooper just happened to mention, I figured he wasn't some guy who dropped in to wash his hands. Besides, he looked familiar."

"I remember you saying that."

"I thought I might have seen him around the neighborhood, but I'd seen him more recently than that, and not from a distance, either. He was the harlequin."

"Huh?"

"On Joan Nugent's easel. A bell went off when Doll talked about posing for Mrs. Nugent. I immediately thought of the harlequin, but all I could remember for certain about him was that he looked sad."

"You'd look sad, too, with a bullet hole in your forehead."

"The harlequin looked sad," I said, "but beyond that I couldn't picture what he looked like. When they're dressed like that all you see is the costume."

"So you went back for a second look."

"I went back for the baseball cards," I said, "or whatever Doll was hoping to find in Luke's apartment."

"And you didn't want her along when you went in."

"No, I figured one's company and two's a crowd. From Luke's place it was easy enough to go back to the Nugents'. I was already in the building, and I knew the locks wouldn't be a problem."

"Except for the one in the bathroom."

"That was still bothering me," I admitted. "The fact that it was clearly impossible. There were two scenarios I could come up with and neither of them made any sense. One, he broke into the apartment, took off all his clothes, locked himself in the bathroom, twisted his arm into a knot to shoot himself in the middle of the forehead, and then ate the gun."

"Couldn't he have dropped it and fallen on it?"

"Sure, why not? Or he could have opened the window, stuck the gun on a ledge, closed the window, then slumped down in the tub and expired. The thing is, nothing about suicide makes sense, even if you manage to figure out a way he could have done it."

"So that leaves murder."

"And that was impossible, too, because the door's locked from the inside. Whoever killed him had to leave the bathroom through the door."

"What about the window?"

"Forget the window. The idea of some Human Fly slipping through that tiny bathroom window and rappelling down the side of the building—well, I'd rather believe he shot himself and then ate the gun for dessert. No, the murderer went out the door, but the door was locked."

"The murderer was a ghost?"

"Either that or there was some way to get around the lock. The more I thought about it, the more I figured that had to be the answer. The last time I flushed the toilet for Raffles, I thought about installing one of those pet ports. You know, you put some sort of hinged flap at the bottom of the door, and that way an animal can get in and out even if the door's closed. If I had one of those, I wouldn't have to remember to leave the bathroom door open."

"Did the Nugents have one of those?"

"No."

"Because I can't believe a cat killed him, Bernie. I draw the line at that."

"No," I said, "although a dog or cat could have moved the gun so that a suicide would wind up looking like murder. But they don't have any pets, and it wouldn't matter if they did because there was no pet port in the bathroom door in the first place. But there had to be something, and then I just happened to think of the light switch."

"Just happened."

"What triggered it," I said, "was flicking a switch in my own bathroom. The light didn't go on."

"Because it was a dummy switch?"

"No, because the bulb had burned out."

"How many burglars did it take to change it?"

"Just one, but while I was changing it I remembered the switch at the Nugent apartment. Now it's not unusual to have a switch that no longer turns anything on or off. A lot of people remove ceiling fixtures when they redecorate, and it's easier to leave the switch plate than plaster over the hole in the wall. Still, I got to wondering what I'd find underneath the switch plate."

"And what you found was a hole in the wall."

"Right."

"And that meant somebody could shoot Luke Santangelo, go out the door, pull it shut, unscrew the switch plate, reach in through the opening, and lock the door."

"Barely," I said. "If my arm had been any shorter I couldn't have reached. And if it had been any fatter it wouldn't have gotten through."

"So we can look for somebody with long skinny arms. But why would anybody go through all that? I don't get it."

"Neither do I."

"So that it would look like suicide? But if you were gonna fake a locked-room suicide, wouldn't you leave the gun behind?"

"Ah, zair you have eet," I said. "No matter how clevair ze criminal, he makes ze leetle mistake."

"But—"

"It doesn't make sense," I agreed, "but so what? It's not my problem."

"It's not?"

I shook my head. "I'm glad I found out about the dummy switch plate, because the impossible-crime element bothered me. I wanted to know how it was done. But I don't have to know *why* it was done, or by whom."

"Or what Luke was doing in that apartment."

"None of that. I put a couple of pieces of jewelry in the tub with him, and I rifled some drawers in the bedroom and took some other jewelry away with me. That was to give the cops an easy answer to some of those questions. He was committing a burglary, he had a partner, the partner killed him. And no, I don't think that's what happened, but I don't honestly care what happened."

"You don't?"

"I've got enough things to worry about," I said. "Like making sure they drop the charges against me. And finding a way to keep from losing the store."

"The store," she said. "I forgot about that, with everything that's been going on. Bernie, your problems are over!"

"They are?"

"You've got the cards, haven't you? All you have to do is give them to Borden Stoppelgard in exchange for a long-term extension of your lease. Wasn't that the deal he offered you?"

"More or less."

"That's why you're all dressed up. You're having lunch with Borden Stoppelgard, aren't you?"

"No, but you're close."

"I'm close? I don't know what that means. Who's close to Borden Stoppelgard?"

"Nobody who can help it."

"But—"

"I'd better get going," I said. "I don't want to keep Marty waiting."

"Marty? Marty Gilmartin?"

"At his club," I said. "Pretty fancy, huh? I'll tell you all about it."

The Pretenders have as their clubhouse a five-story Greek Revival mansion facing Gramercy Park. I walked up Irving Place and arrived no more than three minutes late for my one o'clock lunch date. I gave my name to the liveried attendant at the desk and he informed me that Mr. Gilmartin was awaiting me in the lounge.

I walked down a half flight of carpeted stairs and into a cozy wood-paneled room with a bar at one end and a pool table at the other. Two men stood, cues in hand, while a third took aim at a shot that didn't look terribly promising. Several stood at the bar, and eight or ten others were grouped in twos and threes at dark wooden tables. They were all over thirty-five, they all wore jackets and ties, and one of them was Martin Gilmartin.

Truth to tell, he wasn't terribly hard to find. He was seated by himself with a newspaper and a drink, and he looked up with interest when I entered the room. I approached him and said, "Mr. Gilmartin?" and he got to his feet and said, "Mr. Rhodenbarr?" and we shook hands. I apologized for my late arrival and he assured me that was nonsense, I wasn't late at all. He was an elegant man, tall and slender and silver-haired, splendidly turned out in a tan suit, a deep blue shirt with a contrasting white collar, and a light blue tie. His shoes were cap toes, and looked remarkably like the pair I'd worn home from Harlan Nugent's the previous morning, although those had been black. Gilmartin's were a rich walnut brown.

"I'm awfully sorry," he said. "I told you that you'd need a jacket here, but I didn't think to mention we're stuffy enough to require a tie as well. I see they made you put on one of those horrors they've got hanging in the cloakroom."

"Actually, it's my own tie."

"And a very nice one, too," he said smoothly. "We could eat down here, but it's quieter and a bit more private upstairs in the dining room. Does that sound all right to you?"

I said it was fine and he led me up the stairs and down a hallway to the dining room, pointing out various objects of interest along the way. The ceilings were high, the floors deeply carpeted, and the furniture ran to a lot of dark wood and red leather. The walls were thickly hung with portraits, all of them elaborately framed and almost all of them of actors and actresses.

"Notice the two portraits on either side of the fireplace," he said. "They're in matching frames, although they're the work of two different artists. I don't suppose you recognize the subjects?" I didn't. "We refer to them affectionately as the honorary founders of the club. The chap on the left is James Stuart, and on the right we have his son, Charles Stuart. You may remember him as Bonnie Prince Charlie."

"Pretenders to the English throne."

"Very good. James called himself James III, but history has called him the Old Pretender, and his son the Young Pretender. And so, although the Stuarts are not actors, they seem unquestionably qualified to be of our company. With a single exception, all the other portraits depict members of the Profession."

"Who's the other nonactor?"

"There are four of them, actually, but they're together in the painting. You may have noticed it as you came in, hanging right opposite the cloakroom."

"The four young black men standing around a microphone."

"I don't believe any of them ever trod the boards," he said, "although they'd have been eligible for membership here in that they were unquestionably show-business professionals. They called themselves the Platters, and one of their biggest hits was a song called 'The Great Pretender.' " He smiled, shook out his napkin, and placed it upon his lap. "Well," he said, "what will you have to drink? And then we probably ought to have a look at the menu."

We had a remarkably civilized conversation through drinks and appetizers. When the waiter had served our entrees, a lull settled in. I thought we might get to the business at hand, but after a moment he began talking about a play he'd seen, and that carried us through to coffee. Then it was clearly time, and it was evidently up to me to begin.

"I'm sorry I called you at home this morning," I said, "but I didn't have your office number."

"My home is my office," he said, "although I have more than one telephone line. Here, let me give you a card."

"Thank you," I said. "Here, have one of mine."

"Ah," he said, taking it, turning it over in his hand. "Rabbit Maranville. From the Diamond Stars set of the mid-thirties. I can't recall whether or not he's in the Hall of Fame. Nor can I claim to have seen him play. I'm not quite old enough."

"I was thinking you might recognize the card."

He nodded. "The years haven't dealt kindly with it, have they? I hope they were easier on the Rabbit himself. The card's been folded, one corner's completely gone, and well, it's a mess, isn't it?"

"It would be worth about two hundred dollars in

near mint condition," I said. "But in the shape it's in—"

"No more than five or ten dollars. Assuming someone wanted such a poor specimen." He handed it back, inhaled deeply, exhaled thoroughly. "How on earth did you get hold of this? But I suppose that's a professional secret."

"Sort of."

He sipped his coffee. "Cash," he said.

"You needed some."

"I needed to get some without looking as though I needed it. I have a lot of assets, but none that I could convert to cash invisibly. If I sold paintings off the walls, the sale would be a matter of record and there'd be a blank spot on the wall where the painting had hung. If I sold real estate . . . well, in this market you have to give it away, and the only way to unload anything is to take back mortgages. I wouldn't wind up with anything in the way of cash. And, as you've observed, I needed cash."

"How much?"

"Ideally, a million dollars."

I wondered what it would be like to need a million dollars. I knew people who *wanted* a million dollars, but that's not the same thing.

I said, "So you thought of your baseball cards."

"I've been collecting them for years. My occupation is buying and selling, you know. I began acquiring the cards as a hobby, something to take my mind off weightier matters. Can you believe I've had a higher annual return on them than on stocks or paintings? And don't even mention commercial real estate."

"I won't."

"But what's truly remarkable about the cards," he said, "is the ease with which they can be sold. You walk in with a box of cards, you walk out with a fistful of cash."

"Like stamps or coins."

"I would suppose so, although I think that cards are if anything a little more anonymous. I can tell you this much. In a matter of weeks, without anyone's knowing what I was doing, I had liquidated virtually my entire holdings and raised close to six hundred thousand dollars." He leaned forward. "I should emphasize that there was nothing the slightest bit illegal or immoral or unethical about what I had done. I owned those cards outright. I had bought them, and they were mine to sell."

"And nobody had to know about it."

"And no one did. My collection was housed in a rosewood humidor in my study. The cedar lining that once protected fine cigars from deteriorating is equally efficacious at preserving cardboard rectangles from insect damage. I kept the most valuable cards in acetate sleeves. The rest were loose." He raised a hand, and a waiter hurried over to pour us more coffee. "I would take twenty or fifty or a hundred cards at a time from the box. After I'd sold them, I would stop at another card store and buy late-date commons to replace what I'd sold. Or earlier material in very poor condition, like that unfortunate Rabbit Maranville specimen you brought along."

"So the humidor stayed full."

"That's right. I took a few dozen cards from the box in the morning, and I put back that many or more at night. Nowadays, you know, a full set includes a card for every player in the major leagues. It hasn't always been like that. The 1933 DeLong set had only twenty-four cards in total. The key to it's the Lou Gehrig card. It's worth a little more than the other twenty-three cards combined."

"Did you have one?"

"In VG. In the Goudey set of the same year there were two hundred forty cards, but substantially fewer than two hundred forty different players. The most popular athletes had more than one card. Gehrig had two, and Babe Ruth had four different cards. I owned three of the four Babe Ruth cards, and one day last summer I sold them for a total of twenty-eight thousand dollars. I replaced the Babe with Zane Smith, Kevin McReynolds, and Bucky Pizzarelli." He shook his head. "Babe Ruth started out with the Boston Red Sox, you may recall. He was the best pitcher in baseball, but you couldn't keep a hitter like the Babe on the bench three days out of four, so they had him play the outfield. And the owner of the Red Sox sold him outright to New York. He wanted the money so he could back a Broadway show. Yankee Stadium became the House That Ruth Built, and the Boston fans never forgave that damn fool of an owner, and who could blame them? But I think I know how he may have felt, selling the Babe three times over and filling his slot with the likes of Zane Smith, Kevin McReynolds, and Bucky Pizzarelli."

"And did you use the money to back a Broadway show?"

He smiled at the very thought. "That would be rather like trading the family cow for some magic beans, wouldn't it? No, the stage is many things to me, but not a commercial arena. My wife and I believe in patronage, and I suppose you could say that we err on the side of generosity in our support of the theater. Sometimes our contribution takes the form of an investment, but it's made without much hope of return."

"I see."

"So I gradually sold off my holdings," he said, "deliberately replacing the wheat with chaff and constructing a sort of Potemkin Village of worthless cards in my humidor. Everything good was gone."

"Except Ted Williams."

"You spotted those, did you?" His eyes twinkled.

"Couldn't trade Ted Williams. The Red Sox fans would hang me in effigy."

"That's not why you kept them."

"No, of course not. They were identifiable. The set's scarce, all out of proportion to the price it would bring. And you know my brother-in-law."

"He's my landlord."

"And presumably you know of his passion for the Splendid Splinter. If I sold those cards, there was a fair chance they'd wind up in the hands of a dealer who'd offer them to Borden. One thinks of baseball cards as interchangeable, but Borden's seen my Williams cards enough to recognize them. At the very least, he'd buy the set and then want to compare it to mine. When I couldn't produce them, he'd know I'd sold them. Which is to say he'd know I'd been forced to sell them in order to raise cash."

"Which is what you didn't want to get around."

"Precisely. Easier and safer all around to hang on to the Ted Williams material. But I sold off everything else of value. And, as I've said, what I'd done was entirely within my rights. It was secretive, but one's allowed to have secrets."

"And then?"

"Then I got a telephone call in the middle of the night," he said. "I'd spent an evening with my brother-in-law, always an exhausting experience—"

"I can imagine."

"—and you called, and it was late and I was

tired, and something made me go directly to my study and lift the lid of my humidor. And the cards were gone."

"No," I said.

"I didn't go to my study? I didn't open the humidor? The cards were not gone?"

"You already knew they were gone," I said. "Say my call spooked you and you jumped to the conclusion you'd been burglarized. It's an odd reaction to a late-night nuisance call, but it's not inconceivable. Maybe you'd scout around to make sure your valuables were intact, but your valuables were long gone from the rosewood humidor because you'd already taken them out and sold them. Why would you dash into the study to check on Zane Smith and Bucky Pizzarelli?"

He bought time with a sip of coffee. "You're a very perceptive young man," he said.

"Not that perceptive," I said, "or that young, either, but it's pretty clear what was going on. You already knew the humidor was empty. My phone call was a perfect opportunity for you to go public with the information. You could scoot into the study, open the celebrated rosewood humidor, and discover the cards were gone."

"Why would I do that?"

"To collect the insurance. You had sold the cards, but I don't suppose you canceled your insurance coverage, did you?"

He was silent for a long moment, gazing off at

some dead actor's portrait, gathering his thoughts. Then he said, "It's not like murder, is it? Premeditation's immaterial. Insurance fraud isn't considered a less serious offense if you do it on the spur of the moment."

"No."

"I have to say I didn't plan it from the very beginning. My original intention was merely to sell the cards quietly for the best possible price. And I did a good job of that."

"And?"

"When I'd disposed of perhaps a third of my holdings, the insurance premium came due. A floater on that sort of collection isn't terribly expensive, and I couldn't have saved all that much by asking them to lower my coverage to reflect the diminished nature of the collection. So I paid the premium in full, telling myself that I'd notify the company when I'd sold off the remainder."

"But you didn't."

"No, I didn't. Instead, I laid the groundwork for the commission of a felony. You can't imagine what that felt like. Oh, for heaven's sake, what's the matter with me? Of course you can."

"I've laid a little groundwork in my time."

"Indeed. Bernard, I don't ordinarily have a brandy after luncheon. After dinner, yes, but not after luncheon. But if I could persuade you to join me—"

"What a nice idea," I said.

* * *

"I don't know that I would have gone through with it. You see, I've always been an honest man. In my business dealings I've always tried to be a step ahead of the next fellow, but I've been law-abiding throughout. Still, there's an emotional difference between defrauding an insurance company and stealing the pencils from a blind man's cup."

"I know what you mean."

"I wasn't sure how best to proceed. It seemed to me that the cards couldn't simply disappear. There ought to be the appearance of a burglary. We live in a building with exemplary security, and I understand the locks are on an order that would keep most housebreakers out."

"Most of them," I said.

"So how to create the appearance of a burglary? If I'd known you I might have asked for your professional advice on the matter. I thought I could just leave the door unlocked after having pretended to lock it. But I wasn't sure that would set the stage sufficiently. Oughtn't the premises to look as though they'd been ransacked? What does a house look like after you've been through it?"

"About the same as it did when I arrived."

"Really? Perhaps I was trying to be too thorough, perhaps out of a reluctance to commit myself. The point turned out to be moot. I went to the humidor one day and found it unlocked. I lifted the lid and found it empty."

"When was this?"

"Monday afternoon. I had luncheon here and got home between three and four. I couldn't guess when I'd last looked at the cards. There was little reason to examine them, now that all the decent material was gone. I can't tell you what went through my mind when I looked into that empty box."

"I can imagine."

"I wonder if you can. I began to doubt my own soundness of mind. Had I disposed of the cards and somehow forgotten the episode? Because, you see, I'd planned to get rid of them."

"Who was going to hold them for you?"

He looked puzzled. "No one, for heaven's sake. I certainly wasn't going to let anybody know what I was doing. And why would I want anyone to hold them, anyway? As soon as they were out of my house, I intended for them to disappear from the face of the planet. They'd wind up in an incinerator or a Dumpster, I suppose. I hadn't worked out the details at that point."

"And instead they vanished into thin air."

"Someone had taken them," he said, "but who and why? And what was I to do? Report them stolen? There was certainly not the slightest evidence of a burglary. My policy covers mysterious disappearance as well as theft, and no disappearance was ever more mysterious than this one, but did I dare report it? I was in a quandary. It seemed to me as though I still ought to try to make it look like a burglary, even though the cards were already out of the house." He sighed. "And then we spent the evening with Edna's awful brother, and he was crowing over his triumph in having bought a rare book for a fraction of its current value."

"*'B' Is for Burglar.*"

"Exactly. All I heard was the last word. So burglary was very much on my mind, and we came home and the telephone rang, and it was you. Though of course I didn't know who you were or what you did for a living. You didn't mention your name—"

"Impolite of me."

"—and if you had I'd have thought of you as Borden's tenant, if indeed I chanced to recognize the name at all. I might have, because it's an unusual name, Rhodenbarr. What's the derivation?"

"It was my father's."

"Ah, I see." He lifted his glass of brandy and admired in turn its color, its bouquet, and its taste. "As I was saying, I knew nothing about the identity of my late-night caller, but the opportunity seemed heaven-sent. Edna asked me what was so disturbing. I'm no actor, my membership here notwithstanding, but I had only to be myself. I rushed into the study, I unlocked the humidor, I 'discovered' the loss of its contents, and I called the police."

"Who promptly traced the call."

"I didn't even know they could do that. In the movies and on television they're forever trying to keep criminals on the phone while they trace the call. Now I gather computers keep a record of everything. They did indeed trace the call, and remarkably enough traced it to a known burglar, who turned out to be the very bookstore owner Borden had boasted of outwitting. Ironic, eh? But horribly inconvenient for you, and for that I apologize. Did they go so far as to arrest you?"

I nodded. "I spent a night in a cell."

"No!"

"Not your fault," I said. "Hazards of the game."

"How sporting of you to see it that way. But you hadn't done anything to deserve it, had you?"

"Well," I said, "actually, when you come right down to it, that's not entirely true."

More coffee, more brandy. "When you called this morning," Martin Gilmartin was saying, "I was utterly confounded."

That had been my intention. I'd told him I had been fortunate enough to recover his cards, and wondered if he could let me know the name of his insurance company so that I could see about turning them in for a reward. Unless he thought there might be a mutually advantageous way to handle the matter between ourselves. There had been a strangled pause, then a remarkably graceful invitation to lunch.

"Then I gave it some thought," he went on, "and my position seemed a little less dire. After all, suppose you did go to the insurance company. One of two things would happen. They might look at the cards, assess their value, compare them to the inventory I'd supplied when I arranged the coverage, and conclude that you were trying to pull a fast one. Either you'd already skimmed off the cream of the collection or you'd never taken it in the first place, but in any event they certainly would refuse to have any further dealings with you."

"Possible."

"Or they might have the cards appraised. They're not worthless, after all. The Chalmers Mustard set is worth a couple of thousand, and there are some other Ted Williams items I held on to as well. Say the whole batch is worth ten thousand dollars. I don't think it is, but we'll use that as a figure. After they've run the numbers, they negotiate with you and arrange to acquire the cards. Then they present them to me. 'Here you are, Mr. Gilmartin,' they say. 'We were ever so fortunate as to recover your collection intact. Have a nice day.' 'I beg your pardon,' I reply, 'but these are not my cards at all.' 'Our position is that they are, and that you misrepresented them when you applied for the policy, which we are accordingly canceling as of this moment. If you institute a lawsuit, we'll respond by having you charged with misrepresentation and fraud, but do have a nice day.' "

"They might try that."

"In which case I'd be stuck with a box of junk instead of a six-figure settlement. I could always bring suit, hoping they'd be willing to split the difference, but I might decide it wasn't worth the trouble, not to mention the negative publicity." He furrowed his brow, working it all out. "The best thing to do would be to pay you a finder's fee. What did I just say the cards were worth? Ten thousand at the outside? Well, let's double that. Twenty thousand dollars."

I looked at him.

"No, I didn't really think that would fly. I'm low on cash at the moment, and it would be a strain to pay you even that much. I'll have cash when the insurance company pays up, but they can be sluggish when it comes to settling a claim. Besides, I'm going to need that money. If I hadn't needed it I wouldn't have put in a fraudulent claim in the first place. In a year's time I ought to have more money than I'll know what to do with. Now if you were willing to take a promissory note—"

"You know, I wish I could. But you're not the only one with a cash-flow problem."

"It's the economy," he said with feeling. "Everybody's up against it. But may I say something?"

"Please."

"This may sound like the brandy talking, and perhaps that's exactly what it is, but I can't dismiss the feeling that you and I have the opportunity to do ourselves and each other a great deal of good."

"I know what you mean."

"It's ridiculous on the face of it, and yet—"

"I know."

"Well," he said. "That doesn't change the situation of the moment. Perhaps it would help clarify things if you could tell me just what it is that you want."

"That's easy," I said. "I want to keep my store."

18

When I went out for lunch with Martin Gilmartin I left a little cardboard sign hanging in the door. *Back at,* it says, and there's a clock face. I had set the hands at two-thirty, and when I got back there was a customer waiting. I had never seen her before, although she looked something like my eighth-grade civics teacher. As I was unlocking the door she made one of those throat-clearing sounds that generally gets rendered in print as "harrumph." I looked at her and she pointed first at her wristwatch, then at my cardboard clock face.

"It's three o'clock," she said.

"I know," I said. "That thing's been running slow lately. I'm going to have to get it repaired." I took the sign from the door, moved the big hand to the three and the little hand to the twelve. "There," I said. "How's that?"

For a minute there I thought she was going to send me to the principal's office, but then Raffles rubbed against her ankle and charmed her, and by the time she left she'd picked out a couple of novels to go with the picture book of American folk rugs that had caught her eye in the window, and kept her waiting a half hour. It was a decent sale, and the first of several such. By the time I closed up again at six, I'd punched the old cash register a dozen times. Even better, I'd bought two big shopping bags full of paperbacks from an occasional customer who informed me he was moving to Australia. I took his count and made the deal without even looking at the books, and half of them turned out to be eminently collectible—Ace double volumes, Dell map-backs, and other goodies to gladden the heart of a paperback collector. There were half a dozen spicy novels from the sixties, too, and I knew a vest-pocket dealer in Wetumpka, Alabama, who'd pay me more for those than I'd shelled out for the lot.

Not a bad afternoon at all, and it ended with a phone call from a woman who told me she'd had to put her mother in a nursing home, and would I like to come have a look at the library? From her description it sounded promising, and I made an appointment to see it.

What with one thing and another, I was whistling by the time I got to the Bum Rap. I ordered a Perrier and got a quizzical look from Carolyn.

"It's not what you think," I said. "I had a couple of brandies at lunch. They've just about worn off, and I'd just as soon not add fuel to a dying fire. I had a good day, Carolyn. I bought some books, I sold some books."

"Well, that's the whole idea with bookstores, Bern. How was lunch?"

"Lunch was great," I said. "As a matter of fact, lunch was terrific. I think I'm going to be able to keep the store."

"It's very confusing," she said.

"What's so confusing? It's a perfectly good way for me to wind up with the bookstore."

"Not that, Bern. The whole business with what happened to the baseball cards. According to Doll—"

"I don't think 'according to Doll' is ever going to have the authority of, say, 'according to Hoyle,' or 'according to Emily Post.'"

"I understand that, Bern. But even so, if she's Marty's girlfriend—"

"She's not."

"But—"

"I had a feeling she was making that up. I was pretty sure before I went up to her apartment, but that clinched it. I couldn't imagine why a man crowding sixty would want to climb all those stairs to visit his mistress. A fifth-floor walk-up with a single bed, that's some love nest."

"Then where does she fit in?"

"I don't know."

"And how did the cards wind up in Luke's apartment? And how did she and Luke know each other?"

"Good question."

"Which one?"

"Both of them."

"And what about the Nugents, Bern? How do they fit into the picture? What was Luke doing in their apartment? Who killed him?"

"Beats me."

"Don't you care?"

"Not particularly."

"You've got some ideas, though. Right?"

"Nope."

"But you can't just—uh-oh."

"What's the matter?" I turned and saw the answer to that question, looming over our table like bad weather in the western sky. "Oh," I said. "Hi, Ray."

"Don't mind me," he said, pulling up a chair from another table. "I just thought I'd stop by an' pass the time of day. Had a real funny thing yesterday in your neighborhood, an' I was wonderin' if you had any ideas on the subject."

"Something happened in the Village, Ray?"

"I'm sure plenty of things did," he said, "but the neighborhood I was referrin' to is the one where you live. As opposed to down here, where you got your store, say, or the East Side, where you do the bulk of your stealin'." He turned to favor the waitress with a smile. "Oh, hiya, Maxine," he said.

"Make it a glass of plain ginger ale. You know the way I like it."

"How's that, Ray?" Carolyn asked him.

"How's what?"

"How do you like your plain ginger ale?"

"With about two an' a half ounces of rye in it," he said, "if it's any of your business."

"So why not order it that way?"

"Because it don't look good for a cop to be drinkin' spirits in public."

"But you're not in uniform, Ray. Who's gonna know you're a cop?"

"Anybody who looks at him," I told her. "You were telling a story, Ray. Something happened uptown?"

"Yeah," he said levelly. "An' you're involved, an' I don't know how I know that, but I know it all the same. They got a call on 911 about a bad smell, an' you know what that means. It's never once turned out to be somebody forgot to put the Limburger cheese back in the icebox. So a couple of blues went over, an' nobody in the buildin' knew nothin' about it, an' you couldn't smell nothin' in the hall. The doorman got hold of the super, an' he had keys to the place, an' he let 'em in."

"I think I know what they found," I said, hoping to save us all some time. "There was something on the news last night. There was a man dead in the bathroom, right?"

"That's where the smell was comin' from. The

door was jammed so they had to kick it in, an' there he was. Been dead since the middle of last week, accordin' to the doc."

"Had a Spanish name, if I remember correctly."

"Santangelo," he said. "Spanish or Italian, which is pretty much the same thing. Marginal."

"Marginal?"

He nodded. "Like you wouldn't want your sister to marry one, but it'd be okay for your cousin. Marginal. What you prolly don't know, on account of we just learned it ourselves, is he lived right there in the building. What you also don't know, on account of we been holdin' it back, is he was burglarizin' the place."

"Is that right?"

"Well, somebody was," he said, "an' it sure as shit wasn't me. Was it you, Bernie?"

"Ray—"

"Drawers pulled out an' overturned in the master bedroom. A couple of pieces of jewelry in the tub with him. A bullet hole in the guy's forehead, an' no gun to be found anywhere in the apartment. What's it sound like to you, Bernie?"

"Foul play," I suggested.

"He was no straight arrow, this Santangelo. We got a sheet on him. Mostly drug stuff, but people change, right? Say he's upstairs knockin' off the apartment. Say you're Nugent."

"Come again?"

"Nugent, the guy who lives there. You're Nugent

an' you come home, an' there's this spic or guinea, whatever he is, helpin' hisself to a fistful of bracelets an' earrings. So you grab your gun an' blow him away, which is your right in a free country, him bein' a burglar an' all. What's the matter, Bernie, did I say somethin'?"

"I get nervous when people talk about blowing away burglars."

"I can see where you would. Anyway, here's my question. Say you're a burglar."

"You've been saying that for years, Ray."

"Say you're a burglar, an' you're knockin' off this apartment. Why would you take off your clothes?"

"Huh?"

"He was bareass naked. Didn't that make the news?" I couldn't remember if it had or not. "Naked and dead as the day he was born," he said, "an' I heard of women who do their housecleanin' in the nude, an' I heard of burglars leavin' all kinds of disgustin' souvenirs behind, but did you ever hear of one took all his clothes off before he started huntin' for the valuables?"

"Never."

"Me neither. I can't picture him climbin' two flights of stairs in the buff, either, or ridin' in the elevator that way. But what did he do with his clothes? He wasn't wearin' 'em, an' they weren't in a pile, so what did he do, fold 'em up an' put 'em in the drawers? If you're Nugent an' you shoot the guy, why do you run off with his clothes?"

"If I'm Nugent," Carolyn said, "and I kill him, which I would never do myself because I'm basically nonviolent—"

"Good for you, Carolyn."

"—I pick up the phone and call the police. 'I just defended my home,' I say, 'so will you please send somebody over to get this stiff out of here.' That's what I do. I don't go away and lock the door and hope he'll vanish while I'm gone."

"The elves'll take care of it," I said, "after they're done at my place."

Ray gave me a look. "I thought of that," he said. "Not that shit about elves, but what you just said, Carolyn. Why not report it? What occurs to me, maybe the gun's unregistered. Guy's burglarizin' your premises, you got an iron-clad right to shoot the son of a bitch, but you better make sure you got a license for the gun. Even so . . ."

"It doesn't make a lot of sense," I finished for him. "And didn't I hear that the Nugents were out of the country?"

He nodded. "Due back tomorrow or the next day. Question is, when did they take off?"

"There you go," Carolyn said. "Say I'm Nugent. I'm on my way to the airport, and I wonder did I leave a pot cooking on the stove? So I go back, and what do I find but a burglar. So I pull out my unregistered gun and shoot him, and then I have to leave to catch a plane, so there's no time to call the police. Instead I pull off the guy's clothes, throw him in the tub, take the clothes with me, and catch the next plane to . . . where?"

"Tajikistan," I suggested.

"Forget Nugent," Ray said.

"Done."

"Say another burglar killed him. Say you, for example, Bernie."

"Me?"

"Just for the sake of argument, okay?"

"Fine. I killed him. But you can't quote me on that because you haven't read me my rights yet."

"Oh, for Christ's sake," he said. "This is just a discussion, okay?"

"Whatever you say, Ray."

"He lives right there, he knows the Nugents are out of town, an' he closes his eyes an' sees dollar signs. But he needs somebody who can make a lock sing an' dance, an' that's Mrs. Rhodenbarr's little boy Bernie."

"Why doesn't he just jimmy it, Ray?"

"Maybe he don't know how. But jimmyin' leaves marks, an' there weren't any, so we know he didn't do that. No, he knows you from the neighborhood, whatever, so he tips you to the job, an' the two of you go in together."

"Just my style, Ray."

"When I say you," he said, "I don't mean you. Okay, Bernie? I know you work alone, an' I know you don't shoot people. Forget you, okay? Some other fuckin' burglar is his partner for the day, an' the other fuckin' burglar opens the door for him, an' him an' the other fuckin' burglar both go in, an' then you shoot him."

"It's back to me again, isn't it?"

"It's just too much trouble sayin' it the other way is all. But if it bothers you that much—"

"No, it's all right. Why do I shoot him?"

"So you won't have to split with him. Say you really score big an' it's like the Lufthansa job where there's so much money you can't afford to split it."

"Okay," I said. "Why is he naked?"

"So they won't identify the clothes."

"Get real."

"Okay, maybe you're both naked."

"He seduces me, Ray. Then I realize what I've done. I'm racked with guilt, and instead of killing myself I lash out at him. He's taking a shower, washing away the traces of our evil lust, and I find a gun in the desk drawer and punch his ticket for him."

He sighed. "It don't make a whole lot of sense," he said.

"Gee, Ray, what makes you say that? And why are we even having this conversation? Don't get me wrong, Carolyn and I always enjoy it when you drop around, but what's the point?"

"I don't know."

"Well, that clears it up."

"I don't know," he repeated. "Call it a policeman's intrusion."

"That's exactly what I'd call it," I said, "but I think the word you want is intuition."

"Whatever. There's somethin' tells me you know more about this than meets the eye, an' if you don't you could find out. An' I got the feelin' it could be very good for the both of us."

"How do you mean, Ray?"

"That I couldn't tell you. That's the trouble with feelin's, at least the kind I get. They ain't much on specifics. I don't know what figures to be in it for me, whether it's something as basic as a good collar or something more negotiable. But you an' me, Bernie, we done each other some good over the years."

"And you're just a sentimental guy, Ray. That's why you got all choked up the other day when you threw me in a cell."

"Yeah, I was bitin' back tears." He stood up. "You give it some thought, Bern. I bet you come up with somethin'."

"Ray's right, Bern."

"My God," I said, "I never thought I'd hear you say that. I ought to write it down and make you sign it."

"He thinks you ought to work out what happened, and he doesn't even know you were there. How can you just turn your back on the whole thing?"

"Nothing to it."

"You have information Ray doesn't have, Bern."

"Indeed I do," I said. "About almost everything."

"What about your civic duty?"

"I pay my taxes," I said. "I separate my garbage for recycling. I vote. I even vote in school board elections, for God's sake. How much civic duty does a person have to have?"

"Bern—"

"Oh, look at the time," I said. "Don't rush, take your time and finish your drink. But I've got to get out of here."

"Where are you going?"

"Home to shower and change clothes."

"And then?"

"Got a date. Bye."

19

The car slowed. I pressed a button to lower the window and had a good look at the house in front of me—or as good a look as possible under the circumstances. There were trees in the way, and a vast expanse of lawn, but what I saw through the trees and beyond the lawn was a house not unlike its neighbors. We were, after all, in a subdivision. A subdivision of million-dollar homes, but a subdivision nonetheless. This particular million-dollar home had its porch light on, and light showed through a curtained upstairs window, and in two rooms downstairs as well.

I thought what I've often thought in similar circumstances. How considerate of them, I thought, to leave a light for the burglar.

"Circle the block," I said, and sat back while we did just that. The car was last year's Lincoln, smooth red leather within, hand- rubbed black lacquer without, the air climate-controlled, the engine noise no more than a Rafflesian purr. It was more comfortable by far than a bus, a subway, or a Tajik taxi, but none of those would have got me here. I was north of the city, in Westchester County. The subways don't go this far, and Hashmat Tuktee couldn't have found his way in a million years.

On our second time past the house I reached to take the automatic garage door opener from the driver's visor. I stuck it out the window, pointed it at the garage, and clicked it. Nothing happened.

"You never know," I said, and handed it back. We rode on, and I got out at the first stop sign and walked back. I was wearing a glen plaid sport jacket—it was time, I'd decided, to give the blazer a rest—and a pair of dark trousers. I had a tie on, too, but not the one that had received such good reviews at lunch.

I went right up the front walk, mounted the porch steps and rang the bell, then rang it again. Nothing happened. I had a look at the lock and shook my head at it. New York apartment dwellers know about locks, Poulards and Rabsons and Fox police locks, and gates on the windows and concertina wire at the tops of fences. In the suburbs, where the houses stand apart and each one has a dozen ground-floor windows, it's sort of pointless to knock yourself out making your door hard to get through. And this one wasn't. I was through it in a minute, tops.

The instant I breached the threshold, the alarm went off. It let out that high-pitched whine, that shrill insistent nagging squeal that puts a burglar right off his feed. I'll tell you, if you had a kid who made a sound like that, you'd strangle the little monster.

I had forty-five seconds. I passed quickly through the foyer, angled left through the large cathedral-ceilinged living room, entered the dining room. A Jacobean breakfront on the far wall was flanked by two doors. I opened the one on the right. Within it was a cupboard containing table linen, table pads, and sets of poker chips and mah-jongg tiles. And, right there on the wall, was a numeric keypad, its red light flashing hysterically.

I pushed 1-0-1-5.

The results could hardly have been more gratifying. The flashing red light went out, to be replaced by a steady light of a soothing green. The demonic sound ceased as abruptly as if a celestial hand had placed a pillow over that squalling electronic mouth. I let out the breath I hadn't even realized I'd been holding. I put my set of picks in my pocket—they were still in my hand—and put on my gloves. Then I wiped the few surfaces my unprotected fingers might have touched—the key pad, the closet door and knob, and the door and knob at the front entrance. I closed the door, locked up, and went to work.

The den was on the first floor at the rear of the house, with windows overlooking the garden. I drew the drapes shut before flicking a light on. To the right of the desk stood a three-tiered glassed-in bookcase, and above the bookcase hung an oil painting of a tall ship on the high seas. I took it down from the wall to reveal the circular door of a wall safe with a combination lock.

There is a knack to opening combination locks. A stethoscope is sometimes helpful, but you have to have the touch.

I had that, but I had something better, too. I had the combination.

I spun the dial right and left and right and left again, and damned if the door didn't open right up. I hauled out a dozen boxes, each two inches square and a foot long, all of them chock full of two-by-two kraft envelopes and the odd two-by-two Lucite holder, each of which held a small metal disk.

Coins. Besides the boxes, there were proof sets and uncirculated rolls, a couple of Library of Coins albums, and a custom-made black plastic holder in the shape of a shield, housing an almost-complete collection of Seated Liberty dimes, from 1837 to 1891. And there was some U.S. currency as well, a banded packet half an inch thick.

I emptied the safe, piling the numismatic material on the desk and stacking the other items—wills, deeds, various official-looking documents—to the side. I took the set of dimes with me and found my way to the kitchen. I opened the door leading to the attached garage, entered the garage with the set of dimes, and came back without them, locking up after myself.

In a hall closet I found a bag that would do, a battered leather satchel with nothing in it but memories. It held the coin collection with room to spare. I packed it, zipped it up, and set it down alongside the front door.

Now the part I hated.

From the hardware drawer in the kitchen I equipped myself with a hammer, a chisel, and a mean-looking screwdriver. I returned to the den and proceeded to beat the crap out of the wall safe, prying the dial loose from the door, banging away at the hardware, and making a hell of a racket and a horrible mess. When I'd completed the job of ruining a perfectly satisfactory safe, I took the various documents it had contained, the wills and deeds and all, and left them strewn in and out of the safe, kicking them around the carpet. I pulled out the desk's five unlocked drawers and spilled their contents onto the floor, and I was all poised to open the remaining drawer with hammer and chisel.

"No," I said aloud and laid those crude tools aside and opened the drawer with my picks. It was almost as fast that way. I dumped the drawer, then bent down to pick up a hundred dollars in twenties. I put it in my pocket, where I found the roll of uncirculated 1958-D nickels I'd set aside earlier. They were in a sealed plastic tube, which I cracked open by knocking it sharply against the edge of the desk. I let the coins spill into my palm and tossed a handful of them at the open safe. Some landed inside, while others rained down over the bookcase and onto the floor.

Perfect.

I walked to the front door, checked my watch, and flicked the porch light on and off three times. I hoisted the satchel, opened the door, set the latch so it wouldn't lock behind me, and walked to the street. I got there just as the Lincoln was pulling up. I opened the door, tossed the bag inside, and returned to the house.

One final outrage to perform. I took up hammer and chisel again and had at the poor innocent front door, gouging the jamb, ruining the lock. I went back to the kitchen, put the tools where I'd found them, and went back to the dining room, where I entered 1-0-1-5 on the keypad. The green light went off and the device beeped seven times. I now had something like forty-five seconds to quit the premises and lock the door, after which time the alarm would be armed and dangerous.

I went out on the porch and drew the door almost but not quite shut, counting seconds in my head. I guess my count was a shade fast, because I'd completed it and nothing was happening. I wondered if I'd done something wrong, and then it began, that horrible high-pitched whistling whine.

We'd have forty-five seconds of that, but I didn't

have to stand around and endure it. I walked quickly down the flagstone path to the curb, once again reaching it just as the black Lincoln pulled up. "Twenty-three," I said, opening the door. "Twenty-four. Twenty-five. Twenty-six."

"Everything go all right?"

"Like clockwork," I said, as we pulled away from the curb. "Thirty-one. Thirty-two."

"And the set of dimes in plastic?"

"In the garage," I said. "On a high shelf all the way over on the right, in a box marked 'Games.' About halfway down in the box, between Parcheesi and Stratego. Thirty-eight. Thirty-nine."

By the time I got to forty-five we had turned a corner and covered a couple hundred yards. I had the window down, and when the alarm went off I could hear it clearly. If we'd had Luke Santangelo stuffed in the trunk, it would have been enough to wake him. They'd hear it all over the neighborhood, even as they'd see the board light up in the offices of the security company in the next town over.

But before anybody could do anything about it, Marty Gilmartin and I would be back in Manhattan.

I got out at the corner. No need for my talkative doorman to see me hop out of a Lincoln.

"I'll want to see exactly what we've got here," I said, laying a hand on the satchel. "I know a man who's very good with coins, but even so I like to know what I'm selling. I've got last year's Red Book upstairs, which is all I need to price the U.S. material. I'll have to trust him on the foreign, but there didn't look to be too much of that. Oh, that reminds me." I unzipped the bag, fished around for the packet of currency, and tore off the paper wrapper.

"What's that?"

"Money," I said, dealing out hundred-dollar bills like a hand of gin rummy, one for him, one for me, one for him, one for me. "Something like five thousand would be my guess, but we'll just divvy it up."

"You were just going to take the coin collection. That was the agreement."

"Well, it has to look right," I said. "You wouldn't believe what a mess I made, all for the sake of creating the proper appearance. Did you want me to spoil the illusion by leaving a wad of cash in the safe?"

"No, but—"

"In New York," I said, "if I left cash lying around you could count on the cops to take it. Maybe they're honest here, in which case they'd report it to the IRS and let Mr. McEwan explain where it came from." One for him, one for me, one for him, one for me. "You think he'd prefer it that way?"

"No, you're quite right. But maybe you should keep all the cash for yourself. You found it, after all."

I shook my head. "It's share and share alike.

There, it comes out even. Oh, one more thing." I got five twenties from my pocket. "In the desk. Again, how would it look if I left them? Two for you and two for me, and have you got a ten by any chance? Wait a minute, I've got it. There you go."

He looked at the bills he was holding. He said, "The dimes are in a box of games in the garage? Between the Parcheesi and . . . what was the other one you mentioned?"

"Stratego."

"I'll make a note of that. The dimes are the only collection Jack cares about. His father gave him one he'd found in a drawer when Jack was a boy, and that started him collecting. I think the set's worth forty or fifty thousand dollars. At least that's what they're insured for."

"I didn't examine them too closely," I said, "but the condition looked good, and there were only a couple of dates missing."

"It must have been hard to leave them behind."

I shook my head. "That was the deal. Besides, you'd take a beating fencing anything that specialized. No, the hard part was wrecking the safe and leaving a mess. But I forced myself."

I watched as he put the money in his jacket pocket. He'd already participated fully in a felony, but actually taking the money evidently had some strong symbolic value for him, because he straightened up behind the wheel and gave a little sigh when he had done so.

"Jack's in Atlanta," he said. "He and Betty flew down for the golf. Said he almost didn't go this year, the way the market's been behaving. Said he'd thought about selling the coins, but how would that look? And he'd have hated to part with those dimes."

"Now he won't have to. But he'd better figure on keeping them out of sight for a year or two."

"I'll make sure he knows that." A slow smile spread on his face. "What's the line from *Casablanca*? At the very end, Bogart to Claude Rains."

"This could be the start of a beautiful friendship."

"Indeed. And a profitable one. Get some sleep, Bernie. I've a feeling the next few days are going to be busy ones."

20

He was right. It was a busy week.

Tuesday night, while an eminent cardiologist and his wife were at the Met oohing and ahing over David Hockney's sets for *Die Zauberflöte*, Marty and I were on the way to their house in Port Washington. A security patrol watched over the neighborhood according to a strict schedule; armed with that schedule, we synchronized our own movements accordingly.

There was no alarm this time, just a formidable door with a brass lion's-head knocker and one of those legendary Poulard locks, to which I laid a successful siege. Inside, I dumped a couple of drawers without bothering to see what hit the floor, hurrying directly to the master bedroom, where the doctor's wife kept her jewelry in a handsome dresser-top chest with five inch-deep drawers and a mirrored lid. I grabbed a pillow off one of the twin beds, stripped it of its pillowcase, and scooped all of the jewelry into the pillowcase. I dumped a drawer or two, knocked over a lamp, and hurried downstairs. I was right on schedule, and so were the security forces; I hunkered down by the living-room picture window and watched in admiration as they slowed their prowl car in front of the house and beamed their pivoting spotlight here and there. Then, satisfied that all was well, they pressed on.

For variety's sake, I left the Poulard's pickproof reputation unsullied, picking it shut behind me and scuttling around to the side of the house, where I kicked in a basement window and made a mess of a flower bed. Then I swung the pillowcase over my shoulder, checked my watch, and met the Lincoln out front.

"Poor Alex," Marty said. "A couple of wrong moves in the commodities market put his back against the wall. Unfortunately, frozen pork bellies aren't like stamps and coins and baseball cards. You can't cash them in when times get tough."

"Or arrange to have them stolen."

"Quite. He swallowed his pride and went to Frieda, told her the situation. Pointed out that they had a substantial amount of money invested in her jewelry, and that it could see them through a tight spot. Perhaps they might sell some of the pieces she never wore anyway." He shook his head. "The woman wouldn't hear of it. Well, he suggested, it was only a temporary difficulty. A few triple-bypass operations would set them right again, but in the meantime suppose they pledged the odd tiara as collateral with Provident Loan." He chuckled. "Alex said she was aghast. Pawn her jewelry? Hock her bracelets at some corner pawnshop? Not a chance."

I told him I'd barely had time to look at what I was taking, but the quality looked good.

"The insurance coverage is close to two hundred thousand," he said. "Of course one dresses for the opera, so whatever she wore tonight will have escaped us." I said it was a shame they couldn't have gone square dancing instead, and he smiled at the very idea. "One thing, Bernie. There should be a jade-and-diamond necklace with matching earrings. Everything else is ours to sell, but Alex would like that back."

"No problem," I said, "but how's he going to manage that? Won't it tip her off that he staged the whole thing?"

"Oh, it's not for Frieda," he said. "But Alex is especially fond of that particular ensemble. He wants to give it to his girlfriend."

Wednesday I didn't need the Lincoln, or Marty's company either. I closed the store in the middle of the afternoon, hung the clock face in the window, and told Raffles to take messages if anybody called. I caught a cab and got out half a block from a four-story townhouse in Murray Hill. On the parlor floor, I found what I was looking for in a place of honor over the living-room fireplace. It was an oil painting about twelve inches high and sixteen inches wide, a rural landscape showing some fat cattle taking shelter beneath an enormous tree.

I cut it from its frame and rolled the canvas so that it would fit wrapped around my forearm between my shirtsleeve and my jacket. Minutes later I was on Third Avenue, my hand raised to summon a taxi that took me uptown to Marty's apartment. His eyes widened when I walked in empty-handed. Then I took off my jacket and he smiled and reached for the canvas.

"Here we are," he said, unrolling it. "Many's the time I've admired this little beauty over the years. 'Best investment I ever made,' George Hanley always said. 'Gave ten thousand dollars for it to a little mustachioed froggy art dealer on the Boulevard Haussmann. Barb thought I was crazy, but we both liked it and it made a nice souvenir of the trip. I'll be honest with you, I never even heard of the artist at the time. Courbet? I didn't know Courbet from Beaujolais.' He never tired of that phrase, Bernie. 'I didn't know Courbet from Beaujolais.' "

"Well, it has a nice ring to it."

"It turned out to be worth two or three times what he paid for it, and that was twenty years ago. When the art market went crazy, the value of the little Courbet just kept climbing. A few months ago George realized he had a painting worth several hundred thousand dollars, and that he could use the money and they could hang something else over the fireplace."

"But his wife didn't want to sell it?"

"It was her idea in the first place. George had a chap from Christie's look at it, and that's when he got the bad news. The little Frenchman with the mustache had been the screwer, not the screwee. George had paid ten thousand dollars for a fake. He felt so abashed he couldn't even tell his wife. 'Oh, we can't sell our Courbet,' he told Barbara. 'It would be like auctioning off a member of the family. And it just keeps going up in value. We'd be crazy to sell.' What he said to me, one afternoon at the club when some single-malt scotch had loosened his tongue, was that the most infuriating thing was what he'd paid over the years for insurance. 'The premium kept going up,' he said, 'to reflect the steady increases in value. Turns out I've just been throwing good money after bad. I'll never see a dime of it back.' The other day I took him aside and reminded him of our conversation. 'What you said about never seeing any of the money back,' I said. 'You know, George, that's not necessarily so.' "

"The insurance company won't know it's a fake."

"Of course not. The man from Christie's wouldn't have run off and told them. But if they did know, they'd refuse to honor the claim."

"Obviously."

"But suppose George had told them the truth as soon as he'd learned it. Unwittingly, he'd been insuring a worthless painting for twenty years. That being the case, the company had been taking his premiums without assuming any actual risk. So, now that the actual circumstances had become known, would they agree to refund the premiums he had paid?"

"Obviously not."

"That's why I see nothing wrong with defrauding the sons of bitches," he said with feeling. "They've taken larceny and institutionalized it." He clucked his tongue at the *faux* Courbet and carried it over to the fireplace.

"Wait," I said.

"George never wants to see the thing again," he said, "and I don't suppose you could find a customer for it, do you?"

"I wouldn't know how to sell it even if it were real."

"I shouldn't think so, not without provenance. George gave me ten thousand dollars on signature, as it were, as an advance against half the settlement from the insurance company. The painting's currently insured for $320,000, but they'll very likely stall, and they may even try to chisel." He shook his head. "The swine. If they live up to their part of the deal, you and I walk away with eighty thousand apiece."

"That would be great," I said.

"So I guess we can afford to consign this canvas to the flames."

"We can afford to," I said, "but do we have to? The guy from Christie's could be wrong. It wouldn't be the first time. And even if it is a fake Courbet, so what? It's a real something, even if it's only a real fake. I'll tell you this, it'd look great in my apartment."

"And I imagine it would make a good souvenir."

"That too," I said.

It was a full week, what with the appointments Marty arranged and the follow-up visits I had to make to various gentlemen who would buy choice material even if one couldn't show clear title to it. Coins, jewelry, postage stamps, a Matisse litho, all passed through my hands. The weekend was busy, too, and when I opened up the following Monday I spent most of the morning on the telephone. I had a whole series of conversations with Wally Hemphill, and after the last of these I called time out and looked around for the cat. When I couldn't find him I started crumpling a sheet of paper, and the sound drew him. He knew it was time for another training session.

I had the floor nicely littered with paper balls when Carolyn showed up. "Look at that!" I cried. "Did you see what he just did?"

"What he always does," she said. "He killed a piece of crumpled-up paper. Bern, I went to the Russian deli. I got an Alexander Zinoviev for you and a Lavrenti Beria for myself, but I can't remember which is which. What do you say we each have half of each?"

"That'll be fine," I said. "Look! I swear the training's making a difference. His reflexes are getting sharper every day."

"If you say so, Bern."

"The son of a gun could play shortstop," I said. "Did you see the way he went to his left on that one? Rabbit Maranville, eat your heart out."

"Whatever you say, Bern." She pulled up a chair. "Bern, we have to talk."

"Eat first," I said. "Then we'll talk."

"Bern, I'm serious. Ray stopped by this morning. I was vacuuming a bull mastiff and there was Ray, standing there with his dewlaps hanging out."

"You should report him."

"Bern, it's a sign of how desperate he is. You know how Ray and I get along."

"Like oil and water."

"Like Bosnia and Herzegovina, Bern, but he came into the Poodle Factory because he's concerned about you. And he's convinced you could clear up this case for him if you put your mind to it."

I chewed thoughtfully. "This must be the Lavrenti Beria," I said. "With the raw garlic and the horseradish."

"And I have to tell you I agree with him."

"That's good," I said. "It's even better that garlic agrees with me, because the Zinoviev seems to be laced with it, too. It's probably just as well that I don't have a date tonight."

"He says the Nugents are back. He's been to see them a couple of times. He's really investigating in a big way. It's not like him, Bern."

"He must smell money."

"I don't know what he smells. Not Luke Santangelo, because they must have aired out the place by now. Bern—"

I tossed the Zinoviev wrapper and watched Raffles make his move. He was on it like a pike on a minnow. "He likes sandwich wrappings from the deli best of all," I told Carolyn. "The smell makes him nuts."

"You should get him a catnip mouse, Bern. He'd play with it by the hour."

"You don't get it, do you? I don't want to buy toys for him, Carolyn. He's not a pet."

"He's on staff."

"That's right. The last thing I want to do is play with him. These are training sessions, they're for his reflexes."

"I keep forgetting. I look at the two of you and it looks for all the world like you're having fun, so I forget that the relationship is essentially serious."

"Work can be fun," I said, "if you're goal-oriented."

"Like you and Raffles."

"That's right," I said. "There's something else you should know, besides the fact that Raffles is not a pet, and that's that I'm no Kinsey Millhone."

"You think I don't know that, Bern? You've been

a lot of things in your life, but you've never been a lesbian."

"What I mean," I said, "is that I'm not a detective. I don't solve crimes."

"You have in the past, Bern."

"Once or twice."

"More than that."

"A few times," I conceded. "But it just happened. One way or another I wound up in a jam and in the course of getting out of it I happened to stumble on the solution to a homicide. It was serendipity, that's all. I was looking for one thing and I found something else."

"And that's what happened here, Bern. You were looking for something to steal and you found a dead body."

"And I went home, remember?"

"But you went back."

"Only to go home again. Thomas Wolfe was wrong, you can go home again, and I did. I'm out of it, Carolyn. They dropped the charges, did I tell you that? For me the case is over." I flipped a paper ball, but Raffles was still busy killing the last one. "If you want somebody to solve it," I said, "why don't you try the cat?"

"The cat?"

"Raffles," I said. "Maybe he'll figure it out for you, like in those books by What's-her-name."

"Lillian Jackson Braun."

"That's the one. Everybody's stymied, and then

the genius cat breaks a T'ang vase or coughs up a hairball, and that provides the vital clue that nails another killer. I forget his name, this crime-solving cat."

"It's Ko-Ko. He's Siamese."

"Good for him. He's been doing this forever, hasn't he? Ko-Ko must be getting a little long in the fang by now. She ought to call the next one *The Cat Who Lived Forever.* I can't believe some Siamese is that much sharper than old Raffles here. Go ahead, ask him who did it. Maybe he'll knock a book off the shelves and answer all your questions."

"You think you're pretty funny, don't you, Bern?"

"Well . . ."

"Well, what the hell," she said. "Raffles, what's the solution to the mystery of the stiff in the tub?"

Raffles stopped what he was doing, which was the systematic demolition of one of the sandwich-wrapper mice. He backed away from it, extended his front paws, stretched, extended his back paws, stretched again, and then arched his back, looking like something that belonged on a Halloween card. Then he wagged the tail he didn't have—I can't think of another way to say it—and leaped straight up in the air, grabbing at something only he could see. He landed on all fours, in the manner of his tribe, and turned slowly around, settled on his haunches, and stared at us.

I said, "Well, I'll be damned."

"We all will, Bern, but what's that got to do with

the price of Meow Mix? What was all that about, anyway?"

"Call Ray Kirschmann," I said. "You're the one who won't stop hounding me, so you can be the one to call him." I grabbed a pencil and retrieved a sheet of paper from the floor, uncrumpling it as best I could. I started making a list. "All of these people," I said. "Tell him I want him to have them all at the Nugent apartment tomorrow evening at half past seven."

"You've got to be kidding. How did you—what do you plan to—what did the cat do that—"

"You're not making sentences," I said. "Or sense. Tomorrow."

21

At exactly seven-thirty the following evening I presented myself to the Haitian doorman at 304 West End Avenue. "Bernard Rhodenbarr," I said. "Mr. and Mrs. Nugent are expecting me." I looked over his shoulder while he consulted a little list. I was pleased to note that there was a check mark next to every name but mine.

"Rhodenbarr," I prompted, and he found my name and checked it off, turning to me with a cheering little smile. He pointed my way to the elevator, which was considerate if hardly necessary.

I rode upward to nine, walked the length of the hallway to G. I looked at the two locks, the Poulard, the Rabson.

I knocked on the door, and it was opened unto me.

The doorman's list was accurate. They were all on hand. I didn't know how Ray had managed it, but he had everybody present and accounted for.

They were in the living room. The room's chairs and sofas were ranged in a circle, its circumference swelled by a few chairs brought in from the dining room. It was Ray who had opened the door for me, and he led me through the foyer into the center of things, whereupon whatever conversations had been limping along came to a gratifying halt.

"This here is Bernie Rhodenbarr," Ray announced. "Bernie, I guess you know all these people."

I didn't really, but I nodded and smiled all the same, working my way around the circle with my eyes. As I said, everybody was there, and here's how they lined up.

First was Carolyn Kaiser, my chief friend and poodle washer. Like me, she had gone home and changed after work; like me, she had selected gray flannel slacks and a blue blazer. It was no great trick to tell us apart, however, because there was a silver pin in the shape of a cat on the lapel of her blazer, and she was wearing a green turtleneck. (I had a shirt and tie, in case somebody invited me to the Pretenders.)

On Carolyn's right was the one man present who could have invited me to the Pretenders, but I wasn't sure we'd be speaking by the end of the evening. Marty Gilmartin, sharing a Victorian love seat with his wife, Edna, was wearing a gray suit, a white shirt, and a Jerry Garcia tie, along with a facial expression that hovered somewhere between bemused and noncommittal.

Edna Gilmartin looked more youthful and less formidable than I seemed to remember her from the ticket line at the Cort Theater. I barely noticed the dress she was wearing; what caught my eye was the necklace around her throat. It would have caught anybody's eye, that was the whole point of it, but it had special impact on me because I thought I recognized it as part of the loot from Alex and Frieda's place in Port Washington. A second glance put my mind to rest, but for a moment there it gave me a turn.

Alongside Mrs. Gilmartin, looking long and lean and country casual in boots and jeans and a sweatshirt with the legend GRAMMATICALLY CORRECT, was Patience Tremaine. She looked as though she didn't have a clue what she was doing here, but was determined to be a good sport about it. I knew the feeling. I'd felt pretty much like that myself in the bat cave at Café Villanelle.

Patience was in an armchair. At her right, in one of the dining-room chairs relocated for the occasion, sat our host, Harlan Nugent. I was meeting him for the first time, although it seemed to me as though we had known each other for years. In any case, I recognized him from his photos. He was a big bear of a man, well over six feet tall and perilously close to three hundred pounds. No wonder his shoes had been too big for me. Tonight he wore a black-and-white houndstooth jacket over a black turtleneck, but I couldn't keep from looking at his feet. He was wearing a very attractive pair of black tassel loafers. If they'd been in his closet on my last visit, I must have missed them. I had a feeling they'd made the trip to Europe with him.

Joan Nugent sat beside him. Some of her photographs showed her with graying hair, but evidently she'd had some sort of shock that had turned it black overnight, because there wasn't a drop of gray in evidence at present. She had a long oval face and an olive complexion, and her hair was parted in the middle and gathered into a braid on either side. A Navajo squash-blossom necklace and a couple of silver-and-turquoise rings heightened the American Indian effect.

Ray Kirschmann was next to Joan Nugent, and there's no real need to describe him. As usual, he was wearing a dark suit; as usual, it looked to have been custom-tailored for someone else. He was waiting for me to pull a rabbit out of a hat, and hoping to come out of the evening with something for his troubles. Either the rabbit or the hat, I suppose.

Doll Cooper was seated next to him, at one end of a long couch. She was wearing the very outfit she'd worn the night I first saw her—the dark business suit, the red beret. The only expression on her face was one of keen attention. Her body language reinforced the impression. One sensed that she was poised to cut and run at any moment, but in the meantime she would wait and see.

Borden Stoppelgard had the center of the couch, but he was keeping his distance from Doll and had positioned himself all the way at the other edge of the middle cushion. Borden was wearing a brown suit and a tie with alternating inch-wide stripes of red and green. He was sitting knee-to-knee with a woman with stylish blond hair and eyes the color of a putting green. The process of elimination, along with the fact that Borden was practically sitting in her lap, brought me to the conclusion that she was Lolly Stoppelgard.

There was a chair for me, too, one from the dining room, but I didn't figure to get much use out of it. It was time for me to be on my feet. On my toes, if I could manage it.

"Well, now," I said. "I suppose you're wondering why I summoned you all here."

I'll tell you, no matter how many times you deliver that line, it never fails to quicken the pulse. The game, by God, was afoot.

"Once upon a time," I said, "there were two men, and one of them married the other's sister. That made them brothers-in-law, and they had something else in common. They were both businessmen, they both bought and sold real estate, and they both dabbled in other investments. Martin Gilmartin sometimes took a flier in show business. Borden Stoppelgard stockpiled first-edition crime fiction. And both of them had a passion for baseball cards.

"As far as I know, Borden Stoppelgard still has every baseball card he ever bought or traded for. A week ago this past Thursday, Marty Gilmartin received a telephone call just minutes after he and his wife returned from an evening at the theater. The anonymous caller had evidently paid a lot of attention to Marty's recent movements, and that made him suspicious. He hung up the phone, hurried to his den, and opened the box where he kept his card collection."

"We know all this," Borden Stoppelgard interrupted. "He lifted the lid and the box was empty. Anyway, you took 'em, right?"

"Wrong," I said. "But it's not a farfetched notion, in view of the fact that I was the mysterious caller. The police traced the call to Carolyn Kaiser's apartment, and Officer Kirschmann knew Ms. Kaiser as a close friend of mine. And, much as it pains me to admit it, there was a time years ago when I made occasional forays into, uh, burglary."

"You went away for it once," Ray said helpfully, "an' got away with it hundreds of times."

"Excuse me," Joan Nugent said. "I'm sorry for Mr. Gilmartin, but I don't quite see his connection with our apartment. We had a break-in while we were away. Are you suggesting that the same burglar broke into both his apartment and ours?"

"No," I said.

"Oh."

"There was no burglar."

"No burglar here?" This from Harlan Nugent. "We had a break-in, you know. It's a matter of record."

"No burglar here," I said, "and no burglar at the Gilmartin residence. No break-in at either location."

I caught a glimpse of Marty's face, and he did not look terribly happy at the direction the discussion was taking.

"We'll let that pass for the moment," I said smoothly. "Let's just note that the Gilmartin cards had disappeared. That's one of the reasons we're here. The other phenomenon that has drawn us together is not a disappearance but an appearance, and an astonishing manifestation it was. A man turned up in one of the Nugent bathrooms. He didn't have any clothes on, and he didn't have a pulse, either. He'd been shot, and he was dead."

"Who was he?" Patience wanted to know.

"His name was Luke Santangelo," I said, "and he lived two floors below the Nugents in this very building. Like half the waiters and a third of the moving men in this city, he'd come here to be an actor. Well, *de mortuis* and all that, but I'm afraid Luke was something of a bad actor, and that's irrespective of how he may have acquitted himself on stage. He was a small-time drug dealer and a petty criminal."

"I was so shocked to learn that," Joan Nugent put in. "I knew him, you see. He posed for me, as it happens, in this very apartment." She hazarded a smile. "I paint, you know. He was happy to pose for me, even though I couldn't afford to pay him very much."

Her husband snorted. "While you were painting him," he said, "he was figuring out how to break in."

"Two incidents," I said. "On Thursday, Mr. Gilmartin finds his cards are missing. On Sunday, the police find a dead man in the Nugents' bathroom. But what's the connection?"

"No connection," Borden Stoppelgard said. "Case closed. Can we all go home now?"

"There has to be a connection," Carolyn told him. "You're the one who collects mystery novels, aren't you? It's a shame you don't take the trouble to read them. If you did, you'd know that whenever there are two crimes in the same story, they're related. The connection may not turn up until the last chapter, but it's always there."

"There's a connection," I agreed. "And you're part of it, Mr. Stoppelgard."

"Huh?"

"We'll start with the cards," I said. "Your brother-in-law owned them. And you coveted them."

"If you're trying to say I took 'em—"

"I'm not."

"Oh. But you just said—"

"That you coveted them," I said. "Didn't you?"

He looked at Marty, then at me. "No secret he had some nice material there," he said.

"You wanted the Ted Williams cards."

"I admired them. I wouldn't have minded having a set of them myself. But I didn't want 'em bad enough to steal 'em."

"You thought I stole them."

"Well, yes," he said. "That's what the police were saying, and I didn't have any reason to think they were wrong."

"And, thinking that I'd stolen them, you came to my shop and offered me a deal. If I gave you your brother-in-law's baseball cards, you'd cut me a sweetheart deal on an extension of the store lease."

"Borden," Marty Gilmartin said, his tone one of bottomless disappointment. "Borden, Borden, Borden."

"Marty, he doesn't know what he's talking about."

"Oh, Borden," Marty said. "I'm surprised at you."

And he sounded it, all right. I have to tell you, I was impressed with Marty. I'd told him days ago about his brother-in-law's offer, and what he'd said at the time was along the lines of "That's typical of the avaricious son of a bitch." The Pretenders would have been proud of the show he was putting on.

"I was testing the waters," Borden said now. "Trying to find out for certain if you were the burglar, and laying a little trap for you if you were. Obviously it didn't work, because you never had the cards in the first place, but all it proves now is that I didn't have them either. So I'll ask you again—can we go home now?"

"I think you might want to stick around," I said. "You didn't take them, and it's also true that you didn't know who took them. But the person who did take them got the idea from you."

"Oh, yeah? You want to tell me who that was?"

"You're sitting next to her," I said.

Logically enough, everybody turned to stare at Lolly Stoppelgard, who looked understandably puzzled. *Not that one,* I wanted to cry. *The other one.* But they all figured it out for themselves, and eyes turned to the woman sitting on the other side of Borden Stoppelgard.

"Gwendolyn Beatrice Cooper," I said. "Like Luke Santangelo, she came to New York hoping for acting success. In the meantime, though, she got a job at a law firm called Haber, Haber & Crowell."

"My attorneys," Marty said.

"And your brother-in-law's as well. Ms. Cooper worked there, doing general office work, sometimes filling in as the relief receptionist. She was a natural choice for the front desk because she's personable and eye-catching, and two of the eyes she caught belonged to Borden Stoppelgard. He was a happily married man. She was a young working woman going about her business. So he did the natural thing under the circumstances. He hit on her."

"Oh, Borden," said Lolly Stoppelgard.

"He's full of crap," her husband said. "I may have passed the time of day with Wendy." Wendy! "I'm a friendly guy. But that's as far as it went, believe me."

"You asked her to meet you for a drink," I said. "Then lunch, and then another lunch, and—"

"One drink," he said, "to be sociable. On one occasion, and that's it, total, the end. No lunches. Ask her, for God's sake. Wendy—"

"Oh, Borden . . ."

"Lolly, who are you gonna believe, some convicted felon or your own loving husband?"

"I'm certainly not going to believe you. That's just the way you hit on me, Borden."

"Lolly—"

"You met me when I was working reception, you passed the time of day, you invited me out for a drink, you asked could we have lunch—"

"Lolly, that was completely different."

"I know."

"I was single then. I'm married now."

"Exactly," she said. "Which is why it was okay then, and why it's not okay now, you dirty cheating son of a bitch."

There was nothing much to say to that, and nobody did. I let the moment stretch—rather enjoying it, I have to admit—and then I said that I didn't think it had gone very far.

"One occasion," Borden cried. "One drink, for God's sake!"

"Perhaps a little farther than that," I said, "but I don't think your husband made a very favorable impression on Miss Cooper. I've heard her compare him to pond scum."

"If pond scum had a lawyer," Lolly Stoppelgard said, "pond scum could sue for libel."

"Say, Bernie," Ray Kirschmann said, "this here ain't *Divorce Court,* if you take my meanin'. Whether or not he's been puttin' her away—"

"One miserable drink, dammit!"

"—don't really constitute police business. You were startin' to say somethin' about how she took the cards. He didn't give 'em to her, did he?"

Borden Stoppelgard looked as though he might turn apoplectic at the very thought.

"No," I said, "but he gave her the idea to steal them. Borden's the sort of fellow who likes to brag about what he has. He started out that way with Wendy"—I'd almost called her Doll—"but before he knew it he was off on his favorite theme, his brother-in-law's great collection and how he kept it right out in plain sight instead of tucking it away in a safe deposit vault where it belonged."

Doll raised her eyebrows. She said, "You sound as though you must have been at the next table,

Bernie. It's funny, but I don't remember any conversation like that. Do you, Mr. Stoppelgard?"

"Jesus," Borden said, and turned to his left. "Wendy," he said, "what the hell's the matter with you? Tell the truth. Did I ever say anything to you about stealing Marty's cards?"

"Never," Doll said.

"I said he had some valuable material and he ought to take better care of it. I said there was stuff of his I'd love to get my hands on but he wouldn't sell it to me. I said—"

Doll looked at him, and I guess looks can't kill, because he didn't die. She rolled her eyes, then aimed them at me. "Tell us more, Bernie," she said. "How did I get my greedy little hands on the cards?"

"You found an excuse to go over to the Gilmartin apartment on York Avenue," I said. "My guess is you turned up on the doorstep during business hours with some papers for Marty to sign. It wouldn't have been all that hard for you to hold out an envelope and deliver it yourself instead of giving it to one of the firm's messengers. And then—"

"I knew she looked familiar," Marty said. "I couldn't think why."

"You must have seen me at the office, Mr. Gilmartin."

"No," he said with conviction. "You came over to the apartment."

"Suppose I did," said Doll.

Gotcha!

"As it happens," she went on, "I didn't. But suppose I did. Then what?"

"You took the cards," I said. "One way or another you contrived to be in Marty's den long enough to transfer the cards into whatever you'd brought along for the purpose, a tote bag or briefcase, something like that. You were out the door and gone without arousing any suspicions, and you had a half million dollars' worth of cardboard in your kick. But you also had a problem."

"Oh?"

"You'd met Marty face to face. Suppose he looked in his rosewood humidor an hour after you left. He could hardly fail to remember the cheerfully efficient visitor from Haber, Haber & Crowell. Even if he didn't miss the cards for days, there was no way to be sure your name and face wouldn't come to mind when he tried to think who might have taken them. So you had to do two things. You had to stash the cards where they wouldn't be found while you made arrangements to sell them, and you had to develop some way to misdirect suspicion so it would fall on somebody else.

"The first part was easy. You knew a fellow actor named Luke Santangelo. He wasn't exactly a boyfriend of yours, but he wasn't pond scum either, and you'd been over to his apartment a couple of times. Luke was a shady guy, which was ideal for your purposes. You told him you wanted to leave a briefcase with him for a few days. That way if the police searched your apartment they'd come up empty. You figured you could stand up well enough under questioning, as long as there wasn't any physical evidence to drag you down.

"But you still needed a patsy, and that's where I came in. What put you on to me, Doll?"

"I don't know what you're talking about."

"I can't be sure how my name came up," I said. "My guess would be that Luke mentioned me, and perhaps even pointed me out on the street. I had a little trouble with the law some years back, and I still live in the same neighborhood, so there must be plenty of people around who remember what I used to do for a living."

"Before you saw the error of your ways," Ray Kirschmann drawled.

"In any event, the name registered. And you may have heard it again from Borden Stoppelgard. I know he must have said something about the bookseller he was planning to evict. Did he mention the poor jerk by name?"

Borden started to say that he'd bought the young lady one drink on one occasion, for God's sake, and here I was making a federal case out of it. Lolly said he was just making it worse every time he opened his mouth, whereupon he closed it.

"I think you came to my store once. It would have been after you took Marty's cards but before he found out about it. I can't be sure about the timetable, but I'll try to ballpark it, okay? My guess is you grabbed the cards on Monday and dropped them in Luke's apartment later the same day. Tuesday or Wednesday you came to my store and had a quick look around. Borden had mentioned the books he was buying, so you called him and told him you'd seen something at Barnegat Books that was right up his alley. If he hadn't already told you that was one of the buildings he owned, he told you now.

"Meanwhile, Luke disappeared. You tried to reach him and you couldn't. He didn't answer his phone, and when you went over and pounded on his door, all you got was a sore hand. You started to get nervous. Maybe he'd skipped with the cards. But that didn't seem likely, because the briefcase you gave him was locked and you'd described the contents in a way that wouldn't set dollar signs blinking in his head. Maybe you said they were legal papers with blackmail value, something like that. It would give you a reason to hide them, but there'd be no way for him to cash in on them by himself.

"So he'd probably left the cards behind, but he himself was gone, and this wasn't good. Suppose he got arrested on a dope charge and the police searched his apartment and found the cards while they were at it? Suppose he actually got work out of town and didn't come back for two or three months? Suddenly stowing the cards on West End Avenue didn't seem like such a good idea.

"Now you had more use for me than ever. If I was a burglar, maybe I could do something useful for a change. Maybe I could open his door for you.

"That fateful Thursday night," I said, "I made that silly call to the Gilmartin house. One explanation for my conduct was I had had far too much to drink, and one reason I drank so much is Borden Stoppelgard had just bought a Sue Grafton novel from me for a fraction of its value."

"You're the one priced the book," that gentleman pointed out.

"That's true," I said, "but you didn't have to crow about it. You bragged to the Gilmartins when the four of you went to the theater together that night. Did you do a little boasting to Wendy, too? I'll bet you did. She tipped you off about the book, so it would be only natural for you to call her up and thank her. While you were at it, you could suggest spending some of the money she'd saved you on a nice dinner for two."

That was a shot in the dark, but judging from the expression on his face it struck home. His wife shrank away from him and told him he was disgusting, and all around the room people lowered their eyes in embarrassment.

"You needed me," I told Doll. "You weren't sure what you needed me for, but you needed me. So after you heard from Borden you came downtown looking for me. And you found me, but I had company. I was with Carolyn."

"At the Bum Rap," Carolyn recalled, "and then at the Italian restaurant, and then we wound up at my place."

"And then I kept calling Marty until I reached him around midnight. I don't suppose you stood around on Arbor Court waiting for me to come out. Maybe you gave up, stopped for a cup of coffee on Hudson Street, and got lucky when I turned up. Either way, you must have seen me fail to get a cab and stalk off to the subway, and you knew where I had to be going. All you had to do was jump in a cab and wait for me to come out of the subway entrance at Seventy-second and Broadway."

"This is fascinating," she said. "I had no idea I was such a resourceful woman."

"And a hell of a liar, Doll. I'm going to call you Doll instead of Wendy from now on because that's what I called you that night, once we got around to names. All you wanted me to do was walk you home. You spent a few blocks setting things up so you could make use of me later on, and when we got to the entrance downstairs you decided to float a trial balloon. You made a point of asking the doorman about the Nugents."

"About us?" Joan Nugent demanded. "But how did this young woman even know us?"

"She didn't," I said, "but Luke must have mentioned you. That he used to pose for you, and that you were out of town. So, in the guise of an idle question to the doorman, she let a known burglar know that the tenants in 9-G were out of town."

"Why would I do that, Bernie?"

"I don't know for sure," I admitted. "Maybe you thought Luke was holing up chez Nugent and you were hoping I'd smoke him out. Maybe you figured I'd get caught burgling their place and you could hang the baseball card theft on me at the same time."

"It was spiritual. Blood was calling to blood."

It was Patience who said this, and all of us stopped what we were doing and stared at her.

She put her hand to her mouth. "Maybe I spoke too soon," she said. "Was Luke already in this apartment?" I said he was. "And he was, uh, dead?" Quite dead, I said. "Then that must have been it," she said. "There must have been a strong psychic connection between Luke and . . . I'm sorry, Bernie, is her name Wendy or Doll?"

"Actually, most people call me Gwen," Doll said, "but at this point I don't honestly give a damn what anybody calls me. Could we get on with this?"

"A strong connection," Patience said. "His spirit, freed from his body, was in communication with her. But she didn't know that's what it was, she only felt a sense of urgency relating to this apartment." She held out both hands, the fingers spaced an inch or so apart. "This apartment is psychically charged," she told Joan Nugent. "I don't know how you can possibly live here."

"It's intense," Mrs. Nugent agreed, with a toss of her braids. "But I think the energy is good for my creative work."

"I never thought of that," Patience said. "I'll bet you're right."

I felt like a backseat passenger trying to get a grip on the steering wheel. "Whatever it was," I said, "she baited the trap, bade me good night—"

"With a kiss," Doll reminded me.

"With a kiss," I agreed, "and then you scooted past the doorman and disappeared into the building."

"It was probably Eddie," Harlan Nugent murmured to his wife. "That incompetent."

"Maybe you went upstairs and banged on Luke's door some more," I went on. "Maybe you stationed yourself where you could keep an eye on the lobby to see if I took the bait. Eventually you gave up and went home, which is what I'd already done. I slept off a larger intake of scotch than is my custom, went downtown to open up the store, and the next thing I knew I was under arrest."

"It was a legitimate collar," Ray Kirschmann said. "The phone call you made, your priors—"

"I'm not complaining," I said. "It was a shock, that's all. I spent Friday night in a cell, and Saturday night all I wanted to do was sleep in my own bed. But I got a late-night phone call from you,

Doll. You had a brand-new collection of lies to tell me, and this time you knew just what you wanted me to do. Luke was your boyfriend, you said, and you broke up with him and threw his keys in his face, and you just knew he'd retaliated by stealing your good friend Marty's baseball cards. And all I had to do was open Luke's door for you and we could return Marty's baseball cards and clear my name."

"Hang on a sec," Ray said. "She took the cards an' now she wants to give 'em back?"

"I have a feeling the program would have changed again once she got her hands on the cards," I said, "but it made a good story for the time being. I knew something was fishy, but I figured I'd play out the string and see where it led. One of the first things it did was catch you in a lie, Doll. You'd said you couldn't call me earlier because you didn't know the name of the store or where it was located. So when we split up Saturday night I said I'd meet you the following afternoon at the bookshop, and you said fine. You didn't have to ask where it was or how to find it."

"You had told me earlier."

"Nope. You already knew. And you were there in plenty of time, and we came uptown and I opened Luke's door."

"Breaking and entering," Ray intoned.

"I'll cop to entering," I said, "but we didn't break anything. Didn't find much of anything, either.

Some pills, and what looked like marijuana. A couple of dollars in a jelly jar."

"We found the drugs when we searched the place," Ray said, "but I don't remember no cash in no jam jar."

"Gee," I said, "I wonder what could have happened to it. Oh, and there was one other thing. We found a baseball card. 'A Stand-up Triple!' it was called, and it showed Ted Williams with his hands on his hips."

"From the mustard set," Borden Stoppelgard said. "That was one of Marty's cards, all right. It's a great picture of Williams, too."

"If you like that sort of thing," I said. "Much of its charm was lost on Doll and me. The message I got from it was that the cards had been there and now they were gone. Doll already knew they'd been there, and now she knew that Luke must have forced the lock on the briefcase. Then he'd started to transfer the cards to a backpack, and then he'd evidently changed his mind, but the one card he overlooked in a compartment of the backpack made it clear what he'd done. So that meant he was making a move on his own, and either he'd sold the cards already or he was in the process of doing so, and either way Doll could kiss the money goodbye, at least until Luke turned up again and she got another shot at him."

"But that wasn't going to happen," Carolyn said

helpfully, "because Luke was dead in the bathroom."

"Not anymore," I said. "Oh, he was still dead, but by the time we got into his apartment the cops had hauled him out of here in a body bag. That made the news Sunday night, and after that I never heard another word from Doll. She concluded, reasonably enough I suppose, that any chance she had of making a couple of bucks had just gone down the bathtub drain, so she'd move on to whatever life offered her next."

"What happened to the cards?" It was Lolly Stoppelgard who wanted to know, reinforcing my view of her as an eminently practical woman.

"Gone," I said. "Did Luke sell them? If so, what happened to the money? My guess is he put them, briefcase and all, in a coin locker somewhere while he figured out what to do with them. But there must be half a dozen other things that could have happened to them, and I have a feeling we'll never know where they wound up."

"And what about Luke?"

"I beg your pardon?"

"The young man," Edna Gilmartin said. It was, as far as I could recall, the first time she'd spoken up all night. "The young man who died mysteriously in a locked bathroom. Who killed him?"

"Oh, that's easy," I said. "Harlan Nugent killed him."

22

I had a tense moment there, I have to admit it. Because all Harlan Nugent had to do was tell us to go home and pick up the phone to call his lawyer.

But what he said was, "That's ridiculous. I never even knew the man. Why on earth would I kill him?"

"That's a good question," I said.

"And we were in London," Joan Nugent put in. "Neither of us could have had anything to do with it. We were out of the country."

"You left Wednesday evening," I said. "Doll dropped the cards at Luke's apartment on Monday. Sometime between then and when you left, Luke was up here and Harlan Nugent killed him. If I had to guess, I'd go with Tuesday afternoon." I looked over at Ray. "How does that square with the estimated time of death?"

"No problem, Bernie."

"I think you must be out of your mind," Nugent

said. "That man was never in this apartment on any of those days." A shadow passed over his wife's face, and for an instant it looked as though she was about to say something, but her husband's hand settled on hers and the moment passed. He set his jaw. "I'll repeat what I said before. You admitted it was a good question. Why on earth would I kill him?"

"It's still a good question," I said, "but I've got a couple of good questions myself. Why would a man take off all his clothes and lock himself in somebody else's bathroom?"

"To take a shower," Lolly Stoppelgard suggested.

"That would make sense if it was his own bathroom," Carolyn volunteered, "but it wasn't. Maybe he got all sweaty posing and he needed to wash up."

"He was not here," Harlan Nugent said.

"Or maybe he just needed to use the john, Bern. That wouldn't get him in the tub, though, would it? Ray, has anybody checked if the shower worked in his apartment on the seventh floor? See, if he couldn't take a shower at his own place—"

"Forget the shower," I said. "The water wasn't on and the body wasn't wet."

"Some men tend to lock themselves in the bathroom," Lolly Stoppelgard said, with a glance at her husband. "Did they find any funny magazines in there with him?"

Time to grab the wheel again. "He would lock

himself in the bathroom," I said, "as a way of hiding. Once, years ago, back in the days when I still engaged in occasional acts of burglary—"

"Aw, Jesus," Ray muttered.

"—I was an uninvited guest in an empty apartment when its occupant returned. I hid in the closet, though a bathroom would have done as well had one been close at hand. I couldn't lock the closet, of course." Someone else had locked the closet, with me in it, and when I managed to get out I found a corpse on the floor. I winced at the memory.

"Nor was I naked," I continued. "Last week Ray Kirschmann asked me what kind of burglar takes off his clothes in the course of a burglary. No burglar I ever heard of, I told him, so—"

"He was posing," Patience said. "That's it, isn't it?" She smiled at Joan Nugent. "He was posing for you, wasn't he?"

"I've never painted nudes," Joan Nugent said. "I don't believe in it."

"You don't believe in it?"

"No, I don't. I think we've had entirely too much of that sort of thing down through the centuries. My most recent painting of Luke was in harlequin garb. I assure you he was fully clothed."

"Then he was changing," Patience said. "He'd posed in costume, and—"

"Never in costume. When he posed for me he wore street clothes. I would sketch the lines of his body, and then I'd paint the harlequin costume in later. I didn't need him for that."

"But he was naked," I said.

"Oh, no," she said. "I'd remember that. I'm sure it's not at all the sort of thing I would forget."

"Joan," Harlan Nugent said gently, "shut up."

"You might have remembered," I told her, "if you'd known what was going on. But you were unconscious. You'd been drugged."

"Not a word, Joan," Nugent said.

"If you'll all follow me," I said, leading the way to the studio or guest bedroom, as you prefer. "You were drugged, Mrs. Nugent, and you were unconscious. Your clothes were off. Luke Santangelo's clothes were off as well, and he was attempting to—"

"Oh my God," someone said.

"I suppose you were on the daybed over there, or perhaps on the floor. Then there was the sound of your husband's key in the lock, and seconds later he had thrown open the hall door and announced his presence. He's a big, hearty man. I'm sure he tends to make his presence known."

"Sometimes he'll say, 'Lucy, I'm home.' Like Ricky Ricardo, you know. He does a good Cuban accent. Show them, darling."

Harlan Nugent looked like a man trying to think of a reason to take the next breath.

"You walked in," I said to him, "and found your wife unconscious, or at the very least out of her mind on drugs. You saw the bathroom door, closed. You tried the knob and it was locked."

"And then what did I do?"

"You banged on the door, demanding that it be opened. Luke Santangelo was many things, most of them unsavory, but he was not entirely out of his mind. The last thing he was going to do was open the door."

"Then I'd say we were at an impasse," Nugent said, "since I'm hardly of a size to slither through the keyhole, and the door doesn't have one anyway, does it?" He made a huge fist and gave the door a thump. "Pretty sturdy," he observed, "but I suppose I could have knocked it down *in extremis*. Kicked it in, put my shoulder to it, that sort of thing. But didn't I understand that it was still intact, indeed still locked, when the police were forced to break in?"

"I was wondering about that myself," I said. I went over and tapped on the door, then flicked the switch alongside it. No lights went on or off. I opened the bathroom door and repeated the process, with the same results. "What have we here?" I said. "Doesn't seem to do anything, does it?"

"I think it may control one of the baseboard outlets," Nugent said. "What possible difference could it make?"

"I wonder," I said, and whipped out my ring of burglar's tools and began unscrewing the screws that held the switch plate in place. "*Voilà,*" I said at length, showing them all the rectangle devoid of the usual switchbox. "Once upon a time, this must have been a child's bedroom. And after the child locked itself in the bathroom and couldn't get out, perhaps for the second or third time, one of its parents resolved to make sure nothing of the sort ever happened again. Hence this little safety device."

"Our children were grown when we moved here," Joan Nugent said. "This room has always been my studio. And I've never locked myself in this bathroom. I hardly ever use this bathroom, and I rarely lock the door in the other bathroom, either."

"Joan," her husband said, "nobody cares. And you, sir," he said to me. "What you're suggesting makes no sense at all. Even if all the other nonsense you've suggested were true, which it is not, and even if I had known about this ancient passageway, which I did not, and even if I were sufficiently outraged to want to injure the villain, why would I leave him in the bathroom? If I went in there and killed him, why wouldn't I get rid of the body?"

"Because you couldn't get in the room."

"Bernie," Ray Kirschmann pointed out, "you just showed us how to do it. Remember?"

"Vividly," I said. "But that's not what Mr. Nugent did. Instead he got a gun from wherever he keeps that sort of thing, and he stuck the business end of it through the opening and shot Luke Santangelo right between the eyes. I don't know if Luke was standing in the tub at the time. He may have tried backing away when he saw a gun poking through a wall at him, and who could blame him? But once he was shot the impact would have sent him reeling, and one way or another he wound up in the tub. He was dead, and the door was still locked."

"So, Bernie? He reaches in like you did, unlocks the lock, an' walks out with the stiff draped over his shoulder. Mr. Nugent here's a big guy, the stiff was a wiry little punk, he wouldn't have no trouble doin' it. Your doctor didn't say nothin' about not doin' any heavy liftin', did he, Mr. Nugent?"

"Had any of this happened, Officer, I'd have done exactly what you've just said."

I said, "Oh yeah? Let's see you do it, Mr. Nugent."

"Don't be ridiculous."

"Come on," I said. "Show us how you'd have done it and we'll all go home."

"This is a farce," he said. "Why should I dignify it by—"

"Oh, give it a rest," I told him. "You're too big. You've got forearms like a Bulgarian weightlifter. I don't even know if you could get your hand through the opening, but you'd never get enough of your arm in to reach the lock. And why should you make a fool of yourself now by trying? You already tried once and found out it didn't work."

"And then what did I do, Mr. Rhodenbarr?"

"You tidied up. You screwed the switch plate

back where it belonged. You threw a blanket over your wife and let her sleep it off. When she woke up asking whatever happened to cool bland Luke, you said he must have left before you arrived. 'I guess I must have dozed off,' she said. 'I guess you did at that,' you said, 'but don't you think we ought to start packing? We've got a flight tomorrow evening.' "

"And I suppose I left the corpse in place and trotted off to London."

"Why not? He wasn't going anywhere. Your wife already said she hardly ever uses that bathroom. If she tried to get in there during the twenty-four hours before you left for the airport, she'd find the door locked. 'Seems to be stuck,' you could tell her. 'Wood must have swelled over the summer. Have to get the super to look at it after we come back.' "

"You're forgetting something."

"Oh?"

"Our apartment was ransacked in our absence. Things tossed about, drawers emptied out, jewelry and other valuables taken. How does that fit in with your little scenario?"

"He's got a point," Ray said. "There was even a piece or two of jewelry found in the tub with the deceased."

"I'm sure there was," I said. "Right where Nugent tossed it when he faked the burglary?"

Nugent stared at me. "I faked the burglary?

When did I do that, right after I kidnapped the Lindbergh baby?"

I shook my head. "I have a pretty good idea how you did it," I said. "The only real question is when you tossed the jewelry in the tub. It was a nice touch, and I wonder if you were farsighted enough to do it right after you shot Santangelo or if you had to remove the switch plate a second time later on. I'd guess the latter. The killing was an impulse thing, wasn't it? While the cover-up took some planning."

"You must be out of your mind."

"Here's what I think," I went on. "Late Tuesday night, while your wife was asleep, you realized what you had to do. You got some of her jewelry, came in here, undid the switch plate, tossed the jewels in the tub with the corpse, and closed up again. Then Wednesday the two of you were ready to fly to London. Maybe you were already down on the street loading the bags into the taxi when you contrived to remember something, one bag you'd conveniently left behind. 'I won't be a minute,' you told your wife, and it wouldn't have taken you much longer than that. Scoop up a few valuables, spill out a few drawers, and you're on your way again. You'd already have disposed of whatever clothing Santangelo had removed before he, uh, did what he did. In a pinch you could have tossed them out the window, leaving them for the homeless to scavenge, but I suspect you found an even safer way."

"And what did I do with the jewels?"

"Good question," I said. "That necklace is a beaut, Mrs. Nugent. I've been admiring it all night. I don't suppose it was one of the stolen pieces?"

"I had it with me in Europe."

"I don't know what you're driving at," Nugent said, "and I don't think you do, either. The police have a full and precise inventory of everything that was taken. You can be assured that the pieces my wife is wearing are not on it."

"I'm sure they're not," I said, "but it's good to know about the inventory. Ray, I don't suppose you happen to have a copy of it with you, do you?"

"I do, as a matter of fact."

"And I do if he doesn't," said Nugent. "What possible difference can it make?"

"Well," I said slowly, "if we found some of the pieces on that list here in this apartment, it wouldn't look good for Mr. Nugent, would it?"

"If he took the stuff," Ray said, "he wouldn't leave it here. He ain't stupid, Bernie."

"I could hardly tuck it in my breast pocket and carry it to London and back," Nugent said testily, "and I wouldn't have had time to do anything else with it, would I?"

"That's right," I said. "You'd have had to stash it someplace on the premises. I know what you're going to say, Ray. After the Nugents returned, he could have transferred the goodies to a safe deposit box."

"Words right outta my mouth, Bernie."

"And he could have," I said, "but I don't think he did. Why bother, since the cops had already been in and out of the place in his absence? I think he decided the jewels were perfectly safe right where they were. Now where would that be?" I looked thoughtfully at Harlan Nugent. "Someplace where your wife wouldn't come upon them, because she thought the burglary was genuine. Some private space of yours. A den, say." I led the way, and damned if they didn't all follow me. "A locked desk drawer," I said, having located just such a drawer. "Is this where you put the jewels, Mr. Nugent?"

"What a curious fantasy."

"I don't suppose you'd care to open the drawer for us?"

"Nothing," he said, "would please me more." He opened an unlocked drawer on the opposite side of the desk and rummaged through it. "Damn it to hell," he said.

"Is something wrong?"

"I can't find the fucking key."

"How convenient."

He cursed colorfully and imaginatively. If I'd been a key and somebody talked to me like that, I'd do whatever he wanted me to do. This key, however, remained elusive.

"Bern," Carolyn said, God bless her, "since when did you ever need a key to open a lock? Use the gifts God gave you, will you?"

"Well, I can't do that," I said. "We're guests in Mr. Nugent's home, and it's his desk and his drawer and only he knows what's in it. I couldn't possibly try to open it without his permission."

He looked at me. "You can open a lock without a key?"

"Sometimes," I said.

"Then for God's sake do it," he started to say, and then I think he finally got it, and that made it perfect. "Wait a moment," he said. "Of course you have no legal right."

"No, sir," I said. "We'd need your permission."

"Which if we don't get it, the next step'd be a court order," Ray added.

The big shoulders sagged. "There can't be . . . I can't imagine . . . go ahead, damn you, open the fucking thing."

Guess what we found?

"I completely lost my head," Harlan Nugent said. "Just as you said, I came home that Tuesday afternoon and found Joan sprawled naked on the daybed in her studio. She was unconscious, and in an awkward, unnatural position. I took one look at her and thought she was dead."

"Oh, darling!"

"And there were these clothes piled on the floor, as if they'd been removed in a great hurry. Her clothes, and some male clothing as well. And my eye was drawn to the bathroom door, which was closed. It's usually open when she paints."

"When I use acrylics, I wash my brushes in the sink."

"I tried the door, and of course I couldn't open it. I shouted for whoever was inside to open the door. Of course he didn't. If he had, I think I might have torn him limb from limb."

"So you got your gun."

"From the locked drawer. If I'd misplaced the key a little earlier, Santangelo might be alive." He thought about it. "No," he decided, "I'd have broken down the door and killed him. I was completely beside myself."

"But you remembered a way into the bathroom."

"The switch plate, yes. And I shot him. I don't think I even knew who he was when I pulled the trigger. I didn't care. He'd killed the only woman I ever loved, and he was damn well going to die for it. Then I would call the police and let them take over."

"Instead, she came back to life."

"Thank God," he said. "She moved an arm, she was breathing, she was alive. I didn't know what he'd done, whether he'd knocked her unconscious or drugged her or what—"

"He sometimes gave me these pills," she said, "that made colors a lot richer. They had a very stimulating effect on my painting, but sometimes I would get very tired and have to lie down and take a nap."

"The swine," Nugent said. "I can't say I'm sorry he's dead. It's hard to believe the world's a poorer place for his having left it. But I wish I hadn't killed him. It shook me badly."

"That's why you were so moody in London, darling."

"I tidied up and tried to figure out what to do next. Then Joan awoke smiling and still a little groggy, asking when I'd come in and where Luke had gone. I said I just got in and he must have let himself out. When she turned in for the night I went out and draped his clothes on the gate of the church on Amsterdam Avenue. People leave clothing there all the time, and homeless people help themselves to it. I've left things there before, shirts with frayed collars, trousers that have gone shiny in the seat. I must say I've given away things of my own that were in better shape than what I hung on the gate that night. Dirty jeans gone at the knee, a sweater rank enough to gag a billy goat—"

"Luke was never a dresser," Doll put in. "And he could get a little lax in the personal hygiene area."

"I got rid of the gun as well. I'd bought it to protect our home from prowlers, and, in a manner of speaking, it had done its job. I dropped it down a storm drain."

"An' then you burglarized yourself," Ray said, "an' lit out for London."

Nugent frowned. "I swear I don't remember that part," he said. "Is it possible for a man to do a thing like that and forget it entirely?"

"Darling, you were under a strain," his wife said.

"I've always prided myself on my memory," he said. "And it's not like forgetting a telephone number."

"You did bring two of the bags down, Harlan. And then you went up for the other two, while I waited in the lobby."

"That's when I must have done it," he said. "I could have sworn—"

"What?"

"Nothing," he said. "It doesn't matter. And what earthly difference does it make? I've already admitted to murder. That's a far more serious offense than making a false report of a crime." He heaved a great sigh. "Well," he said, "I suppose I'll call my attorney now. And then you'll want to follow the form and read me my rights, won't you?"

There was a silence, and I started counting to myself. One. Two. Three. Four. . . .

"Let's not be too hasty here," Ray Kirschmann said. "Before we get all caught up in anythin' official, let's see what we're lookin' at here."

Someone asked him what he meant.

"Well, where's our evidence? You made an admission just now in front of a roomful of people, but none of that's admissible in court. Any lawyer'd just tell you to retract it, an' that's the end of it. Far as physical evidence goes, what we got's a lot of nothin'. There's a switch plate with no switch box behind it, provin' somebody coulda been shot in a locked room, but so what?

"An' as for you, young lady," he said to Doll Cooper, "we got no doubt in my mind, an' prolly not a lot in anybody else's either, that you had somethin' to do with the disappearance of those baseball cards. But we ain't got the cards, an' you ain't got 'em either, an' my best guess is they been sold an' split up an' changed hands three times already, an' nobody's ever gonna see 'em again. This gentleman here, Mr. Gilmartin, he might have a bone to pick with you, on account of it's his cards you walked off with. If he insists on pressin' charges, well, I think it'll get kicked for lack of evidence, but I'd have to take you in."

"I don't want to press charges," Marty said. "I just hope Miss Cooper might narrow her range in the future and limit her acting to stage and screen. She would seem to have a considerable talent, and it would be a shame to see it diluted."

"You know," Doll said, "you're a gentleman, you really are. I'm sorry I took the cards from you. I *was* playing a part, that's exactly what I was doing, and I think I fooled myself into thinking it gave me a dramatic license to steal. It's corny to say this, but I may have actually learned a lesson tonight."

Carolyn gave me a "get her" look, but the speech seemed to go over well with everybody else.

"So that's that," Ray said. "Brings us back to you, Mr. Nugent. What we keep comin' back to is there's no evidence, an' I also gotta say the deceased don't sound like no great loss. Of course there's also the matter of makin' a false report to an insurance company, claimin' a loss when there was no loss."

"That bothered me," Nugent admitted. "The idea of making an actual profit on the man's death. But once the burglary was a matter of record I could hardly fail to put in a claim." He thought for a moment. "I could tell them I made a mistake. The jewelry actually turned up."

"You sure you want to do that, Mr. Nugent? You sorta call attention to yourself that way. You're in this deep, the shortest way's straight ahead." He put a companionable hand on the big man's shoulder. "Far as makin' a profit on all of this, believe me, sir, you got nothin' to worry about. The rest of you folks, I'm thinkin' maybe you all oughta clear outta here about now. The show's over, an' me an' Mr. Nugent here need a little privacy to work out some of the details on how we're gonna keep this whole matter private an' personal."

23

I had a lunch date the following day, so I didn't get a chance to sit down and talk with Carolyn until we met after work at the Bum Rap. I was a little late closing—a customer, a devout G. T. Henty collector, may his tribe increase—and by the time I got over there she was already at work on a scotch and soda. I asked Maxine to bring me a beer, and Carolyn told me that was a load off her mind.

"You've been working up a storm lately, Bern," she said. "I was starting to worry about you."

"Not to worry," I said.

"I went on home by myself last night," she said, "because I had the feeling you and Patience might want to creep off into the night."

"On little iambic feet?" I shook my head. "I bought her a cup of coffee," I said, "and put her in a cab."

"I was wondering what she was doing there, Bern. I was trying to figure out how she could have stolen the cards or shot Luke Santangelo, and I came up with a couple of real winners. Why'd you have Ray bring her?"

"To save going through the whole thing another time," I said. "I kind of owed her an explanation, after all the dates I broke and the fibs I told."

"Lies, Bern. Once you're past seven years old, you don't get to call them fibs anymore."

"Besides, I suppose I was showing off a little. And I thought it might cheer her up. She's a nice woman, but she's depressed all the time. She'll come out of it for a minute or two to sing haiku to the tune of 'Moonlight in Vermont,' but then she's off again, sinking into the Slough of Despond."

She frowned. "Isn't that what they called Babe Ruth?"

"That was the Sultan of Swat."

"Right. It's hard keeping them all straight. Bern, you gotta remember that Patience is a poet."

"Who else would sing haiku?"

"And they're all moody like that, especially the women. It's a good thing most of 'em have to live in basement apartments or they'd be jumping out the window all the time. As it stands they kill themselves left and right."

"Sylvia Plath, Anne Sexton."

"That's just the tip of the ice cube, Bern. It's a known phenomenon, poetic depression in women. There's even a name for it."

"The Edna St. Vincent Malaise," I said. "I've heard of it, but this is the first time I ever encountered it in person. And I think Patience and I have had a parting of the ways. Still, it didn't hurt having her there. There were enough chairs to go around."

She took a sip of her drink and asked me what had happened after the rest of them left.

"What you'd expect," I said. "Ray's instincts are pretty good sometimes, I have to say that for him. He had a hunch I could clear it all up, and that there'd be something in it for him. He was right on both counts. You were there to watch me clear it up, and after you left he got his share."

"Harlan Nugent paid him off?"

"That's not the way Ray phrased it. According to him, some money had to be spread around to make sure the investigation didn't go any further. Well, he can make sure of that simply by keeping his mouth shut and not filing a report, so there's not a lot of spreading that has to be done. Ray's idea of sharing is to divide the dough up and put it in different pockets."

"How much did he get?"

"Eighty-three fifty for openers. That's what cash Nugent had on hand. There'll be more when the insurance company pays off on the Nugents' jewelry. My guess is Ray'll pick up another twenty or twenty-five."

"Eighty-three fifty."

"Yeah."

"That's a familiar number."

"Isn't it," I said sourly.

"It's the money you took from Nugent's desk the first time you went there, isn't it?"

"To the penny," I said. "I swear that's the stupidest job I ever pulled in my life. I went in three times. The first time I took some money and jewelry and put back the jewelry. The second time I kept the money and went back for the jewelry. Then the night before last I went in for the last time and put the money back where I found it, and put the jewelry in the same drawer with it. It's like that logic problem with cannibals and Christians."

"I wouldn't trust either of them, Bern. What did you do, go in in the middle of the night?"

"Around four in the morning. Not a Nugent was stirring. I came as Young Dr. Rhodenbarr, with my stethoscope in my pocket. It would have been pretty awful to get caught the one time I was making a delivery instead of a pickup, but I figured I had to set the stage."

"You stole the key, right?"

I nodded. "You'd be surprised how often people keep the key to a locked drawer in one of the neighboring unlocked drawers. Well, it makes sense. Where else would you keep it? I don't usually hunt for the key, because those locks are so easy to open, but I happened to come across it the other night and I figured it would be better theater if Nugent had to say he couldn't open the drawer. It made it look as though he had something to hide. And, much to his own surprise, he did."

"Why put back the eighty-three fifty?"

"I figured there could only be so many jokers in the deck. By the time we left last night, Nugent was beginning to recall moving the jewelry from his wife's dresser to the desk. Since there was no other possible explanation, his memory was obligingly filling in the gaps. Poor bastard."

"Well, he killed a guy, Bern."

"And Doll stole a man's baseball card collection, and how can we let such actions go unpunished? Well, the fact of the matter is that they *did* go unpunished. It didn't cost either of them a dime. Doll walked out of there with her head held high, and Nugent gets to pay off Ray with money from an insurance company."

"It was his money originally, Bern."

"Right, and then it was mine for a while." I shrugged. "I knew there was no point to this. That's why I tried to get out of it. But between Ray's nudging and your nagging, what chance did I have?"

"That wasn't nagging, Bern. That was the advice of a caring friend."

"Well, it had all the earmarks of nagging," I said, "and it worked, so you can take the credit."

"It wasn't me, Bern. It was Raffles."

I looked at her.

"Remember, Bern? Raffles leaped up in the air and arched his back and did all those weird things that he did, and it came to you in a flash."

"Oh, right."

"I mean, let's give credit where it's due, huh?" She waved to Maxine for another round. "Couple of things I'm not completely clear on, Bern. How'd you know Joan Nugent was drugged and unconscious when her husband came home? I never would have thought of that."

"Neither would I."

"Huh?"

"What I thought," I said, "was that she and Luke were having an affair, and that they were going at it when Harlan stuck his key in the door. But wouldn't they have been in the master bedroom? And if so, wouldn't Luke have gone in the other bathroom?"

"Unless they started out posing, and one thing led to another, and they got carried away."

"Or unless she had some compunctions about committing adultery in the very bed she shared with her husband. Still, it became clear that she didn't have a clue how that corpse wound up in her bathroom. And Luke had a whole storehouse of pills in his apartment, and she had the abstracted air of someone who just might have ingested a mood-altering substance sometime or other in the course of her life, and it all came together."

"What a scumbag Luke must have been."

"Well, I don't think he was ever on the short list for the Jean Hersholt Humanitarian Award," I said, "but he wasn't here to give us his side of the story, either. The incident came out sounding like the next best thing to necrophilia, but maybe it didn't start out that way. Maybe he got her stoned and they started necking, and she took off her clothes and they were, uh, embracing, and then the full force of the drug kicked in and she slipped out of consciousness."

"And it didn't occur to him to stop? I suppose he thought she was English. Believe me, Bern, the man was an insect. Look how he betrayed Doll Cooper. She left Marty's cards with him, and he lifted them out from under her."

"That was me, Carolyn. The attaché case full of cards was still under the bed when Luke got shot upstairs."

"Oh, right," she said. "So you're the insect."

"I guess so."

"There was something else I was wondering about. Oh, right. The gun. Couldn't they ever recover it?"

"From a storm drain? Have you got any idea how many guns get tossed down storm drains?"

"Lots, huh?"

"Put it this way," I said. "If there really are alligators in the New York sewers, half of them are armed. Want to get rid of a gun? Just slip it down a storm drain. It's like hiding a needle in a haystack."

"I'd never hide a needle in a haystack," she said. "It's the first place they would look. Bern, why didn't he leave the gun with Luke? I know he couldn't get his arm through, but what if he tossed the gun so it landed in the tub?"

"And it would look like suicide."

"Right."

"Except it wouldn't," I said. "Not if you looked closely. Even if he managed to get his own prints off the gun, how was he going to get Luke's on it? And if they ran a paraffin test on Luke they wouldn't find any nitrate particles on his hand, nothing to indicate he'd fired a gun."

"Oh."

"I don't know what kind of gun it was, so I can't say whether it would have fit through the hole. Even if it would, if I'd just shot a guy and he'd fallen where I couldn't get a good look at him and I had no way of knowing for sure whether he was alive or dead, I don't think I'd be in a big rush to throw him a loaded gun."

"I guess it was a bad idea," she said. "Oh, well. Gotta drink up and go, Bern."

"Already?"

"Got a date."

"Oh? Anybody I know?"

"It's no big deal," she said defensively. "Just a quick drink, a little conversation."

"That's how Borden Stoppelgard described his pursuit of Doll." I looked at her. "It *is* somebody I know, isn't it? Who is it, Carolyn?"

"Somebody I just met the other night."

"Not Doll," I said. "It can't be."

"Jesus, no. Marty would kill me."

"He did seem quite taken with her, now that you mention it. Considering that she stole his baseball cards. Well, he's a patron of the theater. Maybe he'll wind up taking a fatherly interest in her career."

"Or a sugar daddily interest, Bern. Anyway, she's not my type."

"Not Patience. Joan Nugent? What are you going to do, have her paint a portrait of you in a clown suit?"

"Nice, Bern."

"Well—"

"As a matter of fact," she said, "it's Lolly Stoppelgard."

"Lolly Stoppelgard."

"Didn't you think she was nice?"

"Very nice, but—"

"But she's married. That's what you were going to say, isn't it?"

"Something like that."

"You didn't see the looks she was giving me, Bern."

"No, that's true."

"And you didn't hear what she said to me on the way downstairs. 'Call me,' she said."

"So you called her."

"Uh-huh, and in the long run I'll get my heart broken, but that's what hearts are for, and mine's getting used to it. She's really nice, isn't she? Pretty and sharp and funny."

"It's a shame to think of all that wasted on Borden Stoppelgard."

"Well, I look at it this way," she said. "I figure he'll be an easy act to follow."

24

A day or two later I was on the phone with Wally Hemphill when the front door opened. "That's great," I told my lawyer. "So I'll see you then. Listen, I've got to go now, I've got a customer."

It was Borden Stoppelgard.

"I got your message," he said, "and I'd have to say you've got your nerve, asking me to stop by. That was some little show you put on the other night. By the time we got out of there, my marriage was hanging by a thread."

"I'm sorry about that."

"Well, it's all right now. Things blow over, you know? She's a lot calmer the past couple of days. Now what's this item you got that I might be interested in? Early Sue Grafton? Marcia Muller? What?"

I took an acetate-wrapped card from my breast pocket and laid it on the counter.

"You know," he said, "when you talked about finding the Chalmers Mustard card in that schmuck Santangelo's apartment, I wanted to ask whatever became of it, whether you or Wendy wound up with it. But it didn't seem like the right time or place."

"Probably not."

"So you want to sell it? 'A Stand-up Triple!'—right? That's one of the later ones, so it's worth a few bucks. What do you want for it?"

"Take a closer look, Mr. Stoppelgard."

"Jesus Christ," he said. " 'That Home Run Swing.' Card #40. This is the key card of the whole set. Where the hell did you get this?" Even as I was plucking the card from his fingers, light dawned. "I'll be a son of a bitch," he said. "You got Marty's cards!"

"It looks that way," I admitted. "So now all you have to do is draw up that lease we talked about, the one that gives me a thirty-year extension at the current rent."

"Shit."

"What's the matter?"

"Oh, hell. This is embarrassing, all right? I sold the building."

"What?"

"When you're in the real estate game," he said, "you don't marry buildings, you just buy and sell them. Anything's on the block if the price is right. A few days ago I got an offer that was too good to turn down. So I took it."

"But—"

"You should be getting a notice in the mail, where to send the check every month and like that. Your new landlord's something called Poulson Realty. They'll be in touch."

"I hope they like baseball cards."

"Maybe they won't even notice the lease is ready to expire," he said, which didn't strike me as very likely. "Or maybe they'll give you a break in order to keep the space rented to somebody reliable. Of course, the way they came to me and sought out the building, my guess is they want the space for their own purposes. But you're a resourceful guy. You can work something out."

"You sold the building," I said. "Sold it out from under me."

"Dammit, why didn't you say something? How was I supposed to know you had the cards?"

"I didn't want to announce it in front of everybody."

"No, but—"

"And you must have already said yes to the deal on the building by then, anyway."

"Yes, but—"

"So that's that," I said, and put the Splendid Splinter in my pocket.

"Listen," he said, "I still want to buy those cards. The only thing is I'm a little short right now. If you could hold on to them for a couple of months—"

"You can't be serious."

"I guess that's a no. What would you say to a

straight exchange of equity? There's any number of things I could let you have. Could you use a very nice two-bedroom condominium on the Rego Park side of Forest Hills? Look, you could just say no. You don't have to make that kind of face at me."

"If I'm going to have to renegotiate my lease," I said, "or find a place to relocate my store, what I need is cash."

"I suppose."

"And it's not as though baseball cards are hard to move. I offered them to you first because it was a way to save the store, but with you out of the picture I won't have any trouble finding a buyer."

"Sell me the mustard set," he said.

"You just said—"

"I don't give a rat's ass about the rest of the cards. I'm only really interested in Ted Williams. We're talking about forty cards. The book value's what, three grand?"

"Closer to five."

"Really? That sounds high, but screw it. I'll give you five thousand cash. Why not?"

"I'd rather move everything at once."

"Why, for God's sake? Look, forget five. I'll pay a premium, because I really want these cards. I'll give you six thousand dollars."

"Ten."

"That's ridiculous. That's double what they're worth. For Christ's sake, a man buys stolen goods, he expects to get them at a discount. I can't pay ten, that's out of the question."

"Then forget it."

"Seven. I'll hate myself tomorrow, but I'll give you seven."

"Ten."

" 'Ten, ten, ten.' Is that all you know how to say?"

"Eleven?"

"Ten, for God's sake. I can't believe I'm doing this, but I don't care. I don't suppose you want a check, either. I have to go to the bank. I'll be back in twenty minutes. You'll have the cards ready?"

What can I say? He talked me into it.

Borden Stoppelgard wasn't back in twenty minutes, but he was back in twenty-five, and ten minutes later he was on his way, having exchanged a hundred pieces of green paper for forty pieces of cardboard. I went off to flush the toilet—Raffles had used it during our transaction—and I came back to find Wally Hemphill bending over to retie his sneaker. He straightened up, unclasped his briefcase, and handed me an envelope.

"This is what you wanted," he said, "and it took some doing and cost you a ton of money, so I hope you're happy. You're now master of all you survey, and that includes the upstairs and the air rights."

"This is the deed?"

"Indeed it is. You're not just a schmuck with a

bookstore, Bernie. Now you're a schmuck with a building."

"That's great."

"Your friend Gilmartin was very helpful. How we worked it, Hearthstone Realty, which is Stoppelgard's company, sold the land and structure to Poulson, which is a shell we set up. Then the title changed hands three or four times, bang bang bang, just like that. The current owner of record is Winesap Enterprises."

"And that's me?"

"It is," he said, "but the way things are set up, it would be a hell of a job to find that out. The whole thing cost you a hell of a lot of money, my friend. I won't even ask where it came from."

"Good."

"You overpaid for the building. I told you that, but you didn't want to hear it. At the price you paid, you'd have to raise your own rent through the roof to make the thing pay. The florist next door has ten years to go on his lease, and the residential tenants upstairs are all rent-controlled, so what they pay doesn't cover what it costs you to heat their apartments for them. So unless you're planning to try to get some of them to move—"

"I couldn't do that."

"I didn't think so. Bernie, the building won't even cover expenses. It's going to cost you money."

"I know that."

"If you'd taken the same cash and put it in a

good balanced mutual fund, do you know what kind of a yield you'd get?"

"I could have put it in baseball cards," I said. "Wally, suppose you took the hours you spend running and did billable work instead. Wouldn't you make more money that way?"

"Well, yeah, I see your point."

"Money's not everything. I get to keep the store, and that's what's important to me."

"Still," he said, "the building is going to lose money, and your store barely breaks even. How are you going to cover the deficit?"

"Oh, I don't know," I said. "I guess I'll think of something."

When Carolyn came in Raffles was sitting on my lap. "Just an employee," she said. "Not a pet at all, right, Bern?"

"Stroking a cat's fur is an aid to thought," I said. "It's a well-known relaxation technique. There doesn't have to be any affection involved."

"Is that a fact?"

"But here's the big news," I said, and I told her about Wally's delivery of the deed. "So I get to keep the store," I said. "I'll be a landlord, but nobody ever has to know that outside of you and me and Wally. The tenants will just send in their measly checks every month, same as always. And you and I can go on having lunch together and going over to the Bum Rap together after work. And as far as making up the building's annual deficit, well, I got a little installment on that today from Borden Stoppelgard."

I told her about our transaction. "I took pity on him," I said, "and sold him the Ted Williams set for two or three times its value, and of course it was all I had to sell to him or anybody else, because the rest of Marty's good material was gone before Doll lifted it. I was planning on jerking his chain a little more, but I found myself feeling sorry for the man."

"Well, the two of you have something in common, Bern. You're both landlords."

"Don't ever call me that, even in jest. But I looked at the poor slob, doomed to spend his life being outclassed by his brother-in-law—"

"And by everybody else he happens to meet."

"—and trying to cheat on his wife, and screwing that up, and having her cheat on him, and, well, I gave him a break."

"Mr. Nice Guy."

"*C'est moi,*" I agreed.

She reached to pet the cat. "Bernie," she said, "I've been trying not to ask you this, because I'm sure it's obvious, and when you tell me I'm gonna feel like an idiot. How did Raffles solve the case?"

"Huh?"

"Don't tell me you don't remember, because I know you do. We were right here, talking about The Cat Who Lived Forever, and Raffles jumped up in the air and arched his back and chased an imaginary tail or something. I don't know what he did exactly, but it triggered something and the next thing I knew we were all at the Nugents and you were telling everybody who did it."

"Oh."

"Now how did Raffles solve it?"

"Carolyn," I said, "Raffles didn't solve the case."

"Well, I know that, Bern. I mean, I'm not an idiot. I know Raffles is just a cat."

"Right."

"And I don't know what he did, or why he did it, but I know he's not the reincarnation of Nero Wolfe. But whatever he was doing, it made some connection for you and—why are you shaking your head?"

"I had already figured it all out," I said. "I just didn't want to do anything about it, because I couldn't see the point. Then we got into that nutty conversation about the cat, and he picked up his cue and acted as if he was on a hot tin roof, and I just couldn't help myself. What's the matter?"

"Nothing, Bern. I knew I'd feel stupid for asking, and I was right."

"Well, cheer up. This is a special day. I get to keep the store, Carolyn. And we get to go on—"

"Having lunch together," she chimed in, "and having drinks after work, and having doomed relationships with inappropriate people. I was gonna see Lolly tonight, but she had to cancel. She's doing something with Borden."

"He probably wants to show her his new cards. So let me take you out to dinner instead. We'll celebrate."

"I thought I'd go home and reread Sue Grafton. It's been a while since I last read the one about the topless dancer who gets poison injected into one of her implants."

" *'D' Is for Cup.*"

"Right. Bern, you know what I wish? I wish she didn't have to stop at twenty-six. When the alphabet's used up, what happens to Kinsey?"

"Are you kidding? She goes straight into double letters. *'AA' Is for Drunks, 'BB' Is for Gun, 'CC' Is for Rider.* There was a whole list in *Publishers Weekly* a few months back. *'PP' Is for Golden Showers, 'ZZ' Is for Topp*—I can't remember them all, but it looks as though she can go on forever."

"Bern, that's wonderful news."

"You'll be reading about Kinsey fifty years from now," I told her. " *'AAA' Is for Motorists, 'MMM' Is for Scotch Tape.* You'll never have to stop. You'll keep on washing dogs and Raffles will keep on playing shortstop. And I'll keep on doing what I was born to do, selling books and breaking into people's houses."

"And we'll live happily ever after, huh, Bern?"

"Happily ever *now,*" I said, and reached to pet my cat.

Don't miss the next

Bernie Rhodenbarr mystery,

THE BURGLAR WHO THOUGHT HE WAS BOGART,

available now from Dutton.

At a quarter after ten on the last Wednesday in May, I put a beautiful woman in a taxi and watched her ride out of my life, or at least out of my neighborhood. Then I stepped off the curb and flagged a cab of my own.

Seventy-first and West End, I told the driver.

He was one of a vanishing breed, a crusty old bird with English for a native language. "That's five blocks, four up and one over. A beautiful night, a young fella like yourself, what are you doing in a cab?"

Trying to be on time, I thought. The two films had run a little longer than I'd figured, and I had to stop at my own apartment before I rushed off to someone else's.

"I've got a bum leg," I said. Don't ask me why.

"Yeah? What happened? Didn't get hit by a car, did you? All I can say is I hope it wasn't a cab, and if it was I hope it wasn't me."

"Arthritis."

"Go on, arthritis?" He craned his neck and looked at me. "You're too young for arthritis. That's for old farts, you go down to Florida and sit in the sun. Live in a trailer, play shuffleboard, vote Republican. A fellow your age, you tell me you broke your leg skiing, pulled a muscle running the Marathon, that I can understand. But arthritis! Where do you get off having arthritis?"

"Seventy-first and West End," I said. "The northwest corner."

"I know Where you get off, as in get out of the cab, but why arthritis? You got it in your family?"

How had I gotten into this? "It's post-traumatic," I said. "I sustained injuries in a fall, and I've had arthritic complications ever since. It's usually not too bad, but sometimes it acts up."

"Terrible, at your age. What are you doing for it?"

"There's not much I can do," I said. "According to my doctor."

"Doctors!" he cried, and spent the rest of the ride telling me what was wrong with the medical profession, which was almost everything. They didn't know anything, they didn't care about you, they caused more troubles than they cured, they charged the earth, and when you didn't get better they blamed you for it. "And after they blind you and cripple you, so that you got no choice but to sue them, where do you have to go? To a lawyer! And that's worse!"

That carried us clear to the northwest corner of Seventy-first and West End. I'd had it in mind to ask him to wait, since it wouldn't take me long upstairs and I'd need another cab across town, but I'd had enough of—I squinted at the license posted on the right-hand side of the dash—of Max Fiddler.

I paid the meter, added a buck for the tip, and, like a couple of smile buttons, Max and I told each other to have a nice evening. I thought of limping, for the sake of verisimilitude, and decided the hell with it. Then I hurried past my own doorman and into my lobby.

Upstairs in my apartment I did a quick change, shucking the khakis, the polo shirt, the inspirational athletic shoes (*Just Do It!*) and putting on a shirt and tie, gray slacks, crepe-soled black shoes, and a double-breasted blue blazer with an anchor embossed on each of its innumerable brass buttons. The buttons—there'd been matching cuff links, too, but I haven't seen them in years—were a gift from a woman I'd been keeping company with a while back. She had met a guy and married him and moved to a suburb of Chicago, where the last

I'd heard she was expecting their second child. My blazer had outlasted our relationship, and the buttons outlasted the blazer; when I replaced it I'd gotten a tailor to transfer the buttons. They'll probably survive this blazer, too, and may well be in fine shape when I'm gone, although that's something I try not to dwell on.

I got my attaché case from the front closet. In another closet, the one in my bedroom, there is a false compartment built into the rear wall. My apartment has been searched by professionals, and no one has yet found my little hidey-hole. Aside from me and the drug-crazed young carpenter who built it for me, only Carolyn Kaiser knows where it is and how to get into it. Otherwise, should I leave the country or the planet abruptly, whatever I had hidden away would probably remain there until the building came down.

I pressed the two spots you have to press, then slid the panel you have to slide, and the compartment revealed its secrets. They weren't many. The space runs to about three cubic feet, so it's large enough to stow just about anything I steal until such time as I'm able to dispose of it. But I hadn't stolen anything in months, and what I'd last lifted had been long since distributed to a couple of chaps who'd had more use for it than I.

What can I say? I steal things. Cash, ideally, but that's harder and harder to find in this age of credit cards and twenty-four-hour automatic teller machines. There are still people who keep large quantities of real money around, but they typically keep other things on hand as well, such as wholesale quantities of illegal drugs, not to mention assault rifles and attack-trained pit bulls. They lead their lives and I lead mine, and if the twain never get around to meeting, that's fine with me.

The articles I take tend to be the proverbial good things that come in small packages. Jewelry, naturally. Objets d'art—jade carvings, pre-Columbian effigies, Lalique glass. Collectibles—stamps, coins, and once, in recent memory, baseball cards. Now and then a painting. Once—and never again, please God—a fur coat.

I steal from the rich, and for no better reason than Robin Hood did; the poor, God love 'em, have nothing worth taking. And the valuable little items I carry off are, you will note, not the sort of thing anybody needs in order to keep body and soul together. I don't steal pacemakers or iron lungs. No family is left homeless after a visit of mine. I don't take the furniture or the TV set (although I have been known to roll up a small rug and take it for a walk). In short, I lift the things you can live without, and which you have very likely insured, like as not for more than they're worth.

So what? What I do is still rotten and reprehensible, and I know it. I've tried to give it up, and I can't, and deep down inside I don't want to. Because it's who I am and what I do.

It's not the only thing I am or do. I'm also a bookseller, the sole proprietor of Barnegat Books, an antiquarian bookstore on East Eleventh Street, between Broadway and University Place. On my passport, which you'll find in the back of my sock drawer (which is stupid, because, trust me, that's the first place a burglar would look) my occupation is listed as bookseller. The passport has my name, Bernard Grimes Rhodenbarr, and my address on West End Avenue, and a photo which can be safely described as unflattering.

There's a better photo in the other passport, the one in the hidey-hole at the back of the closet. It says my name is William Lee Thompson, that I'm a businessman, and that I live at 504 Phillips Street, in Yellow Springs, Ohio. It looks authentic, and well it might; the passport office issued it, same as the other one. I got it myself, using a birth certificate that was equally authentic, but, alas, not mine.

I've never used the Thompson passport. I've had it for seven years, and in three more years it will expire, and if I still haven't used it I'll probably renew it when the time comes. It doesn't bother me that I haven't had occasion to use it, any more than it would bother a fighter pilot that he hasn't had occasion to use his parachute. The passport's there if I need it.

I wasn't likely to need it tonight, so I left it right where it was. I also left my stash of cash, which I didn't expect to need either. The last time I counted it was down to around five thousand dollars, which is lower than I like it. Ideally I ought to maintain an emergency cash reserve of $25,000, and I periodically boost it to that level, but then I find myself dipping into it for one thing or another, and before I know it I'm scraping bottom.

All the more reason to get to work.

A workman is as good as his tools, and so is a burglar. I picked up my ring of picks and probes and odd-shaped strips of metal and found room for them in a trouser pocket. My flashlight is the size and shape of a fountain pen, and I tucked it accordingly into the blazer's inside breast pocket. I didn't have to keep the flashlight hidden away—they sell them in hardware stores all over town, and it's no crime to carry one. But it is definitely a crime to carry burglar's tools, and the simple possession of a little collection like mine is enough to net their owner an extended vacation upstate, all expenses paid. So I keep them locked up, and stow the flashlight with them so I won't forget it.

Same with the gloves. I used to wear rubber gloves, the kind you put on when washing dishes, and I'd cut the palms out for ventilation. But now they have these terrific disposable gloves of plastic film, light as a feather and cool as a gherkin, and you can buy a whole roll of them for pocket change. I tore off two gloves and put the rest back.

I secured the secret compartment, closed the closet, snatched up the attaché case, let myself out of the apartment, and locked all the doors. All of this takes longer to report than to perform; I was in my apartment by ten-thirty and out of it, dressed and equipped and back on the street, by a quarter to eleven.

There was a cab cruising by as I cleared the threshold, and I could have sprinted and whistled and caught it. But it was hardly the sort of night when cabs were likely to be in short supply. I took my time, walked to the curb at a measured pace, held up a hand, and beckoned to a taxi. Guess who I got.

"What you shoulda done," Max Fiddler said, "was tell me you had someplace to go. I coulda waited. How's your leg now? Not too bad, right?"

"Not too bad," I agreed.

"It's good luck, finding you again. I almost didn't recognize you, all dressed up and everything. Whattaya got, if you don't my asking. A date? My guess, it's a business appointment."

"Strictly business."

"Well, you look very nice, you make a good appearance. We'll take the Transverse, okay? Go right through the park."

"Sounds good."

"Minute I dropped you off," he said, "I said to myself, Max, what's hell's the matter with you, man's got arthritis and you didn't tell him where to go. Herbs!"

"Herbs?"

"You know about herbs? Chinese herbs, like from a Chinese herb doctor. This woman gets into my cab, using a cane, has me take her down to Chinatown. She's not Chinese herself, but she tells me about this Chinese doctor she goes to. When she started with him she couldn't walk!"

"That's wonderful," I said.

"Wait, I haven't even told you yet!" And, even as we entered Central Park, he launched into a tale of miracle cures. A woman with horrible migraines—cured in a week! A man with high blood pressure—back to normal! Shingles, psoriasis, acne, warts—all of them cleared up!

Hemorrhoids—cured without surgery! Chronic back pain—gone!

"For the back he uses the needles. The rest is all herbs. Twenty-eight bucks you pay for a visit and the herbs is free. Seven days a week he's there, nine in the morning till seven at night . . ."

He himself had been cured of cataracts, he assured me, and now he saw better than he had when he was a boy. At a stoplight he took off his glasses and swung his head around, flashing his clear blue eyes at me. When we got to Seventy-sixth and Lexington he gave me a business card, Chinese on one side, English on the other. "I give out hundreds of these," he said. "I send everybody I can to him. Believe me, I'm glad to do it!" On the bottom, he showed me, he'd added his own name, Max Fiddler, and his telephone number. "You get good results," he said, "call me, tell me how it worked out. You'll do that?"

"I will," I said. "Definitely." And I paid him and tipped him and limped over to the brownstone where Hugo Candlemas lived.

I'd met Hugo Candlemas for the first time the previous afternoon. I was in my usual spot behind the counter, seeing what Will Durant had to say about the Medes and the Persians, of whom I knew little aside from the sexual proclivities alluded to in a limerick of dubious ethnological validity. Candlemas was one of three customers crowding my aisles just then. He was browsing quietly in the poetry section, while a regular customer of mine, a doctor at St. Vincent's, searched the adjacent aisle for the out-of-print mysteries she went through like smallpox through the Plains Indians. My third guest was a superannuated flower child who'd spotted Raffles sunbathing in the window. She'd come in to ooh and ahh over him and ask his name, and now she was looking through a shelf of art books and setting some volumes aside. If she wound up buying all the ones she'd picked, the sale would pay for a whole lot of Meow Mix.

The doctor was the first to settle up, relieving me of a half dozen Perry Masons. They were book club editions, a couple of them pretty shabby, but she was a reader, not a collector, and she gave me a twenty and got a little change back.

"Just a few years ago," she said, "these were a buck apiece."

"I can remember when you couldn't give them away," I said, "and now I can't keep them in stock."

"What do you figure it is, people with fond memories of the TV show? I came in the back door, I hated the TV show, but I started reading A. A. Fair and decided, gee, the guy can write, let's see what he's like under his own name. And it turns out they're tough and fast-paced and sassy, not like the television crap at all."

We had a nice conversation, the kind I'd had in mind when I bought the store, and then after she left the flower matron, Maggie Mason by name, brought up her treasure trove and wrote out a check for $228.35, which is what those twelve books came to with tax. "I hope Raffles gets a commission on this," she said. "I must have passed this store a hundred times, but it was seeing him that made me come in. He's a wonderful cat."

He is, but how could the ebullient Ms. Mason possibly know that? "Thank you," I said. "He's a hard worker, too."

He hadn't changed position since she came in, except to preen a little while she'd cooed at him. My irony was unintentional—he *is* a hard worker, maintaining Barnegat Books as a wholly rodent-free ecosystem—but it was lost on her anyway. She had, she assured me, the greatest respect for working cats. And off she went, bearing two shopping bags and a perfectly radiant smile.

She had barely cleared the threshold when my third

customer approached, a faint smile on his face. "Raffles," he said, "is a splendid name for that cat."

"Thank you."

"And appropriate, I'd say."

What exactly did he mean by that? A. J. Raffles was a character in a book, and the cat was in a bookshop, but that fact alone made the name no more appropriate than Queequeg, say, or Arrowsmith. But A. J. Raffles was also a gentleman burglar, an amateur cracksman, while I was a cracksman myself, albeit a professional.

And how did this chap, white-haired, slight of build, thin as a stick, and very nattily if unseasonably turned out in a suit of brown herringbone tweed and a Tattersall vest—how did he happen to know all this?

Admittedly, it's not the most closely held secret in the world. I have, after all, what they call a criminal record, and if it weren't a matter of record they'd call it something else. I haven't been convicted of anything in a long time, but every now and then I get arrested, and a couple of times in recent years I've had my name in the papers, and not as a seller of rare volumes.

I told myself, like Scarlett (another fine name for a cat), that I'd think about it later, and turned my attention to the book he placed on the counter. It was a small volume, bound in blue cloth, containing the selected poems of Winthrop Mackworth Praed (1802–39). It had been part of the inventory when I bought the store. I had, at one time or another, read most of the poems in it—Praed was a virtuoso at meter and rhyme, if not terribly profound—and it was the sort of book I liked having around. No one had ever expressed any interest in it, and I thought I'd own it forever.

It was not without a pang that I rang up $5.41, made change of ten, and slipped my old friend Praed into a brown paper bag. "I'm kind of sorry to see that book go," I admitted. "It was here when I bought the store."

"It must be difficult," he said. "Parting with cherished volumes."

"It's business," I said. "If I'm not willing to sell them, I shouldn't have them on the shelves."

"Even so," he said, and sighed gently. He had a thin face, hollow in the cheeks, and a white mustache so perfect it looked to have been trimmed one hair at a time. "Mr. Rhodenbarr," he said, his guileless blue eyes searching mine, "I just want to say two words to you. Abel Crowe."

If he hadn't commented on the appropriateness of Raffles's name, I might have heard those two words not as a name at all but as an adjective and a noun.

"Abel Crowe," I said. "I haven't heard that name in years."

"He was a friend of mine, Mr. Rhodenbarr."

"And of mine, Mr—?"

"Candlemas, Hugo Candlemas."

"It's a pleasure to meet a friend of Abel's."

"It's my pleasure, Mr. Rhodenbarr." We shook hands, and his palm was dry and his grip firm. "I shan't waste words, sir. I have a proposition to put to you, a matter that could be in our mutual interest. The risk is minimal, the potential reward substantial. But time is very much of the essence." He glanced at the open door. "If there were a way we could talk in private without fear of interruption . . ."

Abel Crowe was a fence, the best one I ever knew, a man of unassailable probity in a business where hardly anyone knows the meaning of the word. Abel was also a concentration camp survivor with a sweet tooth the size of a mastodon's and a passion for the writings of Baruch Spinoza. I did business with Abel whenever I had the chance, and never regretted it, until the day he was killed in his own Riverside Drive apartment by a man who—well, never mind. I'd been able to see to it that his killer didn't get away with it, and there was some satisfaction in that, but it didn't bring Abel back.

And now I had a visitor who'd also been a friend of Abel's, and who had a proposition for me.

I closed the door, turned the lock, hung the BACK IN 5 MINUTES sign in the window, and led Hugo Candlemas to my office in back.